Desert Water

Desert Water

Gary E. Parker

VICTOR BOOKS

A DIVISION OF SCRIPTURE PRESS PUBLICATIONS INC.
USA CANADA ENGLAND

Copyediting: Carole Streeter; Barbara Williams
Design and Digital Management: Scott Rattray
Front Cover Photos: FPG International

1 2 3 4 5 6 7 8 9 10 Printing/Year 99 98 97 96 95

This book is a work of fiction. Names, characters, and incidents are either the product of the author's imagination or are used fictitiously. Any resemblance to actual persons, living or dead, is entirely coincidental.

Section One

This is a hard and precarious world,
where every mistake and infirmity
must be paid for in full.

Clarence Day

Chapter One

Vic didn't plan to act like a hero. Instead, he planned to speed home from his assembly-line job at McDonnell Douglas, take a hot shower, eat a quick bite of supper, and sag down in front of the television and watch a Missouri Tigers basketball game. Energized by his plan, he tapped his thin fingers on the steering wheel in time to the country music pouring out of his radio. He couldn't wait to get home.

From the corner of his eye he spotted a black and white soccer ball hopping into the path of his new Chevrolet Cavalier. The ball jumped through the middle of the road and past him to the opposite curb.

Having fathered three kids himself, Vic instinctively darted his eyes to the right side of the highway, anxiously searching for the child he fully expected to follow the bouncing ball.

Scottie didn't plan to cause anyone any harm. But the soccer ball his daddy had given him last Tuesday for his birthday was his favorite toy. So, when his playmate accidentally kicked the leather treasure into the street in front of the duplex where the two boys were playing, Scottie naturally hustled after it.

The ball stopped on the curb opposite the duplex—trapped by the concrete ledge on one side and a broken tree limb on the other. Scared a car would run over his precious ball, Scottie forgot to look both ways to make sure a car didn't run over him. Into the street he galloped, his carrot-colored hair bobbing like a cork in a wind-churned lake.

Behind the wheel of his Cavalier, Vic spotted the boy as he sprinted into the street, and he acted immediately—slamming down on both his horn and his brakes. Then, he watched with astonishment as time seemed to trip, fall to its knees, and crawl by.

In the slow motion of the milliseconds now passing, he surveyed the right side of the road, wondering if he could swerve in that direction and miss the boy. Nope. He saw a second kid standing there.

Willis didn't plan to start his trip to California with an accident. But, as he well knew from over thirty-five years on the road, trips don't always go as planned. He was scooting down Highway 5, headed toward I-70 for a run to the west coast in his eighteen-wheeler, when he saw the black and white ball, the redheaded boy and the Chevy Cavalier—all at the same time. The boy had stopped dead in his tracks, frozen to the street like an ice cube to the bottom of a tray, in the lane opposite his truck.

Willis watched the Chevy dart away from him, to the right. Good. He would miss hitting it. But wait a second—now the vehicle hesitated.

Willis cursed softly and bit down on the toothpick wedged into the corner of his mouth. Suddenly, he understood.

Vic's green eyes narrowed and the knuckles of his fingers whitened on the wheel as he watched the boy in the road go into paralysis. He scanned the lane to his left and saw the black shadow of the massive transport truck reaching out for him. Glancing down at his speedometer, he wondered if he would survive a crash with a trailer truck going thirty-eight miles an hour.

As if acting on their own, his hands took over and violently twisted the wheel of the car to the left. Though the machine resisted at first, the pressure of the turn forced it to obey and, to his delight, Vic watched the right front fender miss the startled boy.

He breathed out a washtub of relieved air. Then he looked up. Nothing he could do to avoid it. The silver grill of the oncoming truck smiled at him like a happy shark. The words, "Our Father who art . . . " rushed into his mind, but time ran out and he never had a chance to say them.

The smiling grill smashed through his windshield, and a swoosh of raw December wind followed the grill and pinned him momentarily backwards against his seat. The sturdy weight of the truck made the position more permanent.

Hearing a scream, Vic thought at first it was his Cavalier somehow crying out in pain. Then, to his astonishment, he recognized his own voice. But the sound didn't last long. A wave of pain crashed through him and his voice fell silent; a heavy darkness wrapped its fingers around his throat and strangled out the light.

Willis raised his chest off the steering wheel where the crash had thrown him and glanced to his left. He watched as the redheaded boy sprinted back into his yard, his soccer ball tucked safely under his arm. Great! At least the kid wasn't hurt.

Relieved, Willis mentally touched his own body from head to toe. No injuries as far as he could tell. He spat out his toothpick—it was splintered in two. But that seemed to be the only thing broken. He was okay. His truck grill looked like a smashed accordion, but hey, that's why he paid high premiums for good insurance.

Willis pulled a fresh toothpick from his shirt pocket, stuck it into his mouth, and peered over the edge of his truck hood. He wondered about the man in the Chevy.

Zipping his jacket against the December cold, he opened the

door to his cab and gingerly hopped down. Circling to the front of his truck, he peered into the crushed car and saw the crumpled form lying in the seat. The sight made him want to gag, but he fought it back and swore instead, and sweat broke out on his face in spite of the chill. A stream of thick blood oozed from the man's face, and his chest was fused onto the steering wheel.

Willis bit down on his toothpick and suddenly felt scared. The voice of Garth Brooks floated into the air from the cassette deck in the crushed Cavalier and the music mingled with Willis' thoughts and Vic's blood. None of it seemed real, but it was.

The man looked dead. Willis stared for a heartbeat longer, then saw a slight movement of the injured man's chest. The movement jarred him into action. He glanced around for help, but saw none. Then he spotted the duplex into which the boys had disappeared.

Shivering, he hustled to the stoop of the duplex and furiously pressed the doorbell. A chunky woman in a yellow sweat suit answered.

"I need to use a phone," said Willis.

Without hesitation, she nodded and led him to a phone in the kitchen. He dialed 911, reported the accident, thanked the lady, and ran back outside. Waiting impatiently beside the smashed car, he hoped the ambulance would hurry. To cover his own thoughts, he talked softly to the man he didn't know, hoping to encourage him, hoping he was alive enough to hear his words.

The ambulance arrived within minutes—its red light flashing and its siren wailing. Behind the ambulance came a fire truck and a police car. As the fleet of vehicles screeched to a stop, a flurry of feet hit the pavement, and numbers of men and women scurried out of them, frantic to do their work.

A tall, thin man with a black bag approached Willis and a uniformed policeman trailed after him. "You need help, buddy?" asked the EMT.

"Nope, I think I'm okay," said Willis. "I was in the truck. I'm fine."

The EMT stared at him for a second. "You sure?" he asked.

"Yeah, like I said, I'm fine. No cuts and nothing broken. See?" Willis spread his arms out, opening himself for inspection.

The thin man shrugged. "Well, whatever you say. We'll still want to check you out at the hospital."

"Sure, no problem," agreed Willis. "But don't worry about me. Go on and help the guy in the Chevy. He's the one who needs you."

The EMT nodded, turned away from Willis, and hustled toward the rest of the rescue team.

The policeman then pulled a notepad out of his pocket and picked up the conversation. "I'll need to see your driver's license, your registration—"

"Yeah, I know the routine," agreed Willis, pulling out his wallet.

The cop checked out his papers. "It's all in order," he said, writing down the information, then looking back at Willis. "You feel like giving me a statement?"

"Yeah, no problem. I was headed north to I-70. Chevy driver was going south. A kid ran into the road and stopped in front of the Cavalier. I saw the whole thing. Poor guy didn't have anywhere to go. Another kid was in the yard." Willis pointed toward the duplex. "Over there. The man had to choose. Run down the kid and avoid me, or hit me and miss the kid." Willis summed up his report. "The guy in the Chevy swerved to miss the kid and I smashed into him."

"Didn't he see you coming?"

"Sure he did," said Willis. "But it was him or the boy." He nodded his head in admiration. "Gutsy move."

The cop, satisfied with the account, stopped writing and pocketed his pen. "I might need to talk with you again, but that's all for now. Want me to take you home?"

"Nope. I think I'll wait until they get him out."

The cop nodded and the two men together walked closer to the Cavalier. It took almost thirty minutes for the "jaws of life" to rip apart the metal of the car so they could get to the injured man. The two EMTs climbed through the busted windshield and unwrapped the limp body from the steering wheel. The thin EMT checked the pulse. He nodded at his partner and flipped him a thumbs-up. The man was still alive.

Gently, the two men lifted the broken body from the glass-covered seat and hauled it out over the hood. Stretching the man out on the ground, they went to work—covering him with blankets, inserting an IV, getting oxygen to his lungs.

Willis eased toward the crew working on Vic. "Will he make it?" he asked anxiously.

"Don't know," said the thin man.

"If Les Tennet's on duty, he might," said the second.

"Who's Tennet?" asked Willis.

"Best cutter I've ever met," said the thin man.

"Hope he's on duty then," said Willis. "This guy deserves the best. He's a hero."

Chapter Two

Les Tennet, chief trauma surgeon for the St. Louis Medical Center, had planned to be a doctor for as long as he could remember. He had planned to be a surgeon since he was twelve. Especially had he planned to operate on people with heart problems.

Les had managed to see his plan fulfilled. He operated on hearts as a matter of routine now—hearts with clogged arteries, hearts with leaky valves, hearts injured in accidents, and hearts in distress by internal causes. It didn't matter to him how the trauma came; he adored his work either way.

When the ambulance driver wheeled Vic onto the blue-tiled floors of the emergency unit, Les stood ready, dressed in his surgical greens and eager to go to work. Though sorry the man had suffered such severe injuries, Vic's heroism gave Les a chance to do what he most loved. As he met him at the door and rushed him through preparations for surgery, Les felt both a deep compassion and a certain kind of gratitude toward the battered man.

Within minutes, the surgical team handpicked by Tennet had gathered in the quiet, cold operating room. The steel instruments were laid out in precise rows, inanimate soldiers ready to obey the commands Tennet would give them. The patient was tubed and monitored and ventilated and now seemed more like an appendage to the machines than vice versa.

No one spoke. Only the beeps of the heart monitor sounded in the room. Tennet liked it that way; no music cluttered up the airwaves while he worked. He talked to his team once they began, but that was at his discretion, and everyone who worked with him learned quickly to watch for his lead when it came to conversation. If he stayed silent so did they.

Ready to go, Les scanned the man's chart again. Though he saw the name printed on the sheet of paper, he deliberately looked past it. He always ignored the names of his patients until he was certain they were going to live. He believed that calling them by name before they were safely repaired jinxed his efforts.

Everyone at the hospital knew of Les' superstition, and his surgical staff knew it better than the rest. So, they never named a case until the individual was definitely on the mend. Until then, they gave the person a title based on some characteristic of the trauma.

Today, as always, the team waited for Les to start the naming process. He did it quickly because that marked the kickoff for the surgery to begin.

"What exactly happened to this guy?" asked Les, giving them the signal to start thinking.

"A smashup," squeaked Clara Wilson, head surgical nurse at St. Louis Medical and right hand and best friend to Les and his family for over ten years.

"Obviously," said Tennet, rolling his eyes skyward. "Details, Clara, you know I like details."

Clara tried again, her high-pitched voice bouncing off the walls of the sterile room. "EMT guy said he swerved to dodge a boy who ran into the road in front of him. Missed the child but not the eighteen-wheeler in the left lane."

Tennet pushed back a layer of punctured skin and Clara deftly stapled it out of the way with her short black fingers. He examined the wound for several seconds, then cut a mid-

line sternal incision and a midline abdominal incision through
the man's flesh. "Spreaders," Tennet called.

"So what shall we call him?" he asked, gingerly placing the
spreaders inside the chest cavity and prying back what was left
of the ribs. Silence washed over the room as his crew pondered
the question. Les cut silly suggestions to shreds.

While waiting for a response, Les stuck his long fingers into
the open chest and felt them warm up from the heat inside.
Though blood stuck to his hands like pudding, the awe surged
over him again, like it always did when he invaded the forbidden zone.

"What about Child Dodger?" the anesthesiologist suggested.

"Not good," said Les quickly. "Sounds like a guy who
avoids his kids."

After a beat of quiet, the nurse at the heart monitor tried
her luck. "Let's call him Right Choice," she said. "That's what
he did, he made the right choice between himself and that little
boy."

Clara arched her thick eyebrows. "Not bad, doc," she
squeaked. "What you think?"

Les shot it down without reservation. "Nope, can't accept
it. Sounds like an advertisement for a dishwashing detergent. I
can see it now. A pretty young housewife holding up a yellow
bottle and saying, 'You make the best choice for your family
when you buy Right Choice.' No, can't call the man Right
Choice. Let's try again."

Les continued to work as he talked, picking his way through
the chest cavity, assessing the damage. He feared the man
wouldn't live long enough to make many more choices, right
or wrong.

Clara gave it a shot. "Let's call this man Snowball," she
demanded, " 'cause that's all the chance he had to survive that
truck smash. A snowball's chance in you know where . . . and
that's all he's got now. Snowball fits him just fine."

Les hesitated at first, trying to find a way to reject it. But
then he glanced at Clara. The tilt of her two fleshy chins told

him she had made up her mind. He decided not to agitate her. Besides, her name did make a certain kind of sense.

"I can go with that, Clara," he agreed, nodding. "It certainly describes his odds. His ribs are busted up like kindling wood. Pieces of them in his lungs and heart. It's a wonder he's still alive. Look's to me like he's going to—"

"Pressure's going down, chief!" the anesthesiologist interrupted. "Vital signs dropping. Heartbeat erratic. Fading. We've lost it!"

"Here we go." Tennet said it calmly, even as he speeded up his efforts. He touched the man's heart gently, and wrapped his fingers around it, then held it in his right hand—like handling a water balloon. He massaged the fist-sized muscle ever so slightly, probing for the life of it. Though he sensed life running away from him, Les believed that he could catch it before it fled too far, that he could carry it back to its rightful owner, that he could rescue it before it reached the place of hiding where no one could find it again.

Les' eyes widened and he licked his lips under his mask. Though he kept it to himself, he loved moments like these, lived for them. These split seconds when everything hung by a thread gave him power, the ultimate power, not over life and not over death, but the power in between the two, when neither really held sway, when life and death locked in hand-to-hand combat and breathed into each other's faces.

In this in-between world, Tennet ruled like few others. If he did his job right, life usually won. If not, death took home its prey. Both life and death depended on him and he delighted in his ability to determine the victor.

Holding Snowball's heart in his hand, Tennet recalled the first time he discovered his power....

He was on duty at 11 P.M., a first-year resident at the time. The EMT unit had wheeled an oversized man dressed in a black tie and tails through the electric doors of the hospital and into the emergency room. Les sprinted to the stretcher.

"Who've we got here?" he asked, eyes scanning the man's chart.

"A big dog," pronounced the ambulance driver. "The governor of Missouri himself."

For a second Les felt a surge of panic. "Doesn't he have a personal physician?"

"Sure," said the driver. "But he's out of town. You're the man, whether you're up to it or not. By the time anyone else gets here, you'll either show the governor your stuff or he'll be shaking hands with the voters in that great capital in the sky."

Les took a quick, self-conscious look around. Behind the driver and the squad of nurses striding up and down the hallway, a coterie of well-dressed but worried-looking people had gathered. These were people accustomed to the best. If he blew it here, his young career would die in its tracks. He gritted his teeth. But he wouldn't blow it. They expected the best. Well, that's what he was, he whispered to himself. The best. Top of his class at Missouri U. Same story at Johns Hopkins Medical. Already touted as one of the young burners by knowledgeable people in medical circles.

"What happened to him?" he asked, steadied as he remembered his abilities.

"His heart stopped during a late night dinner," said the driver.

"Must have been the broccoli," Tennet joked.

"No time to horse around, doctor," said the nurse beside him. "This is the governor, you know."

"You're right," he nodded. "Let's get him some privacy." The nurse motioned to the ambulance driver and the two shifted into high gear and quickly moved the governor into a private cubicle and stripped off his shirt.

Tennet shook his head as he noticed the man's white skin, white as the underside of a fresh fish. Beneath the clothes and titles, everyone looked pretty much the same.

He turned to the nurse. "You got the needle ready?"

She handed it to him. A needle full of Adrenalin. He hesitated,

but only for a beat. Then, with a deep breath, he plunged the
point of the needle through the governor's skin and into his
heart. The nurse began mouth-to-mouth resuscitation. In time
with her breathing, Les compressed the chest—push down,
pause, push down, pause, push down, pause.

The monitor stayed flat—no pulse. "Give me the paddles,"
said Les. "I'm going to pop him."

The nurse nodded and handed him the electric paddles used
to shock the heart into response.

Tennet grabbed them. "Clear," he shouted. Everyone
obeyed. He slapped the paddles to the governor's fleshy chest
and the electricity jumped into the inert body. The body
flopped as the dual prods jolted him. Nothing.

"Clear," Tennet commanded again. He pressed the paddles to
the body angrily this time. "My first heart attack will not die on
me!" he shouted. "I won't have that on my record." Nothing
moved but the beached man. "Clear," Tennet grunted the word
a third time and the two-inch scar over his right eye raised up
like a mole furrow and turned purple. The veins in his forehead
popped out under his thick, black hair, and his eyes ran away and
left a vacant stare of concentration on his tortured face.

The gray-haired nurse assisting him, a veteran who had
watched scores of young residents lose their first patients,
patted Tennet's sweating back. "Doctor, I think he's gone,"
she said.

Tennet barely noticed. He wasn't in the room anymore. He
was running down a smoky corridor, chasing the beat of a
heart, knowing it was out there in the dark somewhere—afraid
and lost. He dared to think he could locate it, grab it, and
force it to come back. "I said, 'Clear!' "

Nodding, the nurse stepped off. Let him learn the hard way.

Tennet spanked the paddles down, giving the heart a guttur-
al order. "I said, 'Beat, heart, beat!' "

"I've got something." The nurse at the monitor whispered
the magic words. "It's erratic." Everyone stopped and waited.
Nobody breathed.

"Stronger," said the nurse. "It's beating. Leveling out." The monitor registered the return.

"Regular now," said the nurse.

Exhaling heavily, Tennet staggered backward and leaned against the wall. He had found the heartbeat out there, in the tunnel between the emergency room and the funeral parlor. He had recognized it the second he had contacted it. The touch had been warm like an electric blanket, a comforting wrap against the cold of death. Nothing else could ever warm him so. He had caressed a heart and wooed it back. What a feeling!

Tennet had walked out of that emergency room thirteen years ago a man with a future. The media made him a hero. One reporter, citing his academic credentials, his athletic skills as a sometime starting guard on the MU basketball team, and his youthful good looks, dubbed him, "Les the Blest," and the name stuck in the community and at the hospital.

Though gladly accepting the fame, Les had loved the experience itself even more. Saving the governor's life had made him certain at the time that rescuing heartbeats from the shadow world gave him cause enough to live. Lately, though, he had started to wonder. Fame and fortune hadn't made him a happy man. . . .

No time to wonder now. Almost a minute had passed since Snowball's heart had flatlined. Les had only two or three more before brain damage would make saving the man's life a senseless exercise.

"Did anybody meet this guy's family?" Tennet talked like he worked, without panic. He massaged the heart, looking for the damage.

"I did."

Tennet nodded to Clara, the self-designated talker of the operating team. She continued. "They're outside. Four of them. A wife, two teenagers, and a young boy."

"They seem all right?"

"I think so. They've heard of you. Said they're glad you're on duty."

Tennet smiled under his mask. Though not given to much humor lately, and almost never while in surgery, he did enjoy his semi-celebrity status in St. Louis.

He continued to finger the heart as he chatted. He sensed life still fighting there, calling out to him, *Don't give up yet.*

"I'm not sure I'm glad I'm on duty. Don't know if I can help this guy or not."

Clara, all 165 pounds of her, hesitated, but Les saw she wanted to say something else. He nodded again. "Yes, Clara?"

"The family asked me to tell you they are praying for you."

Tennet smiled again. Rare, a two-smile surgery. Didn't remember many of those. "Ah, yes, Clara, the prayers. I should have known you'd squeeze the good Lord in here somewhere. You always do."

Clara smiled too and everyone in the room saw it spread out beyond her mask and cover her jowly face. "I didn't want to disappoint you, doctor."

In that instant, he found it—a puncture wound from the feel of it—in the lower left ventricle of the heart. He placed his thumb over the tiny hole and pressed downward to cut off the escaping blood. The life was fleeing through this open door.

Almost instantaneously, the nurse at the heart monitor whispered, "I've got a blip."

Within seconds, a weak but rhythmic stroke signaled the return of life.

"We've got him." Tennet said it calmly, not boasting. That wasn't his way. Let others boast for him. "Besides," he often said, "if I take credit for those who live, then I've got to take blame for those who die. If I have to trade one to avoid the other, I'll gladly do it."

Tennet didn't lose many. In fact, no one could remember the last patient who had died once they reached his care. He knew his record and so did everyone else. "Les the Blest" was well deserved.

With Snowball's heart thumping consistently again, and the main source of trouble located, Tennet shifted into high gear to clean up the rest of the damage. He sewed four cardiovascular prolene stitches to repair the hole in the heart. Finished with that, he removed Snowball's crushed left kidney and the lower part of his right lung. It took over five hours to complete the painstaking surgery, but Tennet hardly noticed. He was cruising, doing what he loved, barking out orders and saving lives.

He hummed as he worked. The crisis had passed. Les the Blest had saved another one.

"Close it up, folks," he said, finally satisfied. "I think this one's done for now." He pulled his fingers from his rubber gloves and turned to walk out. Then, like a mischievous child, he twirled and tiptoed up behind Clara. Without warning, he bent down, turned her head around, and kissed her wetly on the cheek.

"Clara," he teased, "if I ever end up on this table, get me a surgeon as good as me and skip the prayers."

Clara shook like licorice jello and her laughter pierced the room. "But doc, wherever would we find a surgeon as good as you?"

Les smiled, hugely pleased. A three-smile surgery. Maybe miracles did happen.

Chapter Three

Les switched off the ignition of his black Mercedes as he turned into the driveway of his fourteen-room home. The house, an original by a nationally acclaimed architect he knew from college, was a combination of clear glass and sharp corners.

A house like a huge ski lodge, Clara Wilson had said at the housewarming, almost two years ago.

"With an indoor swimming pool," said Les, proud of the financial success that allowed him to mortgage such a place.

"And a steam bath," Clara agreed, helping him bask in his pride.

At the time he built the house, it seemed to fit his future — precise and impossible for anyone to miss. Now, though, as he let his car coast into the garage, it occurred to Les that the house stood more as a parody of his life than a symbol of it.

Hoping to slip in without waking his wife, Katherine, he quietly eased out of the car, unlocked the door to the house, and stepped inside. Pausing to give his eyes time to adjust to the dark, he breathed a sigh of relief. The lack of light told him Katherine wasn't waiting in the den for him, as she often did. He didn't want to get into another fight tonight. Not at 1 A.M.

Able to see now, he climbed the stairs and reached the landing at the top. But he didn't go straight to his bedroom.

He never did. He always checked on his kids first.

He flipped on the light in the hallway and took two steps to his left, stopping outside his son's room. He creaked open the door and peeked inside. The light from the hall washed over the room and illuminated a clutter of clothes, shoes, and magazines strewn all over the floor. Shaking his head in disgust, Les sucked in his breath and looked at the angular frame of his seventeen-year-old son, John.

The teenager was stretched out, lean and strong, on top of the covers of his bed. He still had on his trademark shoes, size-fourteen black Nikes with the strings untied—as usual. The big shoes dangled over the edge of the bed, and Les marveled again at the athletic talents of his firstborn. Though already six feet, five inches tall—two inches taller than himself—John had none of the awkwardness that characterized most boys his age. He was grace personified, and his combination of size and agility had attracted the attention of dozens of college basketball scouts. Sighing as he gazed at his son, Les wished he would direct some of his drive from basketball into other areas of his life. But he didn't, and that created almost constant conflict between father and son.

Les tilted his head and leaned further into John's room. The sound of rock music poured out of the boy's stereo beside the bed. *Typical,* thought Les.

Easing into the room, he picked his way through the trash on the floor and flipped off the music. Then, wrapping the bedspread over John's legs, he scooted out and hurried down the hall to check on Sherry.

Eagerly stepping inside her room, he took a deep breath and inhaled the sweet smell of his little girl's perfume. For a couple of beats he closed his eyes and just stood there, soaking up the feeling of innocent rest that seemed to rise like morning mist from the covers of Sherry's bed. Of all the people in his life, only Sherry made him feel so vulnerable. And so strong. All in the same moment.

He moved over to her, tiptoeing so she wouldn't awaken.

He leaned over, enjoying, as always, the angelic glow of her face. Her blonde hair glistened in the soft light of the lamp that burned on the table beside her pillow. She clutched a tattered gray rabbit to her chest. Elmer, not Bugs. He'd given Elmer to her on her first birthday, and she never moved without Elmer by her side.

Les smiled, as he always did when he saw Sherry. She created smiles in him because she always smiled herself—and for a good reason. She had been born without the ability to know that life brings lots of reasons to cry. Though she was eight years old physically, the doctors said her mind would never catch up with her body.

She would stay a child for the rest of her life, a simple-minded girl with a brain as uncluttered by adult thought as a blank sheet of paper. But she didn't know any of this and so she kept smiling; and Les smiled because she did, in spite of his grief.

Les smiled with Sherry for a second reason. She reminded him of the only person who had brought laughter to his childhood. With her corn-silk hair and aqua-blue eyes, Sherry looked just like the picture he kept on his desk at the hospital, the picture of his mother, dead since he was twelve. . . .

People who knew him said that's when he had stopped smiling, the day the doctor walked out of the emergency room and told him and his weeping father he had done all he could, but to no avail. "Her heart just exploded," the white-jacketed man said, "like a bomb in her body, and she was gone." The doctor shook his head, lowered his eyes to his chart, and mumbled, "I'm sorry." Then he turned and faded away down the hospital corridor, as nameless as when he had arrived.

Les never forgot the phrase, "She was gone." He remembered it every day of his life, remembered it and swore he would never use it himself. Life didn't just "go," he decided, like a bird heading south for the winter, of its own accord.

His mom didn't just "go." Instead, she died as if a demon

had sunk its talons into her flesh and sought to jerk her away. She fought the hellish beast tooth and nail, with her eyes popping out like a zoom lens on a camera, her hands clawing the air, and her lips twitching, trying to speak to him, trying to tell him something.

Les watched her writhe as the medics lifted her into the ambulance, as they slammed the back doors in his face, as they rushed her into the emergency room a few minutes later at the hospital. That picture stayed with him over the years like a tattoo on his mind and heart. Les couldn't smile too much — not when he still saw his mother's tortured face every day of his life. . . .

Les leaned over Sherry, pushed back a strawy wisp of her hair, and kissed her cheek, grateful for the unconditional love she showered on him. Sherry wouldn't stop loving him, even if everyone else did. No, she wouldn't abandon him like his mother had when she died and like Katherine had threatened to do so often in the last three years.

He stroked Sherry twice on the head, then turned and trudged out. He couldn't put it off any longer. Time to go to bed. Hoping not to awaken Katherine, he undressed in the hallway, edged into the bedroom, and slipped under the sheets. A moist heat from Katherine's body spread over to him and he turned to look at her.

Her tawny hair, not red and not blonde but somewhere between the two, lay gently on her pillow. Her face carried almost no wrinkles and her lips were pert and soft. She wore a pair of gym shorts and a basketball jersey cut off at the midriff. The jersey, given to her by John on her thirty-eighth birthday last July, had a question mark in lieu of a number on the back. The question mark represented the family joke — Katherine had difficulty making up her mind. Under the shorts, her legs stretched out almost as long as the bed.

Staring at her, Les shook his head in amazed admiration. Their years of matrimonial warfare hadn't hurt her appearance any that he could see. She still turned heads, just like she'd turned his twenty years ago as she walked across the basketball field house at the University of Missouri in her cheerleader uniform.

Les gritted his teeth. Though Katherine was still gorgeous, their relationship wasn't, and it seemed to get uglier by the day. Their incessant arguments reminded him of a swamp—pulling them both down, no matter how hard they tried to stay afloat. Lately, he'd felt like giving up and letting the muck pull him to the bottom.

Tonight, as on most nights in the last four years or so, Tennet hoped Katherine wouldn't wake up. Her sleepy voice dashed his hopes.

"What time is it?" she asked, raising up on her elbows.

"You don't want to know."

"I called the hospital at 9." They said you'd already left for home."

"They were right about the 'already left' part." He made a mental note to remind the hospital to keep his schedule confidential.

"But you didn't come home."

Les heard the accusation as she rolled away from him and checked the clock. "No, I didn't," he said.

"Can I ask where you went?"

"Sure you can ask," he said, shaking his head, sadly recognizing the familiar signs of their torturous conversation, but not knowing how to change it. "But I think you know."

"You went to Patrick's Place?" She turned back toward him and propped herself up on her right elbow.

"Yeah, to have a couple of drinks and wind down a little. I had quite a day today. Two gunshot wounds, and an emergency car accident that no one thought would make it."

"But you saved him." He noted her sarcasm.

"I would think you'd be proud of what I do."

"I am proud of what you do. But I don't see much of you because of it. Don't begrudge me my resentment."

Les interlocked his fingers behind his head. "You knew I was going to be a surgeon when you married me."

"Sure I did. But I didn't know your work as a surgeon meant I would see the groundhog's shadow more often than I do you."

Tennet closed his eyes and tightened his grip under his pillow. "Look, Kath, we've walked this ground over and over. We're a cliché for our generation. I'm the husband who's too busy to give proper attention to his wife. Then, I'm unable to connect emotionally with her when I do steal away for a few hours. And you're the upper-class wife who's trying to find herself as she nears forty and sees her children growing up. We're the classic American love story—workaholic, career-focused male, and confused but willing-to-grow female. Only two problems as I see it. One, it ain't working for either of us and two, I don't have a clue how to fix it."

"I'm sure you don't, Les," agreed Katherine, flopping in a huff onto her back. "If you can't cut out the problem with a scalpel or patch it up with a few stitches, then you're lost."

She bit her lip and Les knew she was trying to tone down her anger, to stay away from confrontation. She'd tried that often lately. It was part of her most recent effort to make changes in her life and in her relationship with him. Nothing had worked for years, but Katherine kept plugging away with new ways and approaches.

That was part of his problem with her. Nothing was consistent. She was a tunnel with huge openings on both ends. Thoughts and moods and tangents and trends and fads flowed in and over and through her like daily tides—in and out, in and out—and he never knew which current she'd get swept away with next.

She'd worked diligently early in their marriage to be exactly what he wanted in a wife—an exquisite treasure, perfectly manicured and adorned. Like her mother before her, she had attached herself to an ascending star and she took to the role as one born to play it.

As his career expanded she had kept pace—playing hostess with utmost care. She had birthed John right on cue and together she and John and Les made other couples jealous with their success. Together they made her parents, who had disagreed with their decision to marry, look foolish.

Then came Sherry. A miserable pregnancy marked by high blood pressure and intense vomiting for almost five months. The doctors assured them the unborn child was fine. The birth itself was horrible—twenty-two hours of painful labor followed by a Caesarean section when it finally became evident she couldn't finish the delivery.

For almost eight months no one noticed anything different about Sherry. After that, they couldn't help but notice. Her development slowed and she fell behind other children her age. The doctors never really discovered the cause, but within a year what they at first only feared became a stunning certainty—Sherry would never attain mental normalcy. Her retardation might never institutionalize her, but it would keep her from a full life. And, though the doctors didn't say it, it would also divorce the rest of the family from normalcy.

Both their lives shattered, but Katherine's more than his. At least he still had his work. But she seemed to think she had lost everything. Certainly, a curtain crashed on her old role of wife and mother of the perfect family. The problem was that she hadn't found a new role to play. Les knew that she now recognized the old one for what it was, a fantasy, a charade, a counterfeit. Now she wanted out of any role. She wanted, as she had told him, to "find" herself. He wondered how long this search would last before she turned to something else.

"I wish I knew what to do," said Les, unclasping his hands and turning toward her. "I don't want to go on like this."

"We could try counseling again," she said, reverting her attention back to him. "It helped for a while, didn't it?"

"Yeah, it did," said Les. "But the old patterns came back within months after we stopped going. I don't see it helping right now."

"What will help, Les?"

"Heaven only knows," he said.

He saw the end of the conversation. No use pushing any further. Resigned, he closed his eyes and hoped sleep would provide him an escape from his sadness over a marriage slipping away from him like soap bubbles.

Les rolled onto his side. Katherine tucked her pillow under her head. "One thing before I forget, Les," she said. "You got a notice from your reserve unit today. I put it on your desk."

"I'll check it first thing in the morning. Thanks for remembering." He slipped lower into the bed and feigned sleep. Katherine reached over and touched him on the forehead. "I love you, Les," she whispered. "I always will."

He pretended not to hear. Beside him, Katherine lifted her right hand to her mouth and chewed off the top of each fingernail, one by one by one. Les lay in the dark listening to her chewing and wondered if she had just told him a lie.

Chapter Four

Sherry pushed the covers off her skinny legs and dropped her toes to the floor. She clutched Elmer to her chest, shoved her feet into her Little Miss Mermaid shoes, and padded downstairs. Grinning widely, she quietly opened the door to her parents' bedroom and saw an inert form on her dad's side of the bed. It obviously pleased her to see him still asleep. Though he usually woke her, she took great pleasure in those few times when she got to rouse him after he slept late.

She tiptoed across the room, then squealed and pounced at the same time. Jumping onto the mattress on her mom's empty side, she leapt up and down, up and down, clutching Elmer to her chest. She yelled as she jumped, "Daddee, Daddee, Daddee!"

Shaken awake, Les opened his eyes and sat up. Seeing Sherry, he reached over and grabbed her and pulled her down to him, hugging her and tickling her ribs and rubbing the stubble of his scratchy face against her neck. Sherry squealed louder and louder, and the two of them wrestled and rolled around and under the covers like alligators in water. For several minutes, they laughed and tussled and shrieked together. Finally, though, Sherry's laughter reached the point of exhaustion and Les eased up and let her catch her breath.

"Time to swim?" she panted, gazing at him expectantly.

"Time to swim," said Les, nodding and glancing at his watch. Almost 8. He'd slept two hours later than normal. "Go get your suit on and I'll meet you at the pool."

Sherry hustled out and Les rolled off the bed, stepped to the bathroom, and pulled on a swimsuit. Heading to the pool, he poked his head into the den and spotted Katherine sitting cross-legged in front of the bay window that covered almost half the back wall of the room. A diamond-shaped crystal rested on the sill in the center of the window and Katherine stared blankly into it. The sun blazed through the window and the crystal magnified the rays of light and focused them into Katherine's limpid eyes.

Les opened his mouth to speak but then thought better of it. She didn't like it when he broke her concentration. She'd started this about eight months ago. Morning channeling, she called it. Her mother, always ready with a suggestion for Katherine's improvement, had suggested it to her. "It'll help you center yourself," Beatrice had said. "Find out who you are."

Les had laughed the first time Katherine tried it. It was on a morning like this . . .

She had risen before the sun, climbed into an exercise suit, and worked out on their Nordic Track for thirty minutes. A steam bath followed. So far, new but fairly normal. Then she slipped into an earth-toned linen gown and headband, purchased from a Native American curio shop, and pulled the crystal out of the nightstand by her bed.

She carried the three-pound rock to the den and centered it so it caught the focus of the sunlight that beamed through the glass. Then she sat down and stayed put.

That's how he found her almost an hour later. Surprised, he whispered, "Kath, whatcha doing?" She ignored him. He tried again. "Uh, morning, Kath, coffee ready?" No response. He turned to his all-purpose weapon—sarcasm, "Excuse me, Ms. Ramadan Electra Swami Muhammed Z, but could you step out of the fourth dimension long enough to get a little breakfast?"

Katherine inhaled and exhaled once, twice, three times. She folded her hands in her lap and turned calmly to him. "Go ahead with your swim, Les," she said. "Breakfast will be ready when you get out."

He had walked away, bemused. Let her channel, he thought. So long as breakfast was ready when he got out of the water. Since then, it had been. Every day, without fail. . . .

He left Katherine by the window as he had for almost every day for the last few months. Sherry was waiting for him at the pool. Every morning he was home, he shared this with her. Though she wasn't a particularly good swimmer, Sherry loved the water and for thirty minutes every day they splashed and dove and tossed balls and laughed.

This morning was no different. For half an hour he forgot the pressures of his work, put aside his marital problems, ignored the unrest gnawing away at his gut, shut out the problems he was having communicating with his son, and hung suspended in a buoyant world of water and foam.

Then, far too quickly, it was over. It was time to go. He dried off with Sherry, carried her on his shoulders to her room, and plopped her onto her bed. Leaning over, he snuggled his cheek against hers.

"Who loves you?" he asked.

She answered as he had taught her. "Daddy does."

"And how long will Daddy love you?"

"Always."

"And is there anything you could ever do that would cause Daddy to stop loving you?"

She giggled, "No."

Satisfied, Les hugged her one last time. "Hustle up and get dressed," he said. "Almost time to go." Leaving her, he trooped back downstairs. After a shower and shave, he dressed and joined Katherine—who had finished her meditation and was now busy in the kitchen.

With a day off from the hospital for the first time in nearly a month, he sat down and relaxed in the warmth of the sun slicing through the kitchen window.

Katherine planted a tiny kiss on his cheek and handed him a glass of orange juice.

"You want eggs or pancakes this morning?" she asked, walking back to the stove. "I can't make up my mind."

Les shook his head at her indecisiveness but didn't comment. "Doesn't matter, whatever you want."

She stood still for several seconds. "I don't know, eggs I guess."

"Great," said Les.

"Is Sherry getting dressed?" she asked, setting the pan on the burner.

"Yeah, I told her to get a move on. It's almost time for her gymnastics class."

Katherine glanced at her watch. Almost 9. She'd have to hurry to get Sherry ready and in place on time.

"Does she have to go, Les?"

"Sure she has to go. It's good for her." He sipped from his juice.

"But she doesn't really like it," said Katherine, her voice stiffening with exasperation. "She'd much rather stay here and play with her dolls."

"Don't get upset, Kath," Les said, not wanting to fight. "I just think lying around so much isn't good for her. She doesn't get any exercise and she doesn't learn anything when she's cooped up in her room all day."

Katherine, having heard this complaint more than once, flipped the eggs over in the pan. The anger in her voice rose like the yellow yolks. "Les, it doesn't matter what we do or don't do for Sherry. The doctors have told us she can't learn. It's that simple! She'll never advance much past a five-year-old in her abilities. Why can't you accept the truth and let it rest?"

"Don't you think I have?" Les dropped his eyes and stared at his glass.

"No, I don't," said Katherine, her pace of breathing picking up. "I don't think so at all. You make her go to gymnastics; you make her take swimming lessons; you pay for her tutoring three times a week; you send her to piano lessons even though she'll never be able to play; you push her and push her—all in hopes that somehow, like magic, she'll become a normal child. You torture yourself and you torment me with your insistence on making her better. The sad part is, you know you can't fix her and it's driving you crazy and I'm not far behind you."

Katherine paused to let her body catch up on its oxygen level. "You need to let go and accept her the way she is."

"I want her to have the best opportunity she can to get better. For her sake," Les defended himself.

Katherine hesitated, as if weighing her words, as if trying to decide how far to go. Then, she struck home. "You haven't done it for her sake, Les."

"Whose then?"

"Your own."

"Mine?" Les stared blankly out the window. A robin stood silhouetted against the brown grass in the yard.

"Yes, yours. You want Sherry to get better because she's an embarrassment to you. You don't want people to know you fathered an imperfect child. Your drive for perfection in yourself, in me, in John, and in Sherry is a way to prop up your own ego, even if it destroys us in the process."

"You really believe I'm so selfish?"

"Not selfish, Les, but afraid. I believe you're afraid."

For a beat of an instant, Les fell silent, stunned by a wave of loneliness that surged through him. When he spoke, his voice sounded distant. "Afraid of what?"

"Afraid if you let down for a second, if you don't stay on top, if you don't drive and push and excel in everything, then you'll wake up one morning and you won't have a reason to live. You're trying to prove yourself to someone, and you're afraid if you fail to do it, you'll die."

Les plunked his juice glass down and ran his fingers through his hair, but said nothing. Silence crashed into the breakfast nook and filled it up. Les knew the silence was necessary now, necessary because they were at dead ends. Though it didn't satisfy either of them, the silence provided a respite they recognized. At least in silence they didn't toss word grenades to maim each other.

Les gazed at the robin hopping across the grass outside. "I guess that robin should head south, shouldn't he?"

Katherine looked back at her eggs. "Are you ready to eat? I think these are about finished."

Neither answered the other's question. Two phones went off simultaneously, interrupting their thoughts. Upstairs, in Les' study, his line from the hospital buzzed, and downstairs, an arm's reach from the refrigerator, the family line jingled. Les and Katherine both moved to answer.

She reached hers first.

"Hello."

"Mrs. Tennet?"

"Yes, this is Katherine Tennet."

"Mrs. Tennet, this is the secretary at Archway Academy."

Katherine groaned.

"I hate to bother you, Mrs. Tennet, and I don't really know how to say this, but we have found a pistol in John's locker."

The secretary paused, waiting for a response, but none came. She continued. "The principal would like for you and Dr. Tennet to come down to the school. Given Dr. Tennet's reputation, we'll try to work this out without involving the police." The secretary paused again. Still no response.

"Mrs. Tennet, are you there?"

Katherine jumped and stammered, "Yes, I'm . . . I'm sorry, I'm just stunned. What do I need to do? Is John okay?"

"Yes, he's fine. Mr. Stone's holding him in his office. But we need you and Dr. Tennet to come down immediately. How soon can you get here?"

Katherine looked at her watch. "We can be there in about an hour. Tell John we're on the way." She was already pulling off her robe to change.

"Les," she called, taking the stairs two at a time, brushing her hair with her hand as she climbed.

"Yeah," he answered, from their bedroom. "I'm changing clothes. I've got to get to the hospital. The man I operated on yesterday has taken a turn for the worse. He's losing blood on the inside. I'll have to skip breakfast."

Katherine stopped for a second as his words sank in on her. Then she stalked into the room and grabbed Les by both arms and pinned them to his sides. Her jay-blue eyes searched for his, found them, riveted them in a steel-rigid glare.

"Listen to me," she insisted. "That was the school. They've got John in the office. They found a pistol in his locker. He's in trouble. They haven't called the police yet. They want us down there now. Our son needs us. Your son needs you."

The gaze between them held, his as focused as hers.

"Is John hurt?"

"No, not physically. He's waiting for us in the principal's office."

Les broke the gaze, snapped it like a stick, then pulled his arms away and began to button his shirt.

"You can take care of John for now. I've got a car accident dying on me. The immediate need has to take precedence."

Katherine exploded and the detonation blew away her normal indecisiveness. Her eyes flooded with tears and her voice fired thunder. "Les, this is your son we're talking about, not some hospital triage situation! He's skipped school seven times already this year, they caught him cheating a month ago, and now a gun in his locker. Don't you see a pattern here?"

Les slipped his tie around his throat. "Kath, I don't want to go to the hospital. I want to go with you. You've got to believe me. I know John's trying to get our attention. And, I'm going to start spending more time with him, if he'll let me. When I've tried lately, though, he's rejected me completely. I don't know what else I can do."

"You can go with me to the school."

"I wish I could, Kath, I really do," said Les, finishing his tie and picking up his car keys. "But a man's life is at stake. I've go to help him. I'm the only one at the hospital who can."

"What about your son's life, Les? Aren't you the only one who can help him?"

Les gritted his teeth and shook his head. "You get him home and I'll talk to him tonight," he said.

"I hope that's not too late."

Les hugged her as he walked out. "It'll be fine, Kath. As soon as I get this car accident squared away, I'll get home. You take care of John until then."

As he left the room he picked up the brown envelope lying on his desk—the letter from his reserve unit. He stuck it in his pocket. He would attend to that too, right after he repaired Snowball.

Chapter Five

As he sprinted into the scrub room, Les spotted Clara Wilson. In contact with the hospital through his car phone since he screeched out of his driveway, he already knew the situation. Clara summed it up for him again as he slipped into his operating greens and soaped and scrubbed his hands.

"We're not sure what happened, but the blood pressure started falling about two hours ago. His heartbeat started skipping in and out, stable one minute and sporadic the next. His chart looks like a mountain range. We couldn't get him stabilized."

Impatiently donning his gloves, Tennet bellowed, "Why wasn't I called sooner?"

"We thought we could handle it and we didn't want to bother you on your day off. Figured you might need the time with your family."

Les paused and stared hard at his friend. "How long have we worked together, Clara?"

" 'Bout ten years, I think."

"Then you should know to call me when one of my patients needs me." Les dismissed her and banged the double doors backward and stomped into the operating room.

"You got him under?"

The anesthesiologist nodded.

"Then let's open him up."

Slicing the already zippered skin took far less time than the initial incision. After cutting and pulling out the sternal wires, it took little pressure to spread the puffed scar apart.

"Looks like tire marks." Clara was the only one other than Les who dared talk.

"Yeah, and the question is—can we retread him for a few more miles?" Les picked up her banter but only for an instant. He placed the rib spreaders across the chest for the second time in two days and screwed the body apart.

He went back to work inside the same chest cavity he'd invaded just twelve hours earlier. It was full of blood, and the heart and lungs were drowning in red.

He slid his hands under the heart again, hoping as he did that he was wrong in his assumption about what had gone wrong. He wasn't. He found it, a surgeon's worst nightmare, a loose stitch, the third one from the end. It was an unhinged floodgate and Snowball's life was washing away through it.

Les felt his team's shocked eyes piercing him. Les the Blest had botched it. A stitch he'd sewn had come loose and now a man struggled for his life because of it.

"You okay, Dr. Tennet?" Clara addressed him formally. She didn't usually do that and Les knew it made the situation worse. Everyone in the room would recognize it as Clara's effort to regain some lost status for him. But it was too obvious. He fought to stay calm.

"I'm all right, Clara. Let's see if we can get Snowball fixed up and wheeled out of here."

Did his voice sound squeaky or was it only his imagination?

Tennet pulled out the torn suture and stitched another one. He heard the words before the nurse on the monitor spoke them.

"Trouble, doctor. Blood pressure 60 over 20, heart rate dropping! Still going down. . . . He's flatlined!"

"Get me the needle, Clara. I'm going to inject Adrenalin directly into the heart."

Clara reacted instantly. She pulled the needle from the plastic cover, sucked fluid from a clear bottle into it and shoved it to Les. He took it and plunged the point through Snowball's chest and into his heart muscle. Blinking rapidly, Les pushed the contents of the needle out into the tissue.

He couldn't tell if it was sweat or tears in his eyes. He had lost a patient or two before this one and knew he'd lose others later, but never had a patient died as a direct result of his failure. And that's what he believed had happened—he had screwed it up. His suture had popped loose and the man's blood had seeped through it, and now Snowball was drowning in his own blood. No matter that a thousand things could have caused it—this man's blood was literally on his hands.

Les pulled out the needle and massaged the heart in his hands, loving it like a boy stroking the smooth leather of a new baseball glove. If gentle persuasion could regenerate the damaged organ, he wanted to make sure it happened. For almost five minutes he tried every maneuver, every technique, every trick he'd ever learned. But none of them worked. Nothing he could do to reclaim the life this time.

The heart died in his hands and Snowball's life slipped away. The life walked out into another room—whether a dark room or a bright room, Les didn't know and didn't care to know. All he knew was he couldn't invade this new room. It closed itself to him, hung a "No Trespassing" sign on its portals, and even his abundant skills as a doctor couldn't pry it open.

Everyone else recognized it too. Clara said it for them all. "Les, we can't do anything else. I think he's gone."

Les raised his eyes from the body, already recategorizing it in his mind. Two minutes ago the gaping wound on the table was his patient. Now it was a body, so much bone and hair and blood. The mortician would pump out the blood and replace it with formaldehyde; the hair would continue to grow for a while, fooling itself as if still alive; and the bone would accept its fate and begin the process of returning to the dust which birthed it.

"Would you take care of this, Clara?" Les asked softly. "I need to talk to the family." Slipping off his gloves, he slumped out of the operating suite and headed toward the waiting room.

A bleached blonde dressed in frazzled jeans and a green sweatshirt popped up from her chair to greet him as he trudged through the door. Two teen kids, one a black-haired boy and the other a mother's look-alike daughter, stood up with their mom and draped themselves on either side of her for comfort. A smaller boy stayed seated on a sofa by the wall and stared at the group in the center of the room.

The wife—a widow now, thought Les—shoved a string of her yellow hair into the corner of her mouth and sucked on it as she stared at him. "Doctor?" The widow asked the question in one word.

Les hesitated for a moment, then answered with the words he had sworn never to use. "I'm sorry, ma'am . . . but he's gone." Somehow, the words seemed to fit this time.

The widow moaned and collapsed into Les' arms, a grief-stricken stranger seeking solace, without regard to where she found it. Her tears mixed with the gummed blood on Les' greens and formed a mixture of death and sorrow, and the soggy grief soaked through his shirt to his chest.

The teenagers joined their mother, leeching themselves to both sides of Les—children without a father, and Tennet reached out his arms and embraced them. Then he remembered the child on the sofa. He looked over at him. The boy stared back. Les motioned for him to join the circle. He shook his head—just slightly, and remained glued in place. Les waved him over. The boy refused. A single tear dropped out of the kid's left eye. Les nodded. Okay, let the boy handle it his own way. He squeezed the trio in his arms a little tighter.

For interminable seconds they stayed there as if stuck together—an island of four in the center of the room and a little island of one by himself on the sofa.

Then, with a big sigh, the widow raised her smudged face

and Les smelled her death-saddened breath. "I know you did your best, doctor," she sobbed.

The look-alike daughter turned up to him too. "We prayed for you, Dr. Tennet. We prayed the Lord would help you as you took care of my dad. This must be the Lord's will."

Confused by her logic, Les lifted his arms off the grieving family and fell back a step, and his movement wiped out the web of intimacy that had briefly snared them all. The family stepped back too, suddenly realizing they were strangers to this man.

Les waited for them to turn and leave the room, but they didn't. Instead, they kept staring at him, as if waiting for some signal that it was time to go. But Les had no signal to give. So, he repeated the only words he could muster. "I'm sorry ma'am. I did everything I could . . . but he's gone."

Those words sealed him off. The widow turned to her offspring and they wrapped their arms around each other again and wept bitterly, and this time Les wasn't part of the circle. He glanced over at the boy on the sofa. The boy stared back at him, but said nothing. The tear on his left cheek had dried.

Les swiveled away and headed back to the operating room. He found Clara standing over the body.

"Clara?" Tennet asked, walking up behind her and draping his hands on her broad shoulders. "What was his name?"

Clara pivoted and looked at him hard. "Why you want to know, doc?"

"Don't ask me that, Clara. Just seems I should know who he is, that's all."

"You never wanted to know before," she cautioned. "Not till you knew they were out of the woods. You best leave it that way. This was a car accident that just died. Snowball. He didn't have a chance to live from the beginning. We all knew that. Everybody but you. You think they'll all make it, and with your help and the Lord's they usually do. But not this one. He ain't a man anymore. He's gone and you best not try to hold on to him too tight. Let him go now. That's the way you handle these things."

Les shook his head in confusion. "Maybe my way of handling things isn't the best way, Clara."

"Maybe not, but your way has taken you pretty far, Les Tennet. 'Fore you go changing those ways, you better make sure you got a better one waiting. You got that better way?"

Les pushed his hair off his forehead and felt some of it come loose in his hands. He stared at the strands of black in his palms. Ruefully, he rubbed it with his fingers. Hair loss. Part of the peril of getting older. He grunted. Hair wasn't the only thing falling away from him, he decided.

"Don't have any better way, Clara. Just can't go on with my way." He brushed the hair onto the floor and walked out.

Chapter Six

Her foot pushed harder and harder on the gas pedal and the speedometer slipped up higher and higher. Katherine had stormed away from Les, rushed Sherry to get dressed, and squealed the tires as she sped out of the driveway. Knowing she would need to talk privately with Mr. Stone, Katherine planned to leave Sherry with her parents. That meant she would have to endure her mother's interference, but she couldn't avoid it at this point. That was the price she paid for using a patrician know-it-all as a baby-sitter.

Approaching a sharp curve two miles from the gate to her parents' estate, Katherine slowed down and tried to control her breathing. She loosened her fingers on the steering wheel and forced herself to lean back in the seat. Trying to relax, she reached over and patted Sherry on the leg.

"You mad with Daddy?" Sherry turned her blue eyes on her and asked the question like the answer might really be in doubt.

Katherine tried to smile, but it turned out more like a grimace. "Yeah, baby, I'm mad with Daddy."

"Why?"

What innocence, Katherine thought. "It's hard to explain, Sher, so let's just say we had a disagreement." She patted Sherry on the leg again, trying to shift the conversation. Sherry would have none of it.

"Was it about the cat?"

"The what?" Katherine searched her mind but couldn't remember any cat.

"You know, the cat—you and Daddy always fight about the cat."

Katherine smiled. She and Les did fight about the cat. The cat they didn't own. The cat Les and Sherry wanted, but Katherine wouldn't let them have because she didn't want a cat scratching up her drapes and furniture.

"Yeah, baby, about the cat."

The answer apparently satisfied Sherry and she turned and stared out the window. Katherine only wished the problem was as simple as a nonexistent cat, but it wasn't. Nothing was that simple.

At the gate of the nine-acre Tillman Estate—Katherine's dad, Walter had flourished in his law practice over the years and had invested his earnings wisely—Katherine punched the electric eye and the black, iron gate swung open and let her enter. She wheeled up the curved drive, stopped the car, and hurried with Sherry into the two-story English Tudor house.

Beatrice met them in the kitchen and leaned forward, tilting her pointed chin downward, waiting for a kiss. She always did that, like a queen yielding herself to the demands of the common folk. Katherine knew Beatrice saw herself that way now—as queenly. She had for the last twenty-five years, or ever since Walter had won an acquittal for a cop-killer in the most sensationalized murder trial in St. Louis County in a decade. That case sent him to the top and the top made him wealthy and Beatrice parlayed the wealth into social standing. She dressed like an American queen—silver hair in a tight bun, diamonds on her fingers, gold on her ears, pearls, rubies or emeralds around her neck, and tasteful designer clothes adorning her body.

Katherine and Sherry dutifully pecked her on both cheeks. "Just got a minute, Mother," said Katherine. "Got to get to the school."

"Trouble with John?" Beatrice had good instincts.

"Afraid so."

"What is it this time? Ditching school again?"

Katherine turned to Sherry. "Why don't you go watch television for a moment, sweetheart. I need to talk to Grandmama." Sherry nodded and left the room. Katherine turned back to Beatrice.

"It's worse than ditching school, Mother. A lot worse."

"How much worse?"

Katherine really hated to say more, but knew she couldn't refuse. Her mother wouldn't let her do that; she would press and press until she squeezed the information out, and Katherine didn't have time to make her work for it. Besides, her emotions were running near the edge and she didn't have much strength left. She felt she was about to burst open with anger and she really didn't care much who knew.

"They found a gun in his locker."

Beatrice grabbed her slender throat like she was strangling. "A gun? Katherine, what's gotten into that boy?"

"I don't know, Mother, and I really don't have time to discuss it now. I'll come back as soon as I can and—"

"Where's Les?" interrupted Beatrice.

"I don't have the time, Mother," she said weakly. Beatrice spotted her weakness and plunged ahead to exploit it.

"At the hospital, I guess. Not with you, like he should be."

"No, Mother, he's not with me, he—"

Beatrice pushed her chin out and fired her best shot. "The man never is. Truth is you shouldn't have married him in the first place. It was a disgrace—you could have had any man in St. Louis, in Missouri, for that matter. Somebody with dignity and background." Beatrice paused and patted the back of her bunned hair, conveniently forgetting that neither she nor Walter had any background. As for dignity, well, seats on bank boards and designer dresses and hours of volunteer work can create a lot of dignity. Beatrice continued.

"Les is talented, I give him that, and he's worked hard. But he's from a family with no heritage. A drunk for a father. No mother at all. I don't think it's his fault, but he's an empty briefcase; nothing inside him but blank spaces. Am I right or wrong?" Beatrice stared at her accusingly.

"I don't have time, Moth—"

"Just tell me, am I right or wrong?" Beatrice pushed as usual and Katherine knew by her posture she wouldn't let up until she had an answer. Well, she didn't have time to argue and right now she wasn't sure Beatrice wasn't right.

"You're right. There, I've said what you wanted me to say. You were right all along. I blew it and my life's a mess and I don't know what to do about it."

Triumphantly, Beatrice patted her bun again. "I can tell you what you can do about it."

"What's that?"

"You can call a good divorce lawyer. I can get your father to do it today. You want me to do that for you?"

Katherine threw up her hands in surrender. "I don't care, Mother, I just don't care. Look, I've got to go. I'll see you as soon as I can."

She yelled a goodbye to Sherry and rushed out of the house. Fifteen minutes later she braked her Volvo, freshened up her makeup to hide the splotches under her eyes, and swooshed through the doors of Archway Academy and down the hall toward Mr. Stone's office. She knew the way—she'd been there scores of times since they'd pulled John from the public schools and entered him in the private academy two years ago. She'd been here not only because John had found himself in hot water with discipline problems more than once, but also because she served as the typical upper-class mom. She sold tickets for raffles, ran the refreshment stand at basketball games, and chaperoned dances.

Today, though, the familiar hallway seemed foreign to her, dangerous. She sensed John had crossed a line, a line that even her family name and Les' surgical successes wouldn't easily erase.

She bounded through the open doors of the office and spotted John's slouched form spilling over the edges of the chair outside the principal's door. Hurrying to him, she reached out and gently stroked his hair.

"You okay, son?"

"Never better," he replied, his lip curling up with his typical sarcasm. "What brought you here?"

"I think you can guess that," said Katherine, keeping her voice even.

John leaned over to look past her. "Dad come with you?"

"No, he had an emergency at the hospital. He'll catch up with us when I get you home."

John grunted but said nothing else. Katherine continued, "Mr. Stone said they found a gun in your locker."

"Yeah, they did. Hard to believe they can invade a person's privacy like that. Between classes they announced an inspection, and the next thing I knew one of Stone's secretaries was rummaging through my things. You'd think we lived in Russia or somewhere. But, hey, they don't even do that in Russia—"

"You're missing the point here, John. We're not discussing Russia. We're discussing you having a gun in your locker. Where in the world did you get it?"

"Mrs. Tennet?" Mr. Stone prevented John from answering as he pushed his rotund frame halfway out of his office and motioned her to enter.

She nodded to John. "You want John to wait or come with me?"

"He can wait," said Stone.

She turned to John. "You all right?"

"Never better."

With a grimace playing on her mouth, she left him and walked into Stone's office. The room seemed cramped to her today—cramped because Stone's bulbous frame swelled out in it and because a wad of smell, a cross between oily body odor and bubble gum, filled up every nook and cranny in it. Stone waved his fleshy hand. "Have a seat."

Katherine complied meekly, automatically assuming any resistance on her part would make things tougher on John. For
several seconds, Stone said nothing, Katherine watched him as
he stuck a piece of pink gum into his mouth and squeezed his
mammoth bottom into the metal chair behind his desk. She
knew the only reason an unkempt, overweight manipulator
like Stone kept his job was that his grandfather gave the school
close to $100,000 every year. Several times the school board
had discussed firing him, but no one knew how to make up
the money they would lose, and so he was still there.

He crumpled the gum with his teeth for a beat, then spoke
slowly. "We have what I call a head-scratcher, Mrs. Tennet.
You know what a head-scratcher is?"

She shook her head, noting the half-moons of perspiration
under his arms.

"I didn't think you would." He popped the gum and leaned
forward. His chair squeaked in protest. "So, let me explain it
to you. A head-scratcher is what you get when you don't
know exactly what to do with a given situation. You sit and
think about it and you scratch your head while you're thinking. That's what I've been doing this morning—scratching and
thinking. On the one hand, we don't want your boy in trouble. But, on the other hand, a gun *is* trouble, cop-calling trouble. The only choice we have is in how we report it."

He stopped and shifted in the chair. It groaned as he moved
his ponderous weight.

Katherine furrowed her eyebrows. "I don't follow you, Mr.
Stone. What choice is there in how you report it?"

"Well, it's like this. John's the top gun on our basketball
team and we're about halfway into the season. Got us a good
chance to win the state championship if he stays eligible. Plus,
he's an A student in the classes he likes. Add that to the fact
that you and your good husband contributed $15,000 to our
school's building fund last year and—"

Katherine held up her hand. "I get the picture. So, what
options do we have?"

Stone grinned and leaned back. He folded his meaty hands on his stomach. "Well, we can say we found the gun in an empty locker, or in the cafeteria, anywhere we want. Who's to know? No one gets hurt and John gets another chance. That suit you?"

"It's an offer I can't refuse," agreed Katherine, hating to owe Stone anything, but willing to sell him her soul if it kept her boy out of court. She started to pick up her purse and leave; but then, noticing Stone hadn't moved, she hesitated, sensing he wanted something more from her. He fulfilled her hunch.

"Uh, Mrs. Tennet, one more thing."

"Yes," she looked at him expectantly.

"Well, I hate to bring this up, but you see, it's like this. The car the school furnishes me is almost five years old now and I have a bad back and I really need something a little more conducive to smooth riding and we're a little short right now on the funds we need to buy a new one and I'm sure the trustees would really appreciate a donation—"

"How much, Mr. Stone?" Katherine asked it without visible emotion, though underneath her calm demeanor she wondered how much they could afford. She really didn't know. Les kept most of the family records—including the finances—to himself. Not that he wouldn't tell her if she asked. But so far, she had seen no reason to ask.

"Well, uh, I think $5,000 ought to make a good down payment, you know. The trustees could finish it out, so I have something comfortable for my back. Nothing extravagant, really, but helpful to my back."

Though the first hint of a gag pushed up in her throat, Katherine held it back. "I'll have the check made out to the school for a car. Is that agreeable?"

Stone lurched out of his chair with amazing speed for a man with a bad back and rushed over to shake her hand. "Wonderful, Mrs. Tennet, absolutely wonderful. It's tax deductible, you know, and I am so glad we could work this out in a mutually beneficial way. John has such a future and we certainly don't want to see anything interfere with that, and we don't want anything to smudge your husband's reputation."

Katherine offered him a limp wrist and quickly pulled away from his clammy touch. She felt dirty and wanted desperately to escape Stone's smelly office and find a place to calm herself. She hurried out. John, still sprawled in the corner of the outer office, raised up as she moved toward him.

"Let's go, John," she commanded, grabbing him by the shoulder.

"Through already?" he asked, standing to leave.

"Yes, we're finished."

John's eyes widened. "Really? Am I off the hook?"

"Yes, you are," Katherine said it simply, without explanation.

John punched his fists into the air like he'd just won the Super Bowl, but Katherine's harsh stare toned down his jubilation. "For *now* you're off the hook. At least with Stone. But I wouldn't predict what's going to happen with your dad. I don't want to go into it now, but when we get home you've got a lot of questions to answer."

John dropped his arms but didn't suppress the smirk on his face. He strutted down the hall, tagging after his mom like a puppy with a fresh bone.

They both were silent as they headed out I-70 toward the Tillman Estate.

Leaning his head against the seat, John grinned, happy to be going to Walter Tillman's house. Though Beatrice pretty much ignored him, old Walter liked to have him around. Walter talked to him a lot. Told him about his legal work. Took him quail hunting. Treated him with a little respect.

Though John didn't like to admit it even to himself, he liked Walter and not simply because he bought him things. Fact is, you'd never know Walter had money, except when he spent it on someone else.

Yeah, Beatrice hounded the old man into putting on airs sometimes; but except for when he worked, Walter preferred flannel shirts and blue jeans. Yeah, Walter was okay. Plus, he was rich and that didn't hurt. John figured if he played his cards right, he could get that new CD player he'd wanted for a while. And Walter would buy it for him, not because he was manipulated into it—John knew Walter understood the games he played—but because he wanted to do it.

John's grin widened. All in all, the day still held at least a bit of promise.

Chapter Seven

Dazed, Les slouched down the slick hallway and into the doctors' dressing room. He took a quick shower, slugged down a stiff drink from a brandy decanter he kept in his locker, and walked to the cafeteria. A few minutes later, after a meal of hospital eggs and pancakes, his mood had improved, but only slightly.

He had tried to call Katherine at the school to see about John, but two busy signals had rewarded his efforts. Secretly, he felt relieved. He didn't want to see Stone.

Now sitting in the cafeteria slurping a cup of coffee, he watched the green, blue, white, and tan-clad workers shift and stand and eat and talk and come and leave.

He thought about John and wondered what he could do to change the boy's attitude. John puzzled him and made him angry. John had everything he didn't have as a child. He had a father who never raged at him or hit him or cursed him. He had wealth aplenty and opportunities to do anything he wanted.

But John didn't appreciate the blessings Les and Katherine provided for him. Instead, he seemed to go out of his way to embarrass them, like a ten-year-old sticking out his tongue and defying them to do anything about it.

Les had tried everything. Indulgence—a red Jeep Cherokee

last year for Christmas. Threats—the Cherokee would go if he
didn't straighten out. Man-to-man talks—"Son, why don't you
accept some responsibility?" Counseling—six sessions in the
past year. Nothing worked. Instead, everything got worse, a
train bearing toward a cliff, its bell clanging destruction to
those on board. Les and Katherine heard the warning but neither had figured out a way to turn the train around.

A slap on the back stirred Les out of his reverie. He swiveled and looked up into the flat eyes of Dr. Ned List, the chief
of staff of St. Louis Medical. He always thought that List's
eyes looked as if they had been painted on cardboard, using
pale gray on starry white. Nothing behind those eyes.

List spoke as he threw his leg over an orange seat, mounting
it. "Heard you lost one a little while ago."

Les grunted, affirming the report.

"Want to talk about it?" asked List.

"Not really. Nothing much to say. A suture busted and he
drowned in his own blood."

List lowered his eyes and his voice. "You say anything to
anybody about what caused it?"

"No, nobody to tell. Besides, I don't know what caused it."

"Good. Keep it that way. I've already asked the others in
the operating room to keep what happened to themselves. No
use this getting back to the dead man's family." List bent
toward Tennet. "Look, I know how hard you take failure, Les.
But nobody believes this was your fault. A hundred things
could cause that suture to break. You probably kept him alive
hours longer than he deserved anyway." List paused, waiting
for a response.

Les waited too, trying to decide whether to get up and leave
or to answer. He heard the clock ticking on the wall above
him. Finally, he spoke. "Ned, if nobody believes it was my
fault, then you wouldn't even need to say it. I know how the
system works. You and I and everyone else in this business are
only as good as our last surgery. Save ten lives and you're just
doing your job. Lose one, maybe because you screwed up,

maybe not, maybe because you're human and have other things on your mind, screw up one time and they're looking for ways to nail your backside to the wall. So don't give me that 'Nobody thinks it's your fault' routine. Everyone in that room, except Clara, thinks it was my fault."

Les paused, letting the dust of his anger settle. His voice lowered. "I also know why you're concerned. You're worried the family will sue me and the hospital for malpractice. Well, you can rest at ease over that one. That poor widow and her kids would never think of such a thing. Can you believe it, the daughter said it must be 'God's will.' If it's God's will, then it can't exactly be my fault, can it? If God caused it, then I'm not to blame."

List chuckled, obviously taking his prize surgeon's anger in stride. "I like that, Les. It's all God's will. I like that a lot. Maybe we can use that as a defense at our next malpractice suit."

The two men sat staring at each other. Then Ned picked up Les' coffee cup and took a swallow. He grimaced at the taste of the cold liquid and set the cup back down, rocked his chair again, back this time, and locked his hands behind his head. "When you save one, there's nothing like it in the whole world, is there, Les?"

Les leaned his chair back too and agreed, though grimly. "Absolutely nothing." Then he grinned. "Saving a life is better than sex."

"How so?" asked List, a look of amusement playing on his lips.

"Think about it. Almost anybody can have sex. But you're one of the few people on earth who can hold a heart in your hands and make it live again. Plus, sex happens more often, and everyone knows what's rare is more precious than what's frequent."

List roared his approval and rocked up from his chair to leave. "Neither of the two happens often enough when you get my age, Les." He patted Les on the back. "Look, friend,

you lost one. It happens to everybody, more often to some
than others. But no one gets through life with a perfect record.
Not even you."

"I don't know if I can accept that."

"You'd better learn how," said Ned, getting up and walking
away.

Les waited until List was gone, then stood to leave. At the
register to pay for his meal, he pulled a twenty from his wallet
and cursed under his breath as the girl at the counter walked
off to get change. Drumming his fingers on the counter, he
waited. And waited. He pulled a toothpick from the container
by the register. Still no waitress. Remembering the envelope
he'd slipped into his back pocket as he left the house, he pulled
it out and opened it. The words on the sheet jumped out at
him and shook his 200-pound frame. His knees almost
buckled.

FROM: U.S. ARMY RESERVE UNIT 804.
TO: MAJOR LESLEY EUGENE TENNET.
REGARDING: CALL-UP FOR SERVICE IN THE
    PERSIAN GULF.
REPORTING DATE: DECEMBER 27, 1991.
REPORTING LOCATION: GATE 37.
    LAMBERT FIELD AIRPORT.
ST. LOUIS. MISSOURI

"Doctor?"

Tennet blinked numbly as the checkout girl returned and
spoke to him.

"Here's your change," she said.

Mumbling a superficial, "Thank you," Tennet took the
money and stumbled out of the cafeteria.

Chapter Eight

When he saw Katherine's blue Volvo sitting beside John's jeep in the garage, Les' heart dropped. He had hoped they wouldn't be home yet. He parked and got out quietly, wondering why he felt like he needed to sneak into his own home. He walked quietly into the den and over to the glass-encased liquor cabinet. The sound of voices from the bedroom seeped through the walls, but no one called out to him. Good. They hadn't heard him drive up. He had time for a drink.

He uncapped the brandy and fortified himself with two quick shots of the warm liquid. So braced, he stepped into the bedroom. Sweat broke out on his back as he saw them—Katherine perched on the edge of the canopied bed and John slouched in a reading chair, his right leg slung across the arm of the wingback. Conversation dried up as he entered.

Les nodded to Katherine first. "Where's Sherry?"

"She's at the Y, taking her swim class, like usual on Monday afternoon."

Satisfied, Les moved toward John and placed his right hand on the boy's shoulders, "You okay, John?"

"Yeah, why wouldn't I be?" John pushed Les' hand away and threw his left leg onto the chair's arm. The strings of his black basketball shoes dangled down the side of the chair. Les' face flushed and a thick drop of perspiration crawled to the

edge of his nose. He wiped it away, then clenched and unclenched his fingers, struggling to push back the fury roaring
inside him. Les kept his voice controlled.

"What happened at school today?"

"Nothing that concerns you."

"Everything that happens to you concerns me."

John grinned and it was horrible. "Not hardly, dear old Dad.
You get concerned when my actions reflect badly on you. If I
embarrass you, then you punish me and treat me like scum. If
I stay quiet and out of trouble, you figure that's what I owe
you and you take me for granted. So don't tell me how concerned you are."

The sweat on Les pumped harder now, down his back and
around his knees. He was afraid to argue, afraid he couldn't
control the rage building in him. He pressed to the point.

"What were you doing with a gun?"

"Protecting myself."

"From what?"

John almost snarled. "Why don't you unfreeze your brain,
Dad? For a guy who's supposed to be so smart, you're pretty
dense. You got no clue what happens to me every day and I
doubt you even care, so why don't you give up the pretense?
The hypocrisy doesn't become you. You're the most superficial human being I've ever met and—"

Without realizing what he was doing, Les suddenly raised
his right arm and it coiled back and around his neck like a
slingshot and all the anger of his thirty-nine years rushed to
the knuckles of his fist and perched there, eager to punch
holes in human skin.

John saw the movement, but it didn't stop his tirade. His
eyes glinted, as if he realized that he had pushed his father to
the edge. "You're absolutely useless as a father, and as far as
I'm concerned you can bag your concern along with your
cheap efforts to buy my good behavior."

John paused and waited, apparently expecting Les to hit
him. Instead, Les unclenched his fingers and dropped his arm

to his sides. It wasn't that he didn't want to hit John. In that instant, he wanted to strike back, to hurt the boy like John had hurt him. But he also felt compassion. He wanted to offer comfort, to defang John with a father's love, and he didn't know how. His dad had never taught him. Beaten, he sagged down onto the bed beside Katherine.

"John, I don't know what to say to you," he mumbled. "We've given you everything to try to reach you. Why do you keep hurting us?"

John snorted. "Dad, that's so lame it doesn't even deserve an answer. At least you could be more original."

"Originality is not what's important to me right now, John. Helping you is."

"I'm not the one who needs help, Dad."

"What does that mean?"

John's brow furrowed. He dropped his eyes and stared at his hands. Hands just like his father's, long and thin and strong. Hands to palm a basketball or a scalpel. John looked like he wanted to cry but wouldn't allow it. But he did back off his anger.

"It's you who needs help, Dad," he whispered. "Not me."

Les suddenly felt confused, confused because John's words opened up unhealed wounds, wounds slashed into him by his own father. Confused because he had spoken similar words to his dad over twenty years ago after a beating. It was the last beating he allowed his father to give him, a beating wallowing in the smell of beery breath and stale cigarettes, a beating given because he had refused to bring another beer from the refrigerator to his already stuporous father.

His dad had whipped him down, had knocked him to the floor with the handle of a mop, and Les had curled up with his hands over his head to protect himself from the blows raining down on him.

Only when the mop handle splintered into three jagged pieces did the beating stop. Then, his exhausted father had collapsed onto the sofa.

Stunned, but not bowed, Les had pulled himself up from the floor and glared down at his drunken father. Through bloody lips, he whispered, "Dad, you need help, but I can't give it to you. I wish I could, but I can't. But you need to know one thing. You will never hit me again. If you do, I'll kill you."

He had walked out of the room then, a grown man not by choice but by necessity. Not a great way to live, but at least he had survived.

Les had wanted more than that for his son, but he didn't know how to give it to him.

"John," he said gently, "you may be right. Maybe I am the one who needs help. But I'll have to decide that myself. Not you. And not your mom. And not anyone else."

Les glanced at Katherine. "Honey, I'll be at Patrick's Place. I need some time to think."

Katherine looked as if she wanted to speak, to ask him to stay home, to talk with her, to work things out. But she said nothing. Les walked out. Alone again.

Section Two

To leave is to die a little;
it is to die to what one loves.
One leaves behind a little of oneself,
at any hour, any place.

Edmond Haraucourt

Chapter Nine

Les threw his feet over the side of the bed and rubbed his eyes. Quietly, so as not to wake anyone else, he walked over to the window and looked out at the skin of snow that covered the sidewalk leading up to his front door. The sun was out, but it was weak and sickly. Les didn't know how cold it was, but the weather forecast called for a high of 8°F. The icicles hanging like glass daggers off the corners of the house gave evidence that the forecast had proven correct so far.

He shivered and ran his eyes down the street. Nothing moved. No cars. No people. No pets. It was Christmas Day and a sheen of snow lay on the ground as all the world kept silence.

Almost two weeks had passed since Snowball's death and since the school had called about John and the gun. As promised, Mr. Stone had handed the weapon to the cops, telling them that he found it in an empty locker.

Since then Les and Katherine and John had settled into an uneasy truce, the kind that happens when everyone involved realizes that the only alternative is mutual destruction. Les, though, had found the cold war terribly unsatisfying and he knew the others felt the same. But walls were walls and it wasn't easy to tear them down.

Now it was Christmas and he had only today and tomorrow

left at home. Then it was time to ship out to Saudi Arabia. His orders to go weren't totally unexpected, but they still shocked him. He had hoped his status at the hospital would keep him out of the buildup President Bush had ordered in the Gulf, but these were new days in the military and your turn meant your turn. No deferments.

He hadn't told Katherine immediately after getting the orders. After the episode with John, he hadn't wanted to pile anything else on her. Plus, Katherine seemed more distant every day, getting colder as the calendar moved deeper into winter. Les kept waiting for a good moment, when they were at least civil with each other.

The moment hadn't come quickly. Not until ten days after he received his assignment to Saudi. . . .

On the day he shared the news with her, he came home from the hospital about 6 P.M.—at least two hours earlier than normal. They shared a quiet dinner—not intimate, but at least not stormy. He and John tossed no verbal darts at each other, Sherry didn't spill anything, and Katherine didn't make him feel guilty even once. It wasn't the Waltons, but for the Tennets it had to do.

After putting Sherry to bed and checking in on John, Les headed to the bedroom to relax and read. Katherine joined him. A few minutes later, as they lay beside each other, he broke the news.

"Kath, I've got to tell you something."

She froze instantly, knowing from the tone of his voice to pay attention. "I'm listening," she said.

Les sat up in bed and looked at her. "I've been ordered to Saudi Arabia with my unit."

He waited for a response. She gave none.

"Did you hear me?" he asked.

"Yes," she nodded her head slowly. "I heard you."

"Then why didn't you respond?"

"I don't know," she said. "The whole thing seems so remote. I know we're building up troops in the Middle East, but why you? You're a doctor!"

"And I'm in the Reserve, Kath. They need doctors. If this thing comes to war—and it looks more and more like it will, then trauma surgeons are at the top of the necessary list. In a way, I'm surprised I didn't get called sooner."

Katherine pushed her left hand into her mouth and nibbled at the nail on her index finger. Les waited on her.

She finally asked, "Any way to get out of it?"

"I haven't tried," said Les.

"Why not?"

"Because they're making no exceptions. Can't give deferments like they did in Vietnam. We're all volunteers these days. When I joined ROTC and the military paid for my college education and med school, I became obligated. And rightly so."

He slid back down into the covers, the worst of the announcement over.

"When do you have to leave?" She finished the index finger and started on the middle one.

"December 27."

No explosion. *Good*, thought Les.

"How long have you known?"

Bad question.

"Oh, ten days or so."

She peeled the top of the nail from the middle finger and dropped it into a trash can by the bed. "You didn't think I'd want to know before this?"

"Sure you would, but I wanted time to think before I told you."

"Time to think about what?"

Les gulped, paused a blink, then spewed it out. "About us, where we're going, what this means for us."

"What do you think it means?" she asked timidly, starting on her thumbnail.

"Ten days isn't enough to figure that out."

Katherine fell silent again.

Les waited for the explosion, expecting her to chastise him, make him feel guilty.

Katherine stayed quiet and Les allowed the conversation to end. He turned over and pretended to sleep. She finished her nails and left him alone.

That night had passed and other nights followed it and they made it through them all, even as the space between them on the bed seemed to widen and now they had only two days to go before he left. . . .

Now, Christmas Day had dawned. Les twirled away from the window and gazed over at Katherine, still asleep. Though their estrangement seemed worse every hour, he wanted to make this a good day for her and the children. He owed them one final pleasant day. Funny how he thought of the day as final.

With sudden inspiration, he hurried into the kitchen and hauled out the pots and pans and went to work.

Almost an hour later, Katherine opened her eyes and stretched. The smell of scrambled eggs, bacon and coffee brought her to instant attention. "Les?"

"In here," he called from down the hall.

"Whatcha doing?"

"Don't worry about it. Stay where you are. I'll be there in a sec."

Katherine sat up and raised her eyebrows. She guessed what he was doing and it confused her. With their marriage suffering so terribly, she didn't want him doing anything nice for her before he left for Saudi. Her frustration had reached the point where she had taken her mother's advice and had contacted a divorce lawyer. She thought she owed it to Les to tell him about it before he left. But, then again, she didn't want to send him away to war with such bad news as his last memory of her.

She sighed, listening to him in the kitchen. With him absent for months, she supposed the tension couldn't help but ease. If he didn't come back . . . well, that would mean she would never have to tell him. She would wait.

"Can I help you?" she said.

"No, don't move. I'm on the way."

A couple of minutes later, Les pranced into the room carrying a tray loaded with food. In the center of the tray stood a clear vase holding a silk rose. He placed the tray on the bed in front of her, bowed and said, "Major Les Tennet at your service, ma'am. Enjoy." Then, without another word, he turned and left the room.

Within seconds she heard him banging more plates, getting breakfast for the children.

Outside, the icy air gripped the world with frozen fingers, but inside a momentary thaw warmed Katherine's spirit. She wanted to smile, but her fear refused to let her do it. She'd seen thaws before, but something had always frozen them again.

Chapter Ten

Christmas morning passed quickly into afternoon and afternoon easily yielded to dusk. The sun, tired since the beginning of the day, offered almost no resistance to the shadows. Darkness covered the white snow and lights blinked on in the Tennet house.

Nothing had spoiled their good day. No emergency messages had called Les away to the hospital. No incident had sparked an argument. The family had exchanged gifts lovingly, especially enjoying Sherry's excited squeals as she ripped open package after package from under the tree.

For the first time in months, everyone stayed home all day, soaking up the feeling of togetherness like desert travelers relishing cold water.

After dinner, each split off to their separate interests for a few minutes—John to his room to listen to music, Sherry to the den to play with her new dolls, and Katherine to the bedroom to try on a dress Les had given her that morning.

Les climbed the stairs and pulled down the retractable steps that led to the attic. The heat from the fireplace below drifted up and warmed him as he bent down to enter the storage space.

Flipping on a light switch, he edged to the corner of the dusty room and sat down on an old stool beside a rectangular trunk. As black as a vampire's cloak, the trunk lay like a mammoth coffin on the beamed floor; a padlock the size of a fist kept its contents a secret from everyone but Les. His fingers shaking, Les tugged a six-inch long key from his pocket and inserted it into the lock. As he twisted the key, the lock fell open. He slipped the key back into his pocket.

Raising himself off the stool and getting a good grip on the lid of the trunk, Les lifted off the top of the scarred box. Dust flew through the air, making him want to sneeze.

A hand touched him on the shoulder. Startled, he slammed the lid of the trunk down and twisted around. Katherine stood behind him.

"Whatcha doing?" she asked.

Les choked out a breath. "Nothing much. Just going through some old things."

Katherine peered past him to the trunk, and Les thought for a second about opening it for her inspection. He had brought it with him when they were married, but he'd never shown her its contents and she'd never asked to see. He opened it only on rare occasions—the night he finished med school, the day he saved the governor's life, the nights John and Sherry were born, the day the doctor told them Sherry would never be normal.

The trunk held its secrets like he did, and though he wanted more than anything else to show her its contents, he knew he couldn't. Not yet. Maybe someday. Until then, she'd have to wait.

She waited now, but Les ignored her interest in the trunk. "I'll be down in a minute," he said, discouraging her from staying longer.

She nodded her head, said, "All right," and walked out. He couldn't tell if she was mad or not.

Alone again, Les lifted the lid and peered inside his treasure chest. He pulled up his stool and sagged down on it so he could get to the contents in the trunk.

On top of the stack of well-organized mementos lay his

letter sweater from Lindberg High. He held it up and fingered the golden ornaments hanging on the left side—three in the shape of a football, two for soccer, and three more for basketball. The sounds of cheering crowds echoed from the trunk and Les swelled with pride at the memories.

He wasn't sure what drove him to this trunk on those rare occasions when he opened it, but something always directed him to what he needed when he came. Today, he trusted the same would happen if he searched.

Laying the sweater aside, he picked through the other icons housed in his temple. Old yearbooks. Diplomas from high school and college and med school. Pictures of him from his first birthday and upward. Letters from friends, and plaques and trophies he had won.

The family Bible. Les shook his head as he picked up the weighty book. His mom had inherited it from her mother. And her mom from hers. He opened it and saw the family tree his great-grandmom had traced on the front page, from the late 1700s all the way down to his family. Then his mom had died and the tree had grown no more branches.

Les started to keep the Bible out, then decided against it. He wasn't sure what to do with it anyway. Its mysteries were too abstract for him. He liked what he could see and touch and handle with his hands, and it seemed the Bible described too many airy things like angels' wings and unseen demons. And all that Jesus stuff. Les had watched people die, and he knew they could come back from the dead—but not after three days. No, not even a surgeon as good as he could start a heart again from that distance. He tossed the Bible back into the corner of the trunk.

What he was waiting for happened when he saw his baseball cards, a collection of over 5,000 he had bought between his third and twelfth years. No one knew he owned this stack of cards, their covers graced with the images of Willie Mays and Mickey Mantle, and scores of other heroes and would-be heroes. He picked up a stack and flipped through them, reading the statistics on the back and smiling at the memories of the joy this hobby gave him as a child. He had never shown anyone these cards and he suddenly wondered why he had kept them a secret.

In a split second, he made a decision. He wanted someone to see these cards, to see them and know he had once lived like any boy—full of childish dreams.

Les didn't want to leave these signposts to his boyhood in a trunk any longer. He would give these cards to John before he left.

Consumed now that he knew why he'd opened the trunk, he peeled anxiously through the relics, digging deeper into the stack of treasures, looking for gifts for Sherry and Katherine. Then he found it. The perfect gift for Sherry. It lay like the virgin snow outside, white and glistening. Lovingly, Les rubbed his hand across its silky surface and, for a second, experienced the wonder of a pair of matching tears threatening to climb to the corners of his eyes.

His mother's wedding dress. For Sherry, because she would never wear one herself. Because she kept the visible image of his mother constantly before his eyes. Because Sherry was pure and soft and virginal and because nothing could ever change that.

Les pulled the dress from the trunk and held it up to his cheek. Though he knew it wasn't possible, he smelled the pale fragrance of the perfume his mother always wore. The thought that she had worn it on her wedding day, and that this dress still held her scent, made the threat of tears stronger; the threat of tears scared him and he laid the dress aside and turned his thoughts to Katherine.

What could he give to her? A picture of him from high school? No, she'd met him right after that. Nothing worthy there. His diplomas? No, they would remind her of his work and that wasn't a popular subject since it robbed them of time for each other.

He scrambled through the trunk feverishly, upsetting the

careful order he kept in it, waiting for revelation, searching for insight, but gaining none. Desperate now, he leaned back on his stool and racked his brain. He had to give her something or he couldn't give the others anything. He would have to leave his family and go to war and maybe die and leave nothing of significance behind.

In a blink, it came to him. He knew what Katherine would want most of all. Could he give it to her? Sure, he could, on one condition . . . if she promised to use it only if he died. That would solve all of his problems. He would give it to her if she gave him her promise. He reached into his pocket and pulled it out. He held it up to the glare of the bare light bulb in the attic. The key to the trunk. She could have it . . . if he died.

Chapter Eleven

The jarring ring of the phone prodded Les out of his sleep the next morning. He picked it up quickly, hoping it wouldn't wake Katherine, but it already had. With his other hand, he reached over and stroked her hair as he answered. They had spent a wonderful night together, the best he could remember in a long time, a night of seasoned passion that carried them back to the early days of their marriage. Maybe his leaving could somehow bring them together again. Nothing else had helped.

"Hello," he muttered into the phone, mildly upset at having to wake up and start the day and ruin the spell the evening had cast over him.

"Les? Ned here."

Les raised up in bed at the sound of his boss' voice.

"What's up, Ned?"

"I'm not sure yet, but I think we've got a problem brewing. Remember the guy you operated on a couple of weeks ago, the guy in the car accident who didn't make it?"

"Sure, Ned, I remember," said Les, tightening his grip on the phone. "How could I forget?"

"Well, his family is going to file a malpractice suit against you and the hospital."

Les ground his teeth to match his grip on the phone. "That

doesn't make sense, Ned. They aren't the type. Remember, they're the ones who said it was God's will. We laughed about it in the cafeteria."

"Yeah," grunted Ned, "we did, but I'm not laughing now and neither should you. Unfortunately for us, the guy who died has a brother-in-law who's a lawyer, and he's not as trusting of the Almighty as that dear wife and her kids."

"So the brother-in-law talked the wife into the suit?"

"It appears so, my friend. I spoke to her on the phone a few minutes ago, and she said it didn't seem right to let a wrong go unpunished. So she's filing the suit with her brother-in-law as the attorney."

Les shook his head. He should have known. One mistake and his career could go down the tubes. No matter that he'd done his best. No matter that he'd probably given the man a chance to live, when few others could have done even that. None of it mattered. Doctors were supposed to be infallible. No room for error.

"I'll be there in about an hour, Ned."

"Okay, man. Sorry to call you away from your family on your last day home, but we've got to go over strategy."

"Sure thing, Ned. See you in a few minutes."

He hung up the phone and turned to Katherine. Her eyes were opened wide.

"You heard?" he asked.

"Yeah, I heard," she said sadly. "And I understand you need to go. But it doesn't seem fair. Your last day and you don't even get to spend it with us."

"I know," he said. "But whoever said life was fair?"

He rolled over and picked up his pants lying in a chair beside the bed. Lifting them from the chair, he fumbled inside the pockets until he located the key to the trunk in the attic. Then he leaned back to Katherine. She lay still beside him, clutching her pillow to her chest, looking frail and frightened.

"I want to give you something before I go," he said. "I might not get back from the hospital until late tonight and I won't have much time in the morning. So, I want to give this to you now."

He held the key up in the air. "Do you recognize this?"

"Yes," she said a little fearfully. "It's the key to your trunk."

Les paused briefly, then flipped it like a coin into the air and caught it as it tumbled down. "Well, Kath," he said, "I'm going to give it to you if you'll make me one promise."

Katherine dreaded the promise, knowing she wouldn't like the condition, but also knowing she had no choice but to accept it. "All right," she said. "What's the promise?"

He twisted to her and stared into her blue eyes. "You won't use it unless I'm dead."

She blinked but said nothing.

"Did you hear me?"

"Sure, Les," she said, her eyes filling up and her exasperation building to a cresting point. "But what kind of promise is that? What good will the key to an old trunk do me if you're dead?"

"I don't know, Kath, but there's something about that trunk that always helps me when I'm struggling. Somehow I think it might help you if anything happens to me. I really can't explain it to you. You've just got to trust me on this. If I die, you can open the trunk."

A look of frustration crossed her face as she heard the condition, and she turned belligerent. "What if you live, Les? Can I ever see into it if you live?"

"I can't answer that, Kath," Les said gently. "If I live, who knows what will happen? Maybe my absence will give us both time to make some decisions. Maybe it'll help us get a handle on what we want out of life. Maybe it'll rekindle the spark we've lost. You know what they say, 'Absence makes the heart grow fonder.' "

She shrugged, his words obviously failing to comfort her. "They also say, 'Out of sight, out of mind.' "

"We'll have to wait and see which way it goes with us, won't we," said Les, unyielding.

Both of them fell silent. The clock ticked off, second after precious second, seconds neither of them had to waste. Les reached out and gathered Katherine in his arms and pulled her to him.

"Will you promise?"

Knowing she would never see inside the trunk if she didn't, Katherine yielded. "I promise," she said.

He handed her the key then and he hugged her tighter; but the condition made her feel shut out even more, and she stiffened her shoulders. He felt the message and he let go of her and slid out of bed.

Chapter Twelve

The day at the hospital passed quickly. Les hustled straight to List's office the second he arrived. For two hours they plotted their course of action in regard to the malpractice complaint. They agreed on a threefold strategy. First, they would stall. With the accused doctor serving his country in the Middle East, no one would likely take any action until he returned. "Hey, you might stay gone long enough for the statute of limitations to run out," joked Ned, obviously trying to cover his anxiety with humor. "And when you come back, you'll be a hero."

"*If* we fight a war and win it," cautioned Les.

"And *if* you live through it," said Ned. "But, as I see it, the hospital wins either way. If you die, it would be downright un-American to bring a case against a dead hero."

"If I die, go ahead and let my insurance company pay up," deadpanned Les. "The higher malpractice rates and suspended license won't matter much at that point."

"Good idea," agreed Ned.

"What happens if we have no war and I'm home by February?" asked Les, moving toward seriousness again.

"Then we go with our second strategy. We prove the man didn't have a chance from the beginning. You kept him alive when no one else could. We have plenty of people who will

swear to your gifts as a surgeon. We'll call in the ex-governor
if we need him."

"Will a strategy of telling what I did in the past prove I
didn't screw up in the present?" asked Les, unconvinced he
could get off that easily.

"Not necessarily. But it can't hurt. Competence makes malpractice hard to prove. Plus, your surgical team will swear you
did everything you could have done. That's the third line of
defense. The eyewitnesses in the room with you who know
you did your job."

"We're in good shape then?" asked Les.

"Yeah, nothing to worry about. Just go on over to Saudi,
get yourself a tan, then head back. We'll take care of things for
you here."

The two stood to leave. Ned patted Les on the back. "If
nothing else helps, we can always use the 'God's will' defense,"
he said.

Les tried to laugh but failed. He shook List's hand and
trudged out, headed toward his own office. He spent the balance of the day there, finishing a stack of paperwork on his
desk and saying goodbye to his staff as they stopped in to see
him off. He kept waiting for Clara to poke her head into the
door, but she didn't. The hours sped past and now it was
almost 6 and he still hadn't seen her.

Unwilling to leave without telling her goodbye, he closed
his desk and left the office to find her. It took almost thirty
minutes of paging, but he finally located her at the nurse's
station by the surgical unit. Scared of the emotions surging up
in him, he tried to keep it professional.

"Clara, I've reassigned all my patients, but I'll expect you to
make sure the doctors properly care for them."

Clara rolled her dark eyes up from the computer terminal
she'd been studying. "I'll do the best I can, doctor," she nodded, "but no one can care for them like you."

Les wasn't sure if Clara was being sarcastic or genuine. She
had a way of confusing him. Awkwardly, the two stood and

looked at each other for several seconds. Then, not wanting to leave her, Les stepped past the partition separating them.

"I'll miss you, Clara," he said, dropping his eyes to the floor.

"Don't go getting mushy on me, Les," Clara said.

"Not mushy, Clara, just honest. You've kept me going lots of times when no one else could."

"Don't flatter me. And don't lie to yourself. You don't need someone else to keep you going. You got something burning inside you that keeps you going. You got a fire in you that burns hot like dry wood, and not but a few people have that kind in them. That's the only way you've made it to where you are."

Les opened his arms and walked to her. She stood from her chair. He wrapped her stocky body in a strong embrace and patted her on her broad back. "That fire scares me sometimes, Clara."

Laying her head on his shoulders, Clara squeezed him back.

"I know, doc, I know," she whispered. "You're scared the fire that keeps you alive will burn up the people in your life who get too close. That should scare you. What you got to learn is this—your fire won't burn the people who love you. Let them step inside the fire. Fire can warm us without burning us, if we control it."

"That's hard to do, Clara."

"I know, doc, I know. But you can do it. I know you can." She rubbed his back between his shoulders. "Now get on out of here, Les. Go home to Kath. She needs you. I already got me a man." He laughed and unwrapped his arms from her shoulders, hating to let go of the strength she gave him.

"See you soon, Clara," he said, pivoting to leave.

"You bet you will, doc. I'll be waiting in the operating room for you."

An hour later, Les was home. It was almost 7 o'clock. He found Katherine busy in the kitchen. "Where are the kids?" he asked, pouring himself a cup of coffee.

"In their rooms," she answered, not glancing up from her work.

"I'm going to the study," he said. "Need to get some things in order for you before I leave."

She nodded and he bounded upstairs to his study and started making notes. The location of his will. A printout of their financial status, with account numbers and amounts clearly available to her on the pad. The phone number of their accountant. The keys to the safety deposit box. Another hour passed as he worked.

Working intently, he didn't notice the sound of the doorbell when it first rang. But, as it continued, he looked up from the keyboard. No one downstairs answered it. Though not pleased with the interruption, he finally gave up waiting on someone else, ran down the stairs and opened the front door.

The frigid air slammed into him and he gasped, but he wasn't sure if it was from the cold or not. A baldheaded man with a frayed, brown derby swinging on his index finger stood on his front stoop.

"Dr. Tennet?" said the man.

"That's me," Les nodded. "What can I do for you?"

The man proceeded efficiently. "Dr. Tennet, I'm Lieutenant Tom Clemons." He perched his hat on his head for a second as he pulled his ID out of his pocket and flashed it. "May I come in for a minute?"

Nervously, Les stepped back and allowed Clemons to enter. The two walked into the den and Katherine joined them, wrapping a sweater around her shoulders as she entered the room. "What's going on, Les?" she asked.

"I'm not sure, yet," he said, "but I expect Lieutenant Clemons will tell us shortly." He motioned the man to sit down and all three took chairs. Les reached out for Katherine's hand.

Clemons took off his hat, placed it under his right arm, and rubbed his hands together as if anticipating the opening of a much-awaited gift. His lips curled downward into an exaggerated frown. "I hate to bring bad news so soon after Christmas, but it can't be avoided. A few weeks ago Mr. Bill Stone, the headmaster of Archway Academy, called in to report a .38 pistol found at his school. Said he found it in an empty locker."

Clemons rolled his eyes, and Les digested what he had said. He watched Clemons pull his hat from under his arm and twirl it on his index finger. For some reason he couldn't grasp yet, Les sensed the cop was enjoying his job.

Licking his lips, Clemons continued. "Obviously, we were curious about the weapon, wanting to know how it got in the locker, if a student had anything to do with it, you know, the usual questions. Anyway, the piece lay around for a couple of weeks in a plastic bag, it being the holiday season and everybody being busy and all, until we had a chance to run its numbers through the computers."

He paused again.

Les bit his lower lip, anticipating Clemons' next words.

"When we ran the numbers we made an interesting discovery. The gun came from a pawnshop on Kirkwood Road."

Les jumped at the straw. "So? Nothing wrong with someone buying a gun from a pawnshop."

Clemons twirled his hat again, and Les knew he was enjoying the discomfort his words caused. "No, sir," he said. "Nothing at all wrong with that. But, and here's the tough part, this .38 wasn't bought. It was stolen, along with three more firearms and over $1,000 worth of other merchandise."

Clemons stopped and stared first at Katherine and then at him. Les stood up and spun around as if looking for a way out of the room. Finding no escape, he turned to face the accuser.

"So you're saying a student stole it from this pawnshop?"

"Not necessarily, doctor. A student might have bought it from the one who stole it. Or, he could have found it on a playing field, for all we know. We don't know exactly how it turned up in this locker. That's why we went back to Stone. To find out if he knew anything else about this weapon."

Katherine, silent so far through the exchange, spoke softly. "Obviously, Stone remembered something he hadn't told you before."

"Obviously," said Clemons, rolling the word slowly off his tongue. "The fact that it was stolen caused Mr. Stone to remember they hadn't actually found the .38 in an unassigned locker. Besides, there's one more twist to the saga of this shooter." He paused once more.

Watching the man toying with them, Les wanted to punch him.

"What's that twist?" asked Katherine.

"Three days after it disappeared from the pawnshop, it was used in a shooting in East St. Louis. A high school kid over there got popped after a football game as he walked to his car. This gun Stone found in your son's locker is a murder weapon."

Les and Katherine froze. The tick of the clock over the mantle seemed to grow louder. Clemons spun his hat on his finger. After ten ticks, Les spoke quietly, "No way was John involved with a killing."

Clemons coughed. It sounded like a muffled laugh of derision. "Well, I'm not saying he was and I'm not saying he wasn't. But you can see why we need to take him downtown for a chat. At the least, he either bought a stolen weapon or found one and didn't report it. In the middle, he stole it himself and he's looking at a first offender status—a trial for grand larceny, and probably probation. At worst—"

Les cut him off. "Spare us the rest, officer. We can imagine the worst ourselves."

"I expect so," agreed Clemons. "Can I see the boy?"

"I'll get him," said Katherine. She padded out of the room and up the steps, leaving Clemons and Les to stare at each other.

"Would you like a cup of coffee?" asked Les, trying to control his anger.

"Why not?" said Clemons.

The two men headed for the kitchen. Les busied himself with the water and waited for Katherine to come back with John. Clemons sat down and placed his hat on the table.

The seconds stretched out like miles of telephone wire as Les worked on the coffee. He wondered what was taking so long, why Katherine hadn't brought John down yet. Then, he heard one set of footsteps descending the stairs—Katherine's. Alarmed, he turned and saw Katherine standing there, dead in her tracks, with a glazed stare on her face.

"John's gone," she said blankly.

Chapter Thirteen

Clemons reacted quickly to their futile search. "I'll have to put out an APB for him," he said, scribbling notes on a yellow pad he'd produced from his shirt pocket. "Plus, I'm going to need a list of all his friends, the places where he goes for fun, relatives' addresses, you know."

"I can help you with that," said Katherine.

"Good," said Clemons.

"He might be at a friend's house now," suggested Les. "He doesn't tell us every time he goes out."

"Why don't you check that out while I go to the station and get the search started? Call me if he turns up and I'll keep you informed on progress there."

He picked up his hat, preparing to leave. "Look," he said, "maybe you've got nothing to worry about. Teenagers do some crazy things, you know. Hopefully, your boy John is as sweet as I'm sure you think he is and didn't hurt anybody. But we've got to check it out. You understand." He looked like he wanted to grin but somehow managed to squeeze it off.

Les fought to remain cordial. No use antagonizing the guy.

"Sure, officer. We understand." Les walked him to the door and watched him pull out of the driveway. Then he twirled to Katherine. "Start calling everyplace you can think of where he might be. The movies, the mall, the arcade. . . ."

"What are you going to do?"

"I've got to call Colonel Harper. See if I can postpone leaving for Saudi in the morning."

Katherine nodded and bolted to the den to start her calls. Les headed upstairs to his study. After getting the number, he dialed Colonel Reginald Harper. Harper had served as his unit commander for almost eighteen months now, and he seemed like a reasonable man. Surely he would help him postpone his departure under these circumstances. At the same time, Les realized, Harper also seemed like a thoroughly military man. Head shaved almost to the skin. Big ears flopping on the sides of his naked head. Knuckles covered with thick, brown hair. Over twenty years in the service and still in his forties. Given to upholding rules and regulations. Not prone to go against procedure.

"Hello." A raspy voice on the phone shook Les from his inner debate of his chances.

"Colonel Harper, this is Major Les Tennet."

"Yeah, Les, good to hear from you. Ready to ship out?" The colonel sounded chipper at the prospect.

Les hesitated. "Uh, not exactly, sir. That's why I'm calling. I've got a problem."

On the other end of the line, Harrison raised his burly body up in his chair and brushed his hands over his bushy eyebrows.

"What's the scoop, major?"

"Well, it's, it's my son, sir. John, my seventeen-year-old, well, it's hard to explain, but he's missing and we're concerned about his condition. What's the process for getting a postponement of orders?"

Harper grunted. "Pretty complicated, major. Even under the best of circumstances. And we're awfully close to pulling out. Less than twelve hours. It's practically impossible to do anything with such short notice. Plus, it's getting close to midnight. The authority you need to get a postponement isn't going to take kindly to being bothered at such a late hour. You know—it being the holiday season and all."

"I know it's not easy, sir, but I'm desperate here."

"How long's John been gone?"

Les looked down at his watch and suddenly realized his panic might be unmerited.

"Uh, about three hours as far as we can tell."

"Three hours?"

"Yeah, we saw him at dinner."

Harper cleared his throat. "Look Les, I don't want to sound callous, but just because your boy's been gone for a few hours doesn't mean he's missing. A couple of movies would take longer than that. I'm sure he'll turn up soon."

Les didn't want to say too much, but he felt Harper deserved a little more explanation. "I expect you're right, sir, but . . . we've been having some problems with John."

Harper chuckled. "For Pete's sake, major, you said the boy is seventeen. If you didn't have a few problems with him, then you should be worried. Didn't you have problems with your old man when you were his age?"

"Sure, colonel," protested Les. "But we have good reason to think he's run away."

"I'm sure he has," agreed Harper. "Just like I did and you did and every other teenager has from time to time. Don't worry. He'll be home as soon as he gets hungry and needs his underwear washed."

Les didn't want to go further, but saw no alternative.

"Colonel, let me bottom-line this thing. The cops are looking for John. They found a gun in his locker at school a few weeks ago and it turns out the gun was stolen. Plus," Les took a deep breath, "somebody used the gun to shoot a high school student in East St. Louis."

Harper went rigid in his chair. "Well, uh, Les, that puts a new angle on it, but I'm still unclear about what I can do to help. The Army is desperate for medical personnel. With high casualties anticipated in the war, I expect to fight soon; doctors with your skills are worth more than the oil we're going to protect. Even if my superiors want to do it, which I doubt,

I don't seriously think that I can push this through channels fast enough to get your departure postponed."

"But will you try?"

Harper paused and rubbed his temples. "Tell you what. You go ahead and look for John. At the same time, though, plan on shipping out at 0600 as scheduled. If John's not home by the time you leave, I'll go to work to get you turned around. If he's not back within twenty-four hours after we land in Indianapolis, I'll put you right back on a plane headed home. At worst, you'll be gone a couple of days while the paperwork spins through the cycle."

Les sensed the finality of Harper's suggestion. And, honestly, it made sense. John might walk in any minute. He had no choice but to accept the offer.

"I don't have much choice do I, colonel?"

"No more than I do," said Harper.

"See you in the morning, then," said Les. He hung up and rushed downstairs to see if Katherine had found out anything.

Chapter Fourteen

Katherine dropped the phone into its cradle as Les bounded back into the den. She shook her head. "Nothing so far. I've called every friend I can think of, but none of them are home and their parents don't seem to know where they are."

Les cursed under his breath. "How in the world do we lose touch so completely with our kids? They could all be dead and the parents would be the last to know. Unbelievable." He sagged into his chair, momentarily exhausted. He knew he would stay up all night, if need be, to find John. But just for a second, he wanted respite.

Katherine ignored his question and kept her seat. She bit her lower lip. "What about you?" she asked cautiously. "Can Harper postpone your leaving?"

Les gritted his teeth. "No, no luck. Said it was too late to do anything."

Like a geyser spewing from a bank of underground steam, Katherine exploded. "You talk about unbelievable! You're going halfway across the world and you're leaving me to deal with a missing son who's wanted for questioning in a murder case?"

"You think it's my option?" said Les, standing up and beginning to pace. "I told Harper the situation, but he wouldn't budge. Said he would ship me home as soon as possible after I hit the ground if John hadn't turned up, but he can't move the paperwork any faster than that."

"So what if he does turn up?" pressed Katherine. "Do you go on to Saudi?"

"I expect so."

"And what am I supposed to do with John then? He could end up on trial. Will you get to come back if he does?"

"I have no way of knowing, Kath. It's out of my hands. I'll get started on a release as soon as I can, but if war starts, I have no idea if I'll have an opportunity to come home. All we can do is wait and see. Let's just take it one day at a time."

"That's a good slogan, Les," she snapped, obviously not soothed in the least. "But one day can last a lifetime."

"I know, Kath. I know it's not much. But a slogan is all I've got right now." He walked over to her, hoping to close the gap between them. Katherine wouldn't let him.

"John needs more than a slogan," she pouted. "He needs his father. I need his father." She wrapped her arms around her chest, as if trying to comfort herself.

"I know, Kath, I know." He reached out to her, but she kept her arms folded tightly and refused his hug. He gave up and stepped back from her.

"Look, Katherine, when John shows up, the police will question him. He'll explain how he got the gun, and that'll settle it."

"If he's innocent, that'll settle it."

"I'm sure he's innocent."

"Are you sure he can prove it?"

"Without talking to him, I'm not."

"Then I guess we better find him," she said.

"I guess you're right." He turned to business. "We'll need a sitter for Sherry."

"I'll call Mother. She and Dad should be able to get here in a few minutes."

Les sighed heavily. "I hate to involve them in all this. I feel guilty enough already without hearing your mother's opinions."

"I know," said Katherine. "But I don't see another option right now, do you?"

Les shook his head. "Go ahead and call them. Better you to explain than me. I'll try a couple more of his friends. Maybe we can find him before they get here."

Thirty minutes later Beatrice and Walter pulled up. "Don't worry about Sherry," Beatrice said, shooing Les and Katherine out the door. "We'll take care of her."

"And I'll get on the horn to a couple of guys downtown, see if I can't get some extra manpower looking for John," said Walter, clearly anxious to help.

Les and Katherine hopped into the Mercedes and pulled out of the icy driveway. She tugged her wool coat around her ears and whispered, "I hope he's not out in this cold."

"He's probably curled up in front of a fireplace some-where—making out with some girlfriend he hasn't told us about yet."

"I hope you're right," said Katherine.

Neither of them believed it.

Chapter Fifteen

Seven miles away, John stepped off the elevator on the third floor of the St. Louis Medical Center and tucked himself up against the wall. The scent of freshly waxed floor tiles mixed with the smell of used bedpans and attacked his nostrils. His nose twitched at the aroma as he eased his way down the hall to the last room on the left, his father's office, a cozy corner room with a window view of the Mississippi River.

John edged into the office carefully, not wanting anyone to see him. Closing the door, he flipped on the light and scanned the room. Plaques and awards on bookshelves to his left. Then the window. Past the window, an American flag in the left corner. And a hat tree without any hats on it.

Hiding against the wall and staring past the hat tree, John wrapped his arms around his shoulders and shivered. He'd fled the house without a jacket. When he saw the cop car pull in, he knew automatically it had come for him. Trouble always came to their family because of him.

Sherry couldn't cause any trouble, other than the trouble of caring for her. The kind he caused made teachers and principals call his parents at home and at work. His kind of trouble embarrassed his parents, especially his dad. And it confused him, because he had never meant to cause anyone a problem. But life got confusing sometimes.

Like with Sherry. Why did she have to be retarded? Her handicap sucked up his mom's time like a vacuum cleaner, and she never had any energy left for him. Not since he was nine, right after Sherry was born. Since then, his mom had virtually disappeared from his life.

And his dad?

Well, his dad never had been there. Always somewhere else. Helping someone else. Sure, other people were important, but wasn't he? The thing was, he felt so guilty when he asked for his dad's time. After all, those other folks were knocking on death's door. They needed his dad more than he did, right? So, after a while he'd stopped asking. At least in any verbal way.

John raked his eyes over the wall in front of him, the wall directly behind his dad's desk. The wall had always made him proud, but it angered him too. Lately it had angered him more than it made him proud. The Wall of Fame he called it. A wall of pictures. Fat men shaking his dad's hand. Blue-haired women hugging him by the neck. The grateful governor smiling beside Les Tennet.

They were all here—over seventy-five of them now. People who thought they'd celebrated their last birthday, but who were miraculously alive. Alive due to the wonderful, matchless, incredible care of Les the Blest.

They were thieves, John had decided. All of them. They'd stolen more of life than was due them and they had stolen his dad in the process. They had chained his dad in their illnesses and their injuries and had refused to let him go.

The worst part was that his dad hadn't fought them for his freedom. He had accepted the captivity—gladly, it seemed to John—and had even embraced it, which made his dad the worst thief of all.

John stepped past the desk and reached for the picture on the bottom right hand corner of the display. A tall, thick-shouldered guy wearing a fishing hat covered with lures stared out at him from the frame. The man's arm was draped possessively around his dad's shoulders. "One fish that didn't get away. Thanks," read the inscription at the bottom of the picture.

With a sudden blush of anger, John lifted the photo off the wall and dropped it on the carpeted floor. Then he raised his right foot and slammed the heel of his black shoe downward into the fisherman's face.

The glass broke and the lines from it spread out like tangled ropes and pieces of the jagged glass carved chunks out of the man's smiling face. One slash cut diagonally across his dad's chest, slicing his body in two.

John toed the picture and the frame away from him, under the desk. Then he lifted a second photo off the wall and tossed it on the ground and stomped it too. It shattered into a thousand pieces. He reached for a third one and smashed it. He grabbed for a fourth, but then his anger abated and he blinked his eyes and realized what he had done. Okay, enough of that. Time to think now. He plopped into his father's chair, leaned back and steepled his long fingers together, wondering what to do next. He felt certain the cop had come to ask him about the gun. Trouble was, he didn't think it best to tell the police anything about it. No, the only safe thing was to make himself scarce. And, with his dad leaving in the morning, the one place no one would think to search was the hospital. With any luck at all, he could hole up long enough to get a grip. Long enough to make a decision... a decision that would affect everyone he loved for the rest of their lives.

Chapter Sixteen

Les and Katherine searched all night, growing more frantic as the clock's hands galloped toward 6 A.M.—the time Les had to report. They raced in and out of the late-night movie houses all over St. Louis, forcing attendants to interrupt the feature and page for John Tennet. They scoured arcades and all-night grocery stores. They rushed through loud bars and dance clubs, hoping by some miracle to run into someone who knew the whereabouts of their son. They called every friend they could think of from pay phones in parking lots they'd just combed looking for his jeep. They checked in with the police, but no luck. Too big a city and too little time.

At 2:30 A.M. they gave up and headed back home. Sherry and Walter and Beatrice were asleep and they didn't wake them. Les called Harper again, hoping something could be done to delay his departure. The colonel, not happy about being awakened, would have none of it. "Time insufficient to change orders. See you at 0600."

Katherine made coffee and both took a cup and sagged into chairs at the kitchen table. Les wanted to talk, but there was so much to say that it seemed impossible to say anything. Still, he knew he had to try. He reached across the table and covered Katherine's hands with his.

"I hate to leave you this way," he started.

"It's not exactly ideal, is it?" she said, more weary than sarcastic.

"Not even close," he agreed. "But I don't know what else to do."

"Maybe John will turn up in the morning," she said, a tinge of wistfulness rising in her voice.

"Maybe so. If he's not here by the time I hit the ground overseas, Harper has committed himself to shipping me right back home."

"You think he'll keep that commitment?" Katherine sounded doubtful.

Les rubbed her hands. "Look at me," he said. She put down her coffee and complied. "Harper will keep his promise," he said.

"What if he doesn't?"

Les' eyes went glassy. "Then I will go AWOL and get home myself. Whatever it takes, I'll do it. I will not leave you and Sherry to face this alone. If John's not here, then I will be."

Katherine nodded and Les knew she wanted to believe him. But he suspected she had a hard time doing so. He'd broken too many promises in the past. He hadn't done it deliberately; in fact, he hated himself when he made too many promises to too many people; the promises to his family always seemed the easiest to break.

Desperately wanting to assure her he wouldn't break this promise, he stared into her eyes with a focus he seldom offered, a focus that said he really meant it.

Seeing his gaze, Katherine sighed and nodded and Les realized she understood. He would keep his word on this promise. She pulled her hand away and roused herself from the chair. She glanced at her watch. "Better get you ready, soldier. In two hours, you're out of here."

Les unfolded himself and stood too. But he wasn't ready for activity just yet. He opened his arms to Katherine and she fell into them. They stood that way for almost a minute in the dimly lit kitchen, as if their immobility could stop the click of time.

In those clicks, Les found himself loving Katherine purely again, as purely as he once had, as purely as untouched snow. Then the doubts attacked him, saying it was just the circumstances—he was about to leave for war and a troubled son wandered about on an ice-glazed night.

Angrily, Les gritted his teeth and cast out the intrusive doubts and let himself bask in the warmth of Katherine's embrace. No matter what happened tomorrow, he held her and she held him. And for now, that felt good.

Chapter Seventeen

The noise hit Les first—a chaotic sound no morning should have to endure. But the military had no respect for the quiet of a morning. Shouted commands and equipment being moved and people yelling out loud greetings were the order of the day.

His unit, the Midwest Reserve Evac 804, was tying up in the baggage claim area at Lambert Field for the transport by commercial airline to Ft. Ben Harrison outside of Indianapolis, Indiana. After several days of transition there, they would ship out to Frankfurt, Germany. From Frankfurt they would fly into Saudi.

Almost 300 men and women milled around the area, each one saying tearful goodbyes, checking in with military officers, and gearing themselves up for the uncertain days ahead.

Neither Les nor Katherine had slept. Packing had taken the better part of an hour, a shower for both and a shave for Les had chewed up another half, and then it was time to leave. They'd heard nothing from John, and Lieutenant Clemons had come up empty too.

Not wanting to upset her routine too much, Les had decided to say goodbye to Sherry at home. But parting with her had drained him as much as the evening had. Disturbed by all the commotion, she woke up even earlier than usual and immediately demanded a swim with her daddy.

Trying to please, he obliged her demand, but he was weary and rushed and his heart wasn't in it. Within minutes, Sherry sensed his mood and stopped her splashing. Les pulled her to the side of the pool to say goodbye, hoping some words would surface that would explain it all to her. As if sensing his distress, Sherry reached out and hugged him with her wet arms.

"Why are you sad, Daddy?" she asked, water trickling off the tip of her cherubic nose.

"It's hard to explain," said Les, not wanting to say anything to make her sadder.

"Are you still upset with Mommy?"

"Not really, sweetheart," he said, wiping water out of his eyes. "It's just that Daddy has to go away today and I'm not sure when I'll get home. I'm sad, 'cause I'm going to miss everyone here."

"Will you call on the telephone?"

"When I can, but not every day like I usually do when I'm gone."

"Who'll swim with me?" Sherry changed the subject without warning.

Les shrugged. "I don't know, baby, your mom maybe, or John."

"Will I get to swim alone?" She shuddered in the chill of the morning and snuggled up closer to him.

Les furrowed his brow and pretended to think hard. Tickling her in the ribs, he decided, "Yeah, I think you can swim alone, if you'll promise to stay by the sides. Will you promise me you'll do that?"

"I promise," she said, a wide smile breaking out on her face, obviously pleased with the anticipation of this new freedom. "I'll stay close to the side until you get home to swim with me."

"Good," he said, glad he'd taken these last few minutes with her. "Come on, let's get dressed."

An hour later, everyone gathered at the door to make it

final. Les vaguely heard Beatrice tell Katherine she would take Sherry to her house after they left. Then Walter advised him not to worry—he would take care of his family while Les was gone.

On the front stoop, Les focused his attention on Sherry and paid his in-laws scant attention. He squatted down so he could look her in the eye. A lump the size of an ostrich egg clogged his throat. She kissed him on the cheek. He grabbed her and wrapped her up in one final bear hug.

"Who loves you?" he asked softly, laying her head on his shoulder.

"Daddy does," she said.

"How long will Daddy love you?"

"Forever."

"Is there anything that could happen that could make Daddy not love you?"

"No, nothing."

"Okay," he said. "Remember that."

She raised her head to kiss him again and when she did she saw something she'd never seen before. She saw tears adorning his face, glistening tears like silver bells under each eye. She lifted both her hands and fingered the tears. They burst at her touch and spread out on his face. She touched her fingers to her mouth and tasted the tears, swallowed them into herself.

Les coughed and stood up, squeezed her once more and kissed her on both cheeks, and then turned and left, with Katherine trailing behind him. He hopped into the car and pulled out of the driveway, watching Sherry in the rearview mirror until finally he couldn't see her at all.

Now, he and Katherine slogged like zombies through the duffle bags and backpacks and found an officer with a clipboard who was checking in the unit. Les handed his papers to the officer and, after a quick review, received a nod of approval. All in order.

Les turned to Katherine. "I don't know what to say," he began. "I feel like I'm deserting you, like I'm dumping the garbage of a thousand days on your shoulders and running out."

Katherine lifted a nail to her mouth to bite it, then dropped her hand to her side. "You're trapped, Les. You did all you could. Even if you were here, John would still be gone. You can't make him reappear. He'll come home when he's ready."

"Maybe my leaving will make it easier for him to come home."

"I don't know, Les. Maybe so."

"I just want him safe. He's only seventeen. I never wanted it like this for him. I wanted him to have it easy."

Katherine stepped closer to him. "I know, Les, I know," she soothed. "But we can't make what we want happen all the time. Not even you can do that. Not even Les the Blest."

A twisted smile crossed Les' face. "Especially Les the Blest. I'm beginning to wonder if I can make anything happen the way I want it. I can't think of a worse time for me to leave. A malpractice suit hanging over me, the police after John, a dead patient I should have saved, you and me—" he shook his head and bit his lower lip, refusing to go further.

Katherine pushed a strand of rebellious hair out of her eyes. "I don't guess there's a good time for anybody to go to war."

"Guess not," agreed Les. "Unless you're leaving a worse one behind."

Katherine put her hand on his belt and pulled him toward her. "What are we going to do with each other, Les?"

He had no answer ready and the sound of someone shouting his name gave him no time to manufacture one.

"Hey, Les, Les Tennet!"

Les lifted his eyes from Katherine, recognizing the voice immediately. Roger Tills, the owner of the biggest voice in five states and one of Les' oldest friends from MU.

"Rog!" Les threw up his hand in recognition as Tills bounded over.

The two men seemed about to embrace, then, aware of the other soldiers around them, thought better of it and settled for a double-handed handshake, complemented by lots of back slapping.

"You going over with this group too?" asked Les.

"Absolutely," nodded Tills. "I volunteered for it. I'm bored stiff being the country doctor in Hannibal, Mo. Checking the temperature of snotty-nosed kids has lost its thrill lately. Thought I'd go to the Middle East and serve as the personal physician for some brass-heavy general."

"You doing general practice in Hannibal?"

"Yeah, I decided to be noble, go home and serve the people as a rural doctor. I do a little surgery to keep my hands quick, I deliver babies and give all the boys on the football team a physical at a reduced rate. It's tough work, but somebody has to do it."

"Yeah, with the town guaranteeing you a $100,000 salary in the first year," said Les.

Tills smiled. "Come on, Les, won't you let me impress your lovely wife with my charitable spirit?"

Les didn't get a chance to answer. The loudspeaker blared the announcement. "Attention. Attention. Civilians will need to clear the area in five minutes. All personnel with orders to Fort Ben Harrison should prepare to board their flights at 0600. That's all."

Tills took his cue. "I'll save you a seat," he said, easing away from Les and Katherine.

They looked at each other again.

"I'll miss you," said Katherine, sliding her arms around his shoulders.

Les hugged her closely. "I'll call as soon as I can. And, if John's not back, I'll hop the next plane home."

"You better," sniffled Katherine. "I can't make it without you."

He kissed her then, but he wasn't paying much attention to the kiss. He was wondering if she'd eventually have to find out if her words were true.

Chapter Eighteen

Clara pulled herself up from her seat in front of the computer terminal and waited for the patient reports to spew out so she could sign them and get them filed. These reports, the remainder of the work Les left with her, had added to her normal load and now that her shift had ended she wanted to finish them up and scoot home. As she arched her back, she heard her stomach growl. Still waiting on the printer, she lifted her purse from under the counter, opened it and took out a plastic bag with a Payday bar in it.

The printer stopped and she tore off the sheets. Placing them in a manila folder, she took a bite of the candy and wandered absentmindedly down the hall to Les' office. He'd want a hard copy for his records.

She pushed open the door and walked in without turning on the light. The street lamp outside the window cast enough light for her to leave the folder on Les' desk.

With the first step into the office, Clara sensed something. She wrinkled her nose—the place smelled like a hamburger joint. She squinted her eyes against the darkness and spotted a rumpled white sack and a paper cup near a wastebasket by the corner of the desk.

Growing more curious, Clara went further into the office. Her feet crunched something and she looked down. Shattered glass.

A broken window? Nope. Cautiously now, Clara rounded the corner of the desk and saw the three picture frames on the floor. Each one was mangled into shreds and scattered.

She wedged her manila folder under her left arm and picked up the phone to call security. As she did, John stepped out of the dark corner farthest from the window. The light from the street lamp fell across his face. "Don't do that, Clara," he whispered.

Her report folder fell to the floor and Clara stood silently, staring at John. When she spoke, she stayed calm.

"Why shouldn't I call security, John? Folks are looking for you."

"I know they are. That's why I ran away."

"Why did you run, John? What kind of trouble you in?" She lowered the phone into its cradle.

"Can't answer that one for you, Clara. You heard about the gun?"

She nodded. "Yeah, your daddy called me before he left. Asked me if I had any idea where you'd be. I told him no. So you're here because of the gun?"

"Yeah, that's part of it. I didn't know what to say, didn't know how to answer questions without causing more problems for everybody."

Clara didn't want to spook him, but she didn't want to let him go either. She tried to balance her concerns in her words. "Your folks are worried about you, John. They need to know you're okay." She watched John's face cloud over.

"Yeah, they're worried—worried I'll do something to cause them more grief. Especially Dad."

Clara tried to stay gentle. She didn't want him running out on her before she could convince him to go home.

"Why you so mad at your dad, John? You know he loves you."

He grunted his cynicism. "I guess it's all according to how you define love."

"How do you define it, John? If you going to dismiss your

daddy's kind of love, then tell me, what kind of love do you
want that he hasn't given you?"

John moved toward her and, almost disdainfully, perched
himself on the edge of the desk. He pulled his left leg into an
L across his right knee and wrapped the loose strings of his
black shoe around his fingers.

"I don't know the kind of love I want, Clara, but I know
the kind I don't want."

"Then tell me about that."

"I don't know if I can," he said, dropping his eyes to his
shoes.

Sensing a shift in his attitude, Clara reached her wide, black
hand and stroked John on the back. "It ain't easy to deal with
hurtful things, John, but if we don't deal with them, then they
chew us up and spit us out. I'm here to listen to you. You
know I love everybody in your family. If you want an ear to
listen to you, then I'm your girl. I won't judge you and I
won't advise. Now, tell your Aunt Clara what kind of love it is
you don't want."

"I'll never forget it, Clara. I know it seems so trivial, but I
was only ten. We were playing basketball in the backyard.
Mom and Sherry were out of town. I drove to the basket for a
lay-up and Dad fouled me hard from the back—"

"Dads are supposed—" she interrupted him to defend Les.
He shushed her.

"Don't defend him, Clara. The foul wasn't the problem.
Not at all. I expected that. He always did that, just like I've
learned to do. Anyway, he pushed me into the pole holding up
the basket and I cracked into it with my left shoulder. Broke
my collarbone in half. Part of it was sticking through my
skin."

He pulled the collar of his sweatshirt out from his neck.
"See, I still got a lump from it."

Clara, vaguely remembering the incident, touched the lump
but knew that wasn't the end of the story. She eased her way
into the seat by the desk. "What happened next, John?"

"Well, as you would expect, Dad rushed me to the hospital. He picked me up in his arms and carried me to the car and then drove me straight to the emergency room. Everyone rushed out to meet us, the security cop, the nurses, everybody. We were like celebrities, war heroes or something. It's weird, but I was so proud to be with him, so glad to be his son. I was going to have my famous dad doing his healing magic on me." John paused, remembering, and his eyes moistened. Then they dried up and his face turned hard.

"They carried me into a room and Dad told them to take off my shirt. Then a nurse opened the door and motioned to Dad. He walked over to the nurse and she whispered into his ear and then she left. Dad turned to me. 'John,' he said, 'We've got an emergency that came in right behind us. A heart attack. They want me to take a look at him. So I'm going to turn you over to the resident on call and he's going to take care of you. How's that sound?'

"Well, what could I say? I nodded and he left me there without another word. Within an hour they'd set my shoulder. Though it was throbbing and hurting like crazy, they were finished with me. So, the nurse walked me to the waiting room and left me by myself. There I sat, wondering when Dad was going to come back and take me home. Another hour passed. Though I was scared to bother anybody, I finally went to the desk and asked the nurse where my dad was. She looked at me like I'd asked for a date with Madonna and said, 'Dr. Tennet is in surgery.' That seemed to settle it for her. Not knowing what else to do, I went back to the sofa and fell asleep. Four hours later, Dad woke me up and took me home. Never apologized for making me wait. Never said anything at all. Seemed to think I'd understand."

John wrapped his shoestrings around his fingers. "That's been the story of my relationship with him. He's always leaving me to care for someone else."

Clara let silence play in the room while John caught his breath. Then she spoke. "Look, John, I can't make excuses for your father. That's not my place. But I can tell you this—he's an unusually gifted man. Men like him are rare and they end up with responsibilities far greater than most. I know your daddy doesn't give you the attention you want and deserve. But he does try. He was at least playing ball with you the day you were hurt. A lot of boys don't even have that. Your dad certainly didn't."

John's eyes brightened suddenly and the light from the street flamed up in them. "You know a lot about him, don't you, Clara?"

"A little . . . yeah, I guess I know him pretty good."

"You know him better than I do," John said, momentarily pouting again. "Why is that, Clara?"

"Well, I can't say that I know exactly. But it seems to me that some people talk more to those outside the family than they do to those inside. It's safer for them that way."

John reflected on her words for a beat, then said. "Tell me about him, Clara, tell me about my dad and his father. He's never told me about my grandfather."

"You know your grandpa was a drinking man?"

"Yeah, but not much more."

"Well, your daddy says when he wasn't drinking, he was a good father, as good as any boy could want. But it wasn't often that he wasn't drinking. Especially after his wife died."

"And when he did drink?"

"When he drank, he was a hellish man. Used to whip your daddy, beat him bad. You know that big scar over his eye?"

"Yeah, you can't miss it. It turns purple when he gets mad. What about it?"

"His daddy gave him that scar. Hit him with a mop handle, smacked him right across the forehead, left his mark for all to see. Happened when your dad was about your age."

John stayed still a blink. When he did speak, his voice trembled. "Dad told me he got that scar in a car accident when he was seventeen."

Clara nodded. "That's the official story. Some things you

don't tell the truth about, 'cause the truth hurts more than the lie."

"It scarred him for life."

"Yep, I guess that's a good way of saying it."

"And my dad's mom died when he was twelve?"

"Yeah, she did, John, so it ain't been easy for him. He's doing the best he can with no one ever teaching him nothing about fathering. He's a blind man groping in the dark, stumbling along, trying to save everybody and losing the ones closest to him in the process."

"What happened to his dad?"

"He never told you?"

"Nope, not a word."

"Then you better ask him. It's not my place to say how all that played out."

John stood up and rubbed his palms on the sides of his sweat pants. "Dad's gone now, you know. Shipped out to Saudi."

"Yeah, I know, John. He's gone and your mom's bound to be scared to death—worried about you and him both."

"I better go home," said John as if wanting her approval.

"I expect so," said Clara. "You want me to call her for you?"

"No, you don't need to do that. I'll go home now. I promise you I will."

John started to move, then stopped. "Clara?"

"Yeah?"

"Thanks, for uh, for telling me about him."

"No problem, John. I want to help any way I can."

She opened her arms and John stepped into them and buried his face into her round shoulders. A mama comforting her boy, Clara cooed into his ear, "It's going to be all right, John. Just you wait and see. Just you wait and see."

Section Three

The interval between the decay of the old
and the formation and the establishment
of the new,
constitutes a period of transition,
which must always necessarily be one
of uncertainty, confusion, and error.

John C. Calhoun

Chapter Nineteen

Les climbed aboard the 747 and found Tills seated midway in the plane. After stowing his flight bag overhead, he plopped into the aisle seat beside his old friend.

"Really good of the military to fly us commercial, don't you think?" Tills said, smiling at him like a boy excited over his first camping trip. Les wasn't nearly so delighted about the prospects.

"Guess so," he said.

Tills noticed Les' lack of enthusiasm. "What's the problem, big guy? Glum about leaving your million dollar practice?"

"That's not exactly the issue, Rog, but I don't think now's the time to talk about it. Let's just get where we're going and see what happens."

Tills shrugged. "Fine with me, man. But if I'd known you were going to be so bummed out, I would have chosen another seatmate like—" Tills stopped in dead sentence and his eyes widened. "Like her!"

Les followed Tills' eyes as they shifted to the front of the airliner. His eyes widened too. For a second, the conversation on the plane stopped completely. Then, as if realizing how obvious that was, people started to chatter again, but at a lower decibel than before, as every man in the jet kept one eye on the woman moving down the aisle, looking for a seat.

The air seemed to disappear in her wake as men sucked in gulps of it, trying to breathe. It wasn't that she was beauty-queen pretty. Not that at all. But hair the color of a red maple tree in the fall and a green uniform matching the color of her eyes made for quite a vision. Her body filled the uniform in ways that made Les forget she was military, made him forget anything rigid and unyielding. She walked precisely, not like she wanted people to watch her walk, but like she knew exactly where she wanted to go and would obey her own internal pace to get there.

Les nudged Tills in the ribs as she slipped past them toward the rear of the plane. "Stick your eyes back in the sockets, man. I'm sure somebody else has claims on her already."

"Nope," said Tills, shifting his head to watch her as long as he could with discretion.

"How do you know?"

"I trained with her for two weeks last summer. Her name's Macy Spencer. She's one of our modern Army girls. A graduate of West Point. A career woman. Twenty-nine years old. Her dad's a two-star out of Intelligence at the Pentagon."

"Some folks would say that's not possible."

"Huh?" Roger stared at him blankly, obviously still thinking about Macy Spencer.

"Intelligence at the Pentagon? Come on, Rog, snap out of it. What's with this Spencer woman? Don't act like you've never seen a pretty nurse!"

"Nope, she's not a nurse, smart guy. Guess again."

"Ah, for sure, a doctor then."

"Wrong again, mush brain."

"Then what?"

"A helicopter pilot. Right now she flies a medi-vac copter."

"Likes danger, huh?"

"Apparently so," said Tills.

The noise level edged up again as Spencer chose a seat and everyone settled back down. The pilot taxied the jet onto the runway and revved the engine for takeoff.

"Did you get anywhere with her last summer?" Les asked.

"Huh? Oh, yeah, you mean when we were in camp together. Nope, nowhere. We were in training for only two weeks and I didn't get much chance to work my magic. But I sure haven't given up. Maybe she'll make this escapade worthwhile for me."

Les didn't know whether to laugh or weep at Tills. "Always the skirt hound, aren't you?"

"You know what they say, an old dog can't learn new tricks."

Les remembered Tills' reputation. He viewed women as game animals—he stalked them, brought them to ground, then counted them on his personal tally sheet. It wasn't the politically correct way to look at females, but it was Tills' way. Funny thing, though, he got away with it most of the time. But the one time he didn't, it caught up with him.

"You tried to change, didn't you?" asked Les. "After you married Betty?"

Tills hung his head. "Yeah, man, after we got married, I did. For nine years, no problems. Then I made a mistake and Betty made me pay for it. I didn't love the other woman, but she loved me and decided if she couldn't have me, then Betty couldn't either."

"So she told Betty."

"And Betty told me she believed in one man and one woman and I was one woman over the limit. So she kicked me out."

The two friends nodded their heads. Roger stared out the window for a beat, then turned back to Les.

"What about you, Les? You and Kath? You ever make a mistake with somebody else?"

Les clenched his teeth. "No, Rog, I've never been unfaithful to her. Not the way you mean."

"Is there any other way to be unfaithful?"

"Maybe so," said Les, his voice dropping lower as he considered the question. "You know, when you make promises but then find you can't keep them. When you both agree on something but you don't keep your half of the bargain. When you do exactly the opposite of what you want to do. Maybe that's unfaithfulness too. I don't know. It all depends on how you look at it." He pushed his hands through his hair and leaned back against the seat.

The plane sped up quickly as it spurted down the runway and lifted off the ground. It groaned as it sucked the landing gear into its belly.

Tills stared at Les for several beats. "You look stressed, man. You and Kath having problems?"

Les snorted. "That's the understatement of the year."

"You want to talk about it?"

Les paused, thinking, then decided against it. "No, now's not the time."

"Just let me know, my friend. Maybe I can help. After all, I've been there."

Les leaned his seat back, signaling the end of the conversation. It wouldn't be a long flight. When they touched down in Indiana, the activity would speed up and the days would become a blur and the body would grow weary and the mind numb and no one would have time to talk.

Chapter Twenty

Katherine watched the 747 until it turned into a dime-sized speck in the blue Missouri sky. Then she located a phone in the concourse and called home, hoping that John would answer. He didn't. She tried the call three times, waiting ten minutes between calls, but the noise of the answering machine was her only response. With each call, her hands quivered more and her throat clogged up tighter.

Slightly panicky now, she called Beatrice and asked if Sherry could stay for another couple of hours.

"Sure, no problem. Take as long as you like," said Beatrice.

Katherine hurried to the Mercedes, popped it into gear, and sped out of the airport. She didn't know where she was going, but the flip-flops in her stomach told her she had to go somewhere.

She drove to the Riverfront Mall, parked, and ran inside. She walked around and around the track of the stores for almost fifty minutes. As she walked, she stared into the faces of the people she passed. She searched their faces for something, but she didn't know what.

Though she worked up a hard sweat, the walking didn't calm her nerves. Instead, it simply accelerated her heartbeat. Now, it thudded inside her head and chest like a blacksmith hammering an anvil. Still seeking relief, she left the mall and piloted the Mercedes to the Cardinal Health Club. Changing quickly into workout clothes, she jumped onto a stationary bike and pedaled for thirty minutes. Then she sweated in the sauna for fifteen more. But nothing helped. Her heart thumped harder and she heard it now in her ears, a thump, thump, thump measuring the intensity of her anxiety.

In a rush, she showered, dressed, and headed to the package store near the health center. If exercise couldn't calm her, maybe alcohol would. She bought a quart of Johnny Walker Scotch and hustled back to her car. She almost dropped the bottle as she pulled it out of the sack. Taking a deep breath to steady her shaking hands, she unscrewed the cap and sloshed a stiff shot of the dark liquid down her throat. It burned as she tasted it, but instead of easing her fears, it stoked them higher, fueled them until they threatened to consume her.

Her breathing picked up pace as the Mercedes roared out of the parking lot and onto the highway. She zipped past familiar sights but felt no connection to them. Everything blurred in her vision and her world dissolved like a cloud dispersing before a persistent wind. She thought how all she loved had turned so sour.

Sherry—an angel without a mind, forever locked in time, unable to develop beyond her childish glow. John—maybe dead by now, maybe alive but trapped too, trapped by parents who couldn't love him like he needed, trapped by what shouldn't be but was.

Les—Les the Blest who had become, in many ways, her curse and his own too. Cursed by his incredible talents, cursed by his drivenness, cursed by his willingness to give life to everyone else, even if it meant taking it from his family.

And herself—Katherine, what about her? Guilt-ridden because she blamed herself for Sherry's retardation, scared because she saw John slipping away, and angry because Les had promised so much but had delivered so little.

She screamed. At the top of her voice she spewed out all of the hurt that chewed like a starving hyena at her guts. The scream of her hurt bounced off the windshield of the car, bounced from the windshield back into her face, bounced into her face and almost knocked her out. The scream knocked her hands off the steering wheel and the Mercedes bore left like a stray bullet across two lanes of traffic.

For a second, she didn't react. Confusion and detachment swept over her as the Mercedes slashed through a swirl of approaching vehicles. A woman's face appeared before her eyes, a woman in a blue mini-van. Beside the woman sat a child in a carseat. The woman swerved her van to the right and jammed on her brakes, barely missing Katherine's car.

Katherine's body surged upward as the left front wheel of the Mercedes bounced off the curb and tossed her head toward the ceiling. Only the seat harness kept her safe. The right front wheel slid into a parking lot surrounding a tree-shrouded building. As the car spun around in a circle, the wheels fought to stay on the ground.

Jolted by the crack into the curb, Katherine popped back into reality. She grabbed the wheel, hit her brakes, and brought the car to a skidding stop. The sound of blowing horns receded in the background as traffic resumed its flow in the highway she had just crossed.

Gulping in air, Katherine stared through the windshield and saw a spire dissecting the sky in front of her. A church spire. She glanced around the parking lot. No one there.

A bit calmer now, she eased the car into a white-lined parking space and timidly stepped out of it. Feeling drawn by a force she barely comprehended, much less understood, she stepped to the wooden door of the church and tried the handle. It opened as if it expected her.

She eased inside the vestibule. It was warm and dark with rich wood. Everything fell silent. The thumping in her chest eased a notch. Directly ahead of her, a set of closed, wooden doors led into the sanctuary. She reached for the handle on the doors and opened them and stepped inside the house of worship.

In a flash, the darkness of the vestibule disappeared as a streak of sunlight cut through the stained-glass window that framed the pulpit. Straight as a laser beam the sunshine poured down the aisle from the pulpit to her face and bathed her in shimmering light.

Blinded by the flash of golden sunshine, Katherine raised her hands to her eyes. Then, cautiously, she peered through her fingers to the vision in the light.

She fell to her knees. The knots in her stomach loosened. As the knots untied, her heart broke loose and tears rushed from her heart and perched on the edges of her eyes. Then, like children let out to play, the tears jumped down onto her cheeks. On their backs they carried her fear away.

From the stained-glass window washed in sunlight, Jesus gazed down at Katherine. His hands stretched out to her and she knew instantly that she now bowed in the presence of the Mystery she'd searched for all her life.

It wasn't really Jesus in the window, but no one could ever have convinced Katherine of that. She sensed she should reach for His hands. So, obeying her compulsion, she dropped her hands from her eyes and stretched them out to Jesus. As she did, the sun outside ducked behind a patch of clouds and dimmed the glow in Jesus' face.

Suddenly, Katherine was alone again. Or was she? She stayed on her knees for a moment, wondering and waiting. Nothing happened. The sunbeam stayed hidden.

Though a bit unsteady, she raised herself to her feet, eased to the back pew and sagged into the seat. The picture of Jesus in the window stared back at her, but blankly now. The life had gone out of it.

Strangely, the knots in her stomach were still untied. Her tears, though softer and slower now, still fell. She gladly let them, for she sensed they were washing her pain away as they coursed down her cheeks.

Then it hit her. The life had disappeared from the face of Jesus the exact instant she reached out with her hands to take

His. Maybe the life had not died, but had simply been reborn. Through His hands life had transferred into hers.

Katherine hugged herself. Then, as naturally as if she had done it all her life, she bowed her head and began to pray. She prayed as simply as a child, making simple requests and offering honest commitments. She prayed as one who knew Someone listened; twenty minutes later, when she stopped praying, she believed that Someone had.

She lifted her head, glanced around the sanctuary, picked up her purse, and left the building. She drove calmly to her mother's house and picked up Sherry, enduring the chatter from Beatrice but hearing almost none of it.

In equal quiet she drove home. When she and Sherry stepped into the kitchen from the garage, they found John standing inside, waiting for them. Silently, he came to them and opened his arms and they all embraced in the center of the room.

"I'm sorry, Mom," John said, "but I didn't know what to do. I saw the police car and I knew about the shooting and I had the gun, so I got scared. I needed time to think. So, I ran. But you've got to believe me, mom—I didn't shoot that boy."

Katherine reached up and touched his chin. Then she pulled his face down to her shoulder and hugged both her children close to her. She stroked their heads and shushed John.

"It's okay, John; it's okay, Sherry. Everything's going to be all right." Wrapped up in their warmth, she dared for the first time in years to believe her own words.

Chapter Twenty-one

The bump of wheels on concrete jarred Les from the doze into which he had fallen. He rubbed a smidgen of grit from the corner of his eyes and nudged Tills. "Wake up, Rog," he said. "Time for fun and games."

Tills moaned, turned sideways, and stretched. "Are we there?"

"Open up and see."

He did. Both men stretched their necks so they could see out the window. The stark landscape surrounding Ft. Ben Harrison in the dead of winter stared back at them. "It ain't exactly Disneyland, is it, my friend?" asked Roger.

They laughed and shook themselves awake as the plane turned slowly to a parking area and the rest of their unit stirred to life. The buzz of talk in the cabin notched up for an instant, but then died as quickly as it had started. Colonel Harper had the jetliner's microphone in his hand and now stood in the center of the aisle ready to speak.

Harper braced his chunky frame against the movement of the jet and barked through the intercom. "Okay, boys and girls, we're on the field. You weekend warriors are soldiers again. We're here to do a job and you can be sure we're going to do it right. We don't know what will happen in the next few weeks. Maybe nothing. Maybe we'll all be home for Valentine's Day. But I expect not. They didn't call us up to load on frequent-flyer miles. They called us up for one reason—to fix casualties. That's our purpose. And that means a certain amount of discipline. For everyone, including you doctors." Harper paused and gave his words time to soak.

"We'll only have eighty-four hours before we ship ahead to Frankfurt, Germany. That's a little quicker than normal, I know. But the January 15 deadline set by President Bush is getting here in a hurry and they want us in Frankfurt by January 31 and in Dhahran by February 4. So, we're going to push you through the paces here. You'll get your uniforms, they'll pop shots into your bottoms, you'll receive a short course to update your previous chemical warfare training, and they'll fit you for a gas mask. Plus, you'll get some refresher time on your weapon of choice—a .45 Colt or the 9 mm Beretta. We don't expect you'll ever need it, but . . ."

Harper's voice trailed off for a second and each person in the jetliner reflected on what he'd said so far. Then he continued. "The point is this—we're in the saddle, so get your backsides in gear and get ready. We're the 804 Evac, and when all the shooting breaks loose we're the guys and girls who stitch it back together again. Any questions?"

No one spoke. "Okay, let's get shaking. Get in uniform and get ready. We'll call formation in two hours." Harper handed the microphone to his aide. The plane ground to a halt.

Les and Tills turned to each other. "This is it," said Les.

"Yep, no way out now," agreed Tills, as people in front of them began to unload.

Les reached out his hand to his friend. "Good luck, Rog," he said.

"You too, guy, but I don't think we'll need it. We should be fine."

"I expect you're right, but you never know, what with chemicals and Scud missiles and such."

"Still and all, I don't think we'll face much danger."

"Probably not," agreed Les, standing up to get his overhead

bag. "At least as long as we're still in the States."

They squeezed into the aisles and piled out of the plane. A private pointed them to a barracks compound on the right, but Les veered out of the line of men and women being herded that way.

"Where you headed?" asked Tills.

"To call Katherine."

Confusion crossed Tills' face.

"I'll explain it to you later," said Les. Tills nodded and marched on with the group.

Les found a battery of phones outside the officers' mess. He contacted an operator and placed his call. The phone rang until the answering machine came on. Impatiently, he bit his lower lip and cursed. Where was Kath? Looking for John? At her mom's?

He tried that number. No answer. He tried home again. Nothing.

Les hung up and slouched to his quarters. Going to Harper wouldn't help. For all he knew, John had come home and they were out celebrating, eating pizza somewhere. All he could do was wait.

He entered the barracks soberly, checked at the desk for his assignment, and headed to his room. Inside, he found Roger and one other officer, a lanky man with straw-white hair, putting their gear in place.

Les nodded to the stranger and pitched his gear onto the only bed not taken, the one closest to the door.

Roger turned to the stranger. "Now that we're all here, let me do the introductions. I'll start with yours truly. I'm Roger Tills, family doctor from Hannibal, Missouri, womanizer from forever, boozer from yesterday until tomorrow, and general surgeon from training at Johns Hopkins."

He nodded to Les. "And this is Dr. Les Tennet, also known as Les the Blest, chief cut-and-slice man from St. Louis Med Center. A real live star carver. Best you're likely to see in this man's Army."

Les waved off Tills' comments and directed his talk to the blonde. "Don't pay any attention to him. He's mouthy, but it's usually harmless. What's your story?"

The blonde man grinned and his white teeth sliced through the room and it seemed to Les like they picked up the light of the bulbs overhead and intensified it tenfold. The whole room brightened in the glare of his grin.

When he spoke, his voice surprised Les. It seemed to start at his toes and rise up, getting deeper every inch it climbed, until it finally erupted as if from an underground cavern—deep and wide. "Name's Nelson Reed. I'm from Chicago. The Lake Michigan Hospital."

"What's your area, doctor?" asked Tills. "Orthopedics? Surgery? Proctology? Gynecology? Come on, tell us how you make your millions."

"If you'll shut up and give him a chance, maybe he will," groused Les.

Reed laughed out loud and the tone sounded like a happy lion's roar. "I don't work on anything you can see, gentlemen," he said. "My job's less tangible than that. I—"

"A shrink!" interrupted Roger. "Just what I need—somebody to analyze my tangled mind."

Reed chuckled again, like a boy about to pull a joke. "Afraid you're a tad off the mark. I'm not a shrink." Reed's smile widened even further and his crystal blue eyes danced. "I'm a chaplain."

The color drained from Tills' face. "A chaplain?"

"Yep, a chaplain, of the American Baptist variety. Sent here to analyze your soul."

"Well, I'll be—!"

"Better not say it, Rog," warned Les. "With a chaplain here, it might come true."

Nelson Reed tilted back his head and roared his thunderous laugh again. Les joined with him—the first full laugh he'd enjoyed in a long time. Amazing, he thought. In the midst of preparation for war, he'd found someone with whom to laugh.

Chapter Twenty-two

The ponderous clouds that rolled in a few hours after Les' departure were filled with warm moisture. When they collided with a frigid air mass hovering above St. Louis, the two formed a patchy weather front that included pockets of ice, snow, and rain.

About the time the clock hanging outside First Missouri Bank hit struck 4 P.M., the clouds disgorged their heavy moisture. A large portion of the ice in the clouds hit warm air as it plummeted downward and melted into harmless sprinkles of rain. But in certain areas the ice survived the fall and encased the land underneath it in a clear glaze.

Where it did stick it caused problems... like on the main telephone terminal less than a half mile from the Tennet home. The ice settled on the terminal like a glass cloak and the weight of the cloak grew heavier as the afternoon temperature dropped and the ice pellets pounded more intensely. A few minutes before 6, the weight sagged down on the lines connecting to the terminal and the ice snapped the line, instantly shutting off almost 1,000 phones.

Katherine discovered the outage when she tried to call out for pizza for supper. She ran next door and found her neighbors had the same problem. She wondered if the outage had hit her parents. No way to tell. They were in New York on their annual after-Christmas shopping spree. After finding John home, Katherine insisted they go ahead with their trip. Beatrice resisted at first; she didn't think she and Walter should leave Katherine alone at such a crucial time, but Katherine promised to call immediately if she needed their help, and Beatrice finally accepted her promise.

With the lines out, Katherine worried most about Les, knowing how desperately he would want news of John. But since she didn't know how to reach him and couldn't do anything about the downed lines, she accepted the situation with a surprising calm.

One thing about it — the bad weather and the phone outage and the holiday slowdown kept Clemons from bothering her. The first day after John came home, she thought about going to a phone outside the neighborhood and calling Clemons. Then she considered going to the Kirkwood Station. But then she decided against both. If Clemons wanted to find out about John, he could come to the house.

She also decided to leave John alone about the gun. He would have to answer plenty of questions soon enough. If he wanted to tell her without prodding, fine. But in a way, she hoped he wouldn't talk about it. Not yet, anyway. That wasn't what she needed right now.

What she needed now was quiet, to sort out her experience in the church. Needed it to assure John. Needed it to thrash through her emotions about Les. Needed it to dig deeper into herself.

What was happening to her? What did the scene in the church mean? Another fad? Another effort to escape the harsh realities of her life? She didn't know the answers to her questions, but she wanted to know, and the ice had given her a window of time to begin to sort it all out.

To her relief, the phones weren't fixed the next day or the next or even the third. She figured the holiday season caused the delay and, since she wanted the time alone anyway, she didn't bother to contact the phone company to speed them up.

For three days she hibernated with John and Sherry, seldom venturing out. After the ice and rain fell, the temperature dropped again and stayed intensely cold; the cold wrapped around the house like a frozen cocoon and Katherine snuggled down in it with her children.

John and Sherry embraced the interlude too. No one talked very much. Sherry busied herself with her morning swims and her dolls and John spent hours in his room listening to his music.

Even when they ate their meals, words were sparse. Somehow it seemed as if words weren't particularly necessary. Without discussing it, they reached an accord of quiet and all of them felt stronger for it when it was over.

It ended far too soon for Katherine, on December 31 to be exact, right before 8 P.M. It ended with the jangle of the phone. Katherine stared at it for a second before she picked it up, knowing it meant her retreat had ended. Then she sucked in her breath and answered.

"Hello."

"Officer Clemons here, Mrs. Tennet. Look, I'm sorry to bother you on New Year's Eve and all, but since I've had court all week and your phone's been out, I've not had a chance to contact you."

"You don't need to apologize, officer," Katherine said wryly. "I'm doing fine."

"Uh, good, Mrs. Tennet, glad to hear it. Look, I need an update from you on John. Has he gotten home yet?" He stopped and waited on her to fill him in.

Katherine hesitated, reluctant to begin the hell she knew would follow.

"Mrs. Tennet, any sign of John?" Clemons repeated.

Katherine pushed back her hair. "Oh . . . yes, sorry, officer. Yes, John is here with me." She didn't volunteer the information that he'd come home almost four days ago. "The phone company only fixed our phones today and I've had no way to call you."

On the other end of the line, Clemons said nothing for a second. He didn't ask when John came home. No need to make a stink about that now. Enough time for that later. Right now he wanted to revel in the fun he would have interrogating the privileged white kid. What a break from his usual suspects. He hoped John wouldn't want to drive to the station himself. He much preferred to pick him up in the squad car. A better scene for the neighbors that way. More scandal for the Tennet family.

"Good, Mrs. Tennet, good. This way John's safe. We can question him, get this mess clarified, and get him home. Would you like for us to pick him up?"

"Uh, no, I don't think so, officer. I can bring him down. Is the morning soon enough? It's fairly late already tonight. And it is New Year's Eve."

Clemons shrugged. Though anxious to get John into custody, the day had tired him and he didn't want fatigue to cause any mistakes when he questioned the kid. Besides, he had no doubt she would bring him in and he hated to start the paperwork on an arrest at this time of night.

"Yeah, sure, I think that'll be fine. But we'll certainly pick him up ourselves in the morning, if that would help you out."

"No," insisted Katherine. "I'll have him in your office tomorrow if that fits your schedule. Will you be in on New Year's Day?"

Clemons paused, but only for a short beat. "Sure, I'll be right here. Crime doesn't pay much attention to the calendar. I'll see you then." Clemons put down the phone and rubbed his bald head, puzzling out how best to frighten John. He didn't want to ruin this rare chance.

Katherine laid the phone down and pushed back her hair, wondering how best to navigate John through this quagmire. She'd never faced anything like this and didn't know the first thing about the process. She needed help, but Les was too far away to do anything.

She didn't have but one place to turn. Though she knew Les would dislike her doing it, she had no choice. If they had kept the schedule they'd given her before they left, then they were home by now. She dialed the number. Beatrice answered.

"Mother, when did you and Dad get back?"

"Earlier today. We didn't want to spend New Year's Eve in New York. Figured it would get too crazy for us. What's up with you? Everything okay with John?"

"Well, not exactly. I'm need to talk to Dad on this one."

Beatrice hesitated for a skip. "Isn't it something I can help you with?" she asked, nosy as usual.

"No, I need to talk to Dad."

Beatrice grunted, but then acquiesced. "All right, Katherine, hold on a minute." She called, "Walter, it's Katherine. He's coming, dear. Now, what is it? Why do you need to talk to your father?"

Katherine sighed and started to answer. But then, amazingly, she didn't. Beatrice could wait.

Chapter Twenty-three

Les had tried one final time to call Katherine before he flew out of Ft. Ben Harrison the morning of December 31, headed to Frankfurt, Germany. Still no answer. The operator repeated the refrain he'd heard often in the last few days. "The phones are still out. You'll have to try again later."

Failing to reach home, he had also fought one more round in his ongoing argument with Colonel Harper. He had tried every day, but so far had not won a single point.

Harper kept stalling. "Wait until the phones are working again," he said over and over. "If I send you back and John's home, then I look like a fool. I'll keep my word and send you back if he's missing, but we don't know anything yet. So, you're going nowhere but where the 804th goes."

Now the 804th had landed in Germany just long enough to receive their orders, enjoy New Year's Eve, and finish the final preparations to jump off to Saudi Arabia. "Just be glad you're here," Harper encouraged him. "Here you can still celebrate."

Les didn't feel much like celebrating. Not while he remained in the dark about John. He hurried to a phone as quickly as possible after they landed in Frankfurt. No result. Phones still out of order.

Finally, resigned to his fate, Les decided to make the most of it. He'd try calling again tomorrow. Within an hour of landing, he carried his pack into his temporary quarters and joined Roger and Reed.

Roger gushed over the accommodations. "Lucky, lucky, lucky," he beamed, as they tossed their gear down on the floor. "New Year's Eve on a U.S. base. Let's get a bite to eat and then let the party roll." Les didn't dispute his recommendation.

Two hours later, they finished their supper in the central mess hall and headed for the lobby of the building where the TVs were located. Roger saw Macy Spencer in front of one in the right corner of the room and he directed Les and Nelson to her. "My lucky night," he gloated, rubbing his hands together. "I'm finally going to get some time with the woman of my latest dreams. New Year's Eve and Macy Spencer. What a combination."

She glanced up as the three sat down around her in the otherwise deserted area. "Roger Tills," she said, greeting him professionally, but with no particular warmth.

"Ms. Spencer, what a pleasure to see you again. Let me introduce my bunkies." He went around the circle and each man greeted Spencer, filling her in on their specialty and home base.

Macy Spencer nodded to each one, but kept her primary attention focused on the screen. Les and Nelson took the hint, but Roger missed it. "What you watching?" he asked.

"*Sound of Music*," said Macy, not looking up from it.

"A love story!" groused Roger. "In the middle of a military base? What's come over you? If Saddam His Insane could see us watching this mama's apron stuff, he'd know he didn't have anything to worry about."

Roger pounced from his chair as if about to turn the channel. Macy Spencer's steely voice chopped him off short. "This movie is about over, and if you touch that dial you won't live to turn another one."

Roger swallowed hard and sat down. "Excuse me, Ms. Spencer, I didn't mean to offend your highness. I forgot we were fighting the first war known to the human race without John Wayne as its patron saint."

A trace of a smile flicked onto Macy's full lips. Watching her, Les decided she was playing with Roger, teasing him. She said, "I accept your apology, Tills, but don't let it happen again. If it does, you can join Wayne in that male chauvinist haven in the sky."

The group laughed in unison and settled down to watch the end of the Von Trapp family adventures. Within minutes the Von Trapps were climbing the mountain to freedom and the movie ended.

"What next, gang?" asked Roger, eager to shift the tone of the evening.

"It's barely 9," said Les. "Far too early to turn in."

"Anybody for poker?"

They all turned in surprise to Nelson.

"You play?" asked Les cautiously.

"A little," said Nelson, pulling a deck of cards from his jacket pocket.

"Good man!" shouted Roger. "Maybe we'll remember this party after all. Boys and girls, let me make a suggestion. Let's move the party back to our room. We can have a bit of privacy there and I can offer my contribution to the war effort." He raised his eyebrows. "Any problem with that?"

They all turned to Macy. Les wondered if she would join them, or if her playful distaste for Roger's aggressiveness would separate her from their threesome.

"If we protect you from Roger, will you play?" asked Les.

"Can I trust you to do that?" she said.

"You can trust me," said Reed. "After all, I'm a chaplain."

Macy nodded. "That's sufficient, I suppose. Count me in."

Roger slapped his knees and stood up. "Okay, it's settled. Let's get the festivities underway."

Fifteen minutes later Les finished centering a table in the middle of their square room. Macy set four plastic cups on top of the table. Then Roger, wearing a cockeyed grin, pulled a brown paper sack from the bottom of his pack and unwrapped it. Triumphantly, he held aloft a fifth of Jack Daniels.

"Man, don't you know that stuff is off-limits?" said Macy.

"Sure it's off-limits, but what's a party without a little party mix? Besides, this is New Year's Eve. What would it be without a little joy juice?"

"I guess that would be un-American," agreed Les.

"And unhealthy," concluded Macy.

"None for me," said Nelson.

They all looked at him. "Your religion?" asked Roger.

"Well, partly. But more my health. The stuff makes me nauseated."

"Yeah, me too," agreed Roger. "But it takes a heap more than one glass for that to happen."

They all laughed. "Go ahead," said Reed. "I'll drink water."

Shrugging, Roger picked a cup off the table and blew into it. "Who's first?"

"Ladies first," said Macy, raising her hand.

"Hey," argued Les. "You come up with that 'ladies first' stuff when it's to your advantage, but stick with the liberation line when it's not. That's not fair."

"All's fair in love and war," cracked Macy. "And this is war."

Roger poured her drink first. Then he took care of Les and himself. Nelson pulled a bottle of water from his gear, filled his cup with it, and offered a toast. "To the 804th," he said. "May she send all her soldiers home alive."

"Salute," they all said, clicking their cups together.

"Time to play cards," said Nelson, taking a swig and knocking the deck against the tabletop. "Everybody chip in or ship out."

All chipped in. He dealt the cards with a surprisingly practiced hand and the poker game began. Within a couple of hours, Nelson had demonstrated an uncanny skill at the game.

Pile after pile of money ended up on his side of the table. As his stack heaped taller, the whiskey line in the bottle edged lower and lower. Several cigars had appeared from Roger's pockets and Les and Macy took one, sticking them equally unlit into their teeth.

"Good grief, Nelson," griped Les as he tossed in his losing cards yet again. "Are you cheating?"

"Would a man of the cloth sink to cheating to win a few measly bucks off his friends?" asked Reed in mock chagrin.

"Don't know," said Les. "Depends on how much the man of the cloth needed the money."

"Well, I can tell you for sure, this one needs it badly," said Nelson, sweeping the cash to his side of the table. "Men of the cloth don't make the big bucks you body carvers do."

"What about female helicopter pilots?" pouted Macy. "They don't make bucks either, but that hasn't stopped you from picking me clean."

"He's just treating you equally, dear Macy," jibed Les. "You wouldn't want him to discriminate against you, I'm sure. That's not the modern way. No, I expect the Reverend Reed believes in equality all the way down the line. No quarter asked and none given. Male or female, looks like he's an equal opportunity poker player." Les turned to Nelson. "Am I right, reverend?"

"Couldn't have said it better myself. Now, who's in?"

He dealt another hand and the night stretched longer. Midnight passed and they stopped briefly to yell and toast the start of 1992 and go to the bathroom. Then they wandered back to the poker table. The cards kept coming.

"How long you been a preacher?" Roger asked Reed, as he tossed a card on the table in front of him.

"About fifteen years." He dispensed cards to everyone at the table.

"You're how old now?"

"Thirty-seven."

"Started early then."

"Yep, pretty early. In my last year of college I took a pastorate of a small church. Started preaching every Sunday. Been doing it ever since." Everyone checked their hands and made opening bets.

"What made you decide to be a reverend?" Les eased into the conversation.

"Oh, I don't know, not really. I've got a few ideas why I ended up doing this, but I can't say for sure. What made you become a doctor? What makes anyone become anything?"

"Give me two cards," said Les. Nelson obliged and Les turned back to the question Reed had asked. "I thought preachers were different. You know, they are what they are because something special happens to them."

"How do you mean?" asked Nelson, playing the part of the devil's advocate as he tossed Roger and Macy three cards apiece. He took only one himself.

"You know what I mean," said Les. "Don't you believe God has something to do with your being a minister?"

"Don't you believe God has something to do with your being a doctor?" countered Nelson, "I'm in for five bucks."

Roger and Macy flung their hands on the table simultaneously and folded. Les covered the bet.

Les was stumped. "It's possible God had something to do with my becoming a doctor, but I never considered it from that angle."

"Maybe you should."

"Raise you ten, " said Les, slyly slipping the bill onto the table.

"Getting steep in here," grinned Roger.

Les continued Nelson's train of thought. "Only one problem with thinking God had a hand in my life's occupation."

"What's that? And I up you ten more." He tossed his money into the pile.

"I'm not sure God even exists." Les rubbed his tongue over his front teeth, a windshield wiper swishing back and forth, back and forth. Then, deliberately, he slapped the cash down.

"You an atheist?" Nelson asked it gently.

"Yeah," Les said. "Swear to God I am." His eyes widened

with pleasure as he lowered his full house—queens over threes—onto the table.

Nelson swallowed hard and stared at the cards in front of him. Roger slapped Macy on the back and she gagged on her cigar. All waited to see Nelson's hand. He grinned too and his grin split open the room and made Les certain he had lost again. He laid out his cards. Four fours.

Les threw his hands up in surrender. "I give up, Nelson. Either you're cheating or there really is a God and He's on your side."

"Or She," suggested Macy, flashing her green eyes at Les.

Nelson leaned over and rounded up his winnings, pulling the money to him like a fishing net hauling a catch out of the water.

"Where did you learn to play like that?" asked Les, his tone one of admiration.

"The army, of course. After all, they don't teach this at the seminary."

"Isn't gambling a vice for you religious guys?"

"To some it is," agreed Nelson. "But I never saw it that way. Seems to me gambling is a way of life. Everybody gambles."

"How so?"

"Well, take me and you for instance. I say God does exist. That God cares for us, loves us even. That God gives us courage and hope and strength and grace to make life meaningful. You, on the other hand, say God doesn't exist. That we're rotating around all alone on this rock called Earth. That we're chance circumstances spawned out of some primordial chemical soup. That no purpose lies behind our creation. Does that say it right?"

"Yeah, pretty much so. What's the point?"

"Think about it. We're both gamblers. You're gambling no God exists and I'm gambling one does. Neither of us can prove what we believe. As a trained physician you know you can't get behind the starting point of life. Even with a Big

Bang you have to have a Big Banger. Who created the dust particles that supposedly exploded? Who created the space in which those particles swirled for aeons? You can't answer that. So, your theory of life rests on faith—on a possibility you can't demonstrate in a laboratory."

"And yours?" Les whispered his question.

"Same thing. I can't show God in a lab. God won't yield to a CAT scan, so I have to deduce God . . . from the order of the natural world. A honey bee pollinating a flower. A human brain interpreting electrical signals and telling my eye I'm seeing a waterfall. A child suckling a mother's breast. Life, as fouled up and fallen as it is, gives me reason to have faith."

"A reasonable faith?" Les sounded incredulous.

"Absolutely reasonable. Where did we even get the notion of God? Someone or some being had to plant the notion in us. Where did we gain our sense of right and wrong? A moral law written into our genes? Who wrote it down first? Sure it's reasonable. At least as reasonable as your gamble that it all happened by pure accident."

Les rubbed his teeth over his tongue again. Then he raised his shoulders in a shrug. "I guess we'll never know who's right, will we?"

Nelson's smile brightened the room again. "Oh, that's where you're wrong, good doctor. We'll know all right."

"How so?"

"We'll know when we've played our last hand. We'll know when we die." Reed cut the cards and tapped them onto the table. "Now, who's still playing?"

Chapter Twenty-four

Lieutenant Tom Clemons stood at the window of the Kirkwood Police Station and watched as the wheels of the Jeep Cherokee stopped against the curb outside. He licked his lips as Katherine and John Tennet climbed out of the jeep and walked toward him. Leaving the window, he walked to his desk and sat down. Didn't want to appear too anxious.

From the desk, he saw Katherine and John enter the building, glance around to get their bearings, then head for the check-in desk in the center of the room.

Clemons tried to stay calm, but it wasn't easy. After staying up most of the night anticipating his visit with John Tennet, he had come to the station at 7 A.M. Then, not wanting to chance missing their entry, he never left his desk, not even to go to the bathroom. Now, watching them walk toward the desk sergeant, he leaned back in his seat and enjoyed the spectacle—two rich snobs getting what they deserved. He smiled to himself, pleased by the somber stares on the faces of John and Katherine Tennet.

Standing slowly, Clemons picked up his hat, perched it on his middle finger, and spun it around three times. He always did that when he wanted good luck on a case. Though he had never actually calculated whether it made any difference in the outcomes of his arrests, spinning his hat made him feel lucky.

And that's what counted.

Finished spinning it, he laid his hat on his desk and, with feigned concern etched on his face, stepped across the room to intercept John and Katherine.

"Mrs. Tennet."

Katherine saw Clemons coming and slowed to speak. "Yes, Lieutenant Clemons," she said, extending her hand. "What do we do now?"

Ignoring her question, he took her hand, shook it firmly and smiled. Then he turned to John. "And you must be John."

John nodded but didn't take the hand offered to him. *Arrogant smart aleck,* thought Clemons. *Let's see how superior you act after you've spent a few hours pacing the floor of a jail cell.*

His attention on Katherine again, Clemons spoke smoothly. "Here's what happens now, Mrs. Tennet. You wait here while I take John back for questioning. I think I can move you in and out of here without too much trouble."

Katherine hesitated and swiveled her head to the door. "We're waiting for an attorney," she said, her voice a bit timid.

Clemons' spine straightened, but only for a thin instant. He regained his relaxed posture before Katherine noticed the slip.

"Certainly, Mrs. Tennet, we can wait for your lawyer if you wish. But I don't think we'll need one right yet. We only want to question John, not arrest him. But, if you think he needs a lawyer . . ." He left the sentence hanging like a spider web about to entangle them, the accusation plain enough for all to see. If John needed an attorney, then maybe he had something to hide.

John cleared his throat and spoke for the first time to Clemons. "I don't need to wait." He turned to his mom. "I don't have anything to tell him, so he can question me all he wants. It won't make any difference whether a lawyer's here or not."

Clemons wanted to spin his hat and felt sorry he'd left it on his desk. The kid was going to walk right into it.

Katherine started to protest but John cut her off. "Really,

Mom, what's the big deal? It's only questioning, and if I didn't do it, then what can happen? Send Granddad in when he gets here, if you want; but I don't want to waste the whole day, so let's get this started."

Clemons paused for a moment, wondering who the Granddad was. No matter, he thought, pushing ahead was what mattered. "The sooner we begin, the sooner you both can leave for home," he said, keeping his anxiety under wraps.

Katherine questioned him. "As soon as Mr. Tillman arrives, he can come in?"

"Absolutely," said Clemons. *So Walter Tillman is her dad.* Reason for caution, but Tillman had retired from criminal practice quite a while ago. Out of the loop for sure. No worry.

Katherine shrugged. "All right, John, go ahead if you feel comfortable." She leaned in for a skip, as if to hug him, but John stiffened and she backed off. Clemons placed his hand on John's elbow and led him out of her vision. She gulped, found a seat, and sat down to wait.

Steering John into a soundproof cubicle out of view of the main office, Clemons squeezed John's arm tighter and pressed him down into a hard-backed chair. A second chair sat less than five feet away, with only a square table between the two. The light in the room was muted but glaring, and a slight hum filtered into the cramped quarters from the air conditioning system somewhere below.

Seated now, John rubbed his elbow, as if trying to clean off the touch of Clemons' hand. Clemons watched him for a second, then, like a falcon with open talons, pounced.

"Now listen up, rich boy," he hissed. "You can make this easy or hard on yourself. It's your choice. I prefer that you make it hard, if you want to know the truth. I want you to lie, to cover up, to pretend you don't know a thing. You see, that's good for me. I get to harass you longer when you do. And that's my whole pleasure in life—to get on the cases of pretty boys like you and make their silver-spooned lives a little less like heaven. So what's it going to be? You tell me right now about your part in this drive-by shooting and be done with it and make me miserable, or you stonewall the whole thing and give me a reason to get up tomorrow morning."

John showed no emotion as Clemons made his speech. When he spoke, his words were measured. "I found the gun in an alley a couple of blocks from the school. I don't know anything about a drive-by shooting."

Clemons wanted to shout for joy, but he circled John's chair instead. A buzzard waiting for its prey to fall.

"What were you doing in the alley? A guy with your cash flow wasn't in there looking for a new winter coat."

"No, I cut through the alley as a shortcut home."

"I thought you owned a jeep."

John winced and Clemons saw it. John covered. "My jeep had a flat tire."

"Where did you get it fixed?"

"I fixed it myself."

"Why didn't you fix it immediately instead of walking home?"

"I didn't have a spare with me."

"And would you like to tell me where your spare was?"

John smiled. "Yes, sir, my spare was at home."

Clemons bowed slightly at John, acknowledging the loss of this round. The kid was sharp. Good. That would make it all the more gratifying when he finally brought him down. He tried another direction.

"What about Trevor Mashburn, the murdered boy? Did you know him?"

"Yeah, I knew him, played ball against him a few times."

"How long did you know him?"

"I don't know, a couple of years, I guess."

"Ever have any problems—"

Sharp knuckles rapped on the door and interrupted Clemons' question. Clemons stalked over and flung it open. A stocky block of a man followed the knocking and plunged ahead to where John sat in the center of the room.

"You okay, John?" Walter Tillman asked, obviously anxious about the boy's safety.

"Yeah, Gramps, doing fine."

Walter swiveled around to Clemons with an agility that belied his age. He pointed a stubby finger into Clemons' chest and roared like an injured elephant. "Clemons, you know better than this. You don't question a client of mine outside of my presence. Especially this client. You make a mistake and harm this boy and I'll have your fanny in a sling so fast you'll wish your mother had left you out in a St. Louis snowstorm to die young."

Clemons threw up his hands. "Mr. Tillman, calm yourself. An older gentleman like you can have a stroke if you stay stoked up like this too long. John and I were having a simple chat. That's all. As you can see, he's perfectly all right." He turned both palms up and motioned toward John. John sat nonchalantly in his chair and fiddled with his loose shoestrings.

Walter hesitated and his thick, gray eyebrows settled down on the stoops of his brow like a hunting dog lying down for a nap.

He switched his attention to John again. "That right, John?"

"Yeah, pretty much so," said John, tying his left sneaker.

"See," urged Clemons, relieved at John's attitude. "The boy's fine."

"You done with him?"

It was Clemons' turn to hesitate. He had a weak hand so far. Not enough to go to the D.A. and ask for an arrest. He had no choice but to cut John loose. He eased back. "For now I am." He switched his eyes back to John and his voice hardened just a beat. "But I'll probably need to chat with John again at some point in the future. That suit you, John?"

"Absolutely." He tied his right shoe, never taking his eyes off the string.

"Then you're free to go."

Walter touched John's shoulder and John raised himself up to leave. With a final stare toward Clemons, he stalked out.

Got to like his attitude, mused Clemons. He would really enjoy breaking him.

Chapter Twenty-five

Les woke with a jerk, snapping up in his cot and trying to remember where he was. Holding his head in his hands, he immediately regretted he had moved so fast. He remembered the evening. New Year's Eve had turned into a blur of card games and animated conversation and warm booze. From somewhere Roger had kept bringing it out, bottle after bottle, and Les and Macy and Roger had kept drinking, and all of them had talked and played and watched as the night passed.

Les focused his swollen eyes on his watch. Almost 10 A.M., 3 A.M. back home. He'd have to wait awhile to call.

Feeling the pounding of his head, he wished he had more than a couple of hours before he had to report for final preparations for Saudi. He had a feeling the last-minute details wouldn't give him much time to recover.

Slowly, he showered, dressed, and shaved, and then headed to the mess hall for a bite to eat. Holding a tray full of cereal and muffins, he spotted Macy alone at a table and sat down with her. Surprisingly, she showed no effects from the evening's escapades. Eyes as green as Coke bottles—no red streaks anywhere. Face smooth as liquid butter. Les stared at her and she locked her gaze with his.

"Excuse me," he said, "but weren't you up past 2 with me?"

Macy laughed and it sounded like a spring bubbling up. She

lifted a juice glass to her lips, taking a skinny sip. "Sure, Les, I lost all my money to Nellie, just like you did."

"Then why do you look like Rebecca of Sunnybrook Farm?" He munched off one of his muffins.

She placed the glass on the table. "Good makeup, a girl's best friend."

Les scanned her face from forehead to chin. High cheekbones. A nose and chin a plastic surgeon would kill to create. Lips full as fresh strawberries and equally as red. A thin gap between her two front teeth the only imperfection he could see. But instead of detracting from her beauty, the gap in her teeth added to it, made her seem girlish and accessible. And, contrary to what she had said, she wore no makeup that he could see. But he didn't comment on that.

"Well, I feel like death warmed over in a microwave," he said, sipping from his coffee.

"And you look it too."

"Hey, thanks for the compassionate bedside manner."

Macy snorted. "Hey, don't forget, I'm not a doctor. Just a pilot. No one pays me for bedside manner."

Les rubbed his forehead and noticed his headache had disappeared since he started talking to Macy.

"You ready to go to Saudi?"

"As much as possible, I guess. You?"

"Yeah, pretty much so." He spread butter on a piece of bread.

"You excited?" she asked.

"Not really, leaving too much behind." He shoved the bread into his mouth and picked up a napkin to wipe his lips.

"Your family?" She asked the question gently, as if careful not to pry.

"Yeah," nodded Les. "Two children, John and Sherry, and my wife, Katherine."

"Sounds beautiful," said Macy, swallowing a spoonful of cereal.

Les chuckled slightly. "Not always."

"How so?"

Les put down his coffee and focused on her eyes. "You know, problems."

"Yeah, we all have them, don't we?"

"Not like mine."

Macy reached over and touched his arm. "You want to talk about it?"

Les lowered his eyes and rubbed his tongue over his top teeth. "I don't know, you sure you want to hear it?"

Her touch on his arm tightened. "Yeah, Les, I think I do."

Why not, he decided. It wouldn't hurt to tell her. It would do him good to talk. Besides, talking with Macy had erased his headache, and if she could do that for him, then he could trust her with his story.

He took another bite of bread, chewed it, and swallowed. Then he began to talk, slowly at first, but with increasing pace. He poured out the situation. All of it. From the beginning of their marriage.

Though he tried to keep the emotion out of his voice, the steady gaze of Macy's green eyes made him feel safe, and the touch of her hand on his arm told him she cared. By the time he finished she knew more about him than anyone but Katherine, and she was an ocean away. Macy rested only inches away and her touch felt so good and—

And then Roger plopped down beside them and groaned and Les stopped talking. Mumbling only a short good morning to his pal and a quick goodbye to Macy, Les picked up his tray and left. He could feel Macy's eyes on his back as he walked away and he looked forward to talking with her again.

For the rest of the day, Les joined the rest of the 804 in a scurry of activity. A final battery of shots, two hours of review on operations at the Saudi hospital where they would serve, another hour on procedures in case of chemical attack.

The day hurried past and before he could blink, the moon had risen and he had finished supper. Only one more night before he landed in the Middle East.

Though not hopeful, he decided to try the phone once more. On the fourth ring, he got an answer. "Hello."

Les felt like leaping. It was John! "John," he shouted, as if trying to make his voice heard in St. Louis without the phone. "This is Dad. I've been trying to call, but the lines have been out and I've been on the move and haven't been able to get you. I've been going crazy wondering about you. Are you okay?"

"Yeah, Dad, I'm fine," said John. "It's good to hear your voice."

"Thanks, man, you too. How's Sherry?"

"Great, Dad, she's doing fine. She's playing at a friend's house right now."

Les was disappointed he wouldn't get to talk with her, but maybe it was best. Gave him more time to find out about John. He plunged into the questions he wanted answered, hoping John would understand his need to know.

"Look, John, I don't want this to sound like an interrogation, but I'm dying to know what's happening with you. When did you get home? Where were you? What's the story with this gun they found on you?"

Les heard John sigh, as if trying to decide how to respond. Les said, "I'm not accusing you of anything, John. Please know that."

John cleared his throat. "Okay, Dad, I'll give it to you straight. I was in your office at the hospital, trying to decide what to do. I came home the same day you left."

"You were at my office?"

"Yeah, didn't figure anyone would think of looking there."

"Pretty smart of you," said Les.

"Yeah, I thought so." John chuckled slightly.

Les switched ears with the phone, not certain what to say next. He didn't want to probe too deeply, but he wanted so many answers and he didn't feel he had time to get them. He decided to ask the most pertinent one.

"John, have you contacted the police about the gun yet?"

John didn't hesitate. "Yeah, Dad, I went down this morning with Mom. Talked with a cop named Clemons. But I didn't help him too much. Then Granddad came in and asked Clemons if he was pressing charges. Clemons said no and he cut me loose. That was that."

"What did you tell him about the gun?"

"Told him I found it in an alley near the school."

Les sucked in his breath. He didn't know if John was telling the truth or not. But now wasn't the time to demonstrate any lack of trust.

"Then that's the end of it?"

John hesitated and then answered, "Wouldn't count on that. I have the feeling Clemons will try to pin me to that shooting somehow. He seemed pretty hostile. I don't think he'll give up easily."

"Probably not," agreed Les. "We'll have to wait and see on that. For now, at least, you're okay. You don't know how relieved I am to hear your voice."

The line went silent. Les rubbed his forehead, then continued. "John, when I get home I want us to go back to square one. I want things to be better between us. Are you willing to try?"

For a brief moment, John didn't answer. Les knew his son didn't trust him.

"Are you willing?" he asked again.

"Yeah, I'm willing," said John. "But Dad—"

"Yeah?"

"Well, I don't know how to say this, but um, I've heard you say this before and then something always happens and your attention gets diverted and we fall apart again. If that changes, maybe things can get better."

"You blaming it all on me?" Anger rolled into Les's voice.

"I'm not blaming it on anyone. I'm only trying to tell you how I feel."

Les bit his lower lip and his face flushed. Suddenly his headache returned. "I can't go into it with you now, John, I need

.o talk to your mom. Is she there?"

"Sure, Dad," said John. "She's here, hang on a sec."

John dropped the phone. A few moments later Katherine picked it up.

"Les, is that you?"

"Yeah, it's me and I can't talk but a minute or so more, but I wanted you to know I'm alive and kicking. I'm thrilled John's home. That takes a load off, I can tell you."

"He tell you we went to the police station?"

"Yeah, he said everything was fine."

"For now, at least."

"Hopefully, from now on. He said you'd gotten your dad's help?"

Katherine caught her breath, then answered. "Yeah, I didn't know where else to turn."

Les considered her situation. He and Walter weren't on the best of terms. Never had been, though he didn't really understand why. Both were self-made men. But, maybe that made them competitors and that competitiveness kept them distant. Or maybe it was Beatrice, always chopping away at Les for his lack of sophistication and family standing.

"Isn't he a little rusty?" he asked, hoping not to sound defensive. "He's almost retired and hasn't done criminal work for almost ten years. Are you sure he's the best we can get?"

"No, Les, he's not the best criminal attorney we can get, but I don't see that we need that. Dad did fine today. Clemons let John go the second Dad walked into the office. Don't forget, Dad has a pretty strong reputation here in St. Louis."

"You're comfortable with the situation?"

"Yes, completely, so let's drop it for now. I'm sure you don't have much time and I want to visit with you for a minute about something that happened to me."

Not wanting to argue with her, Les stayed quiet as she gulped in her breath and continued. "Les, on the day you left St. Louis the most remarkable thing happened. I left the airport . . ."

With increasing excitement in her voice, she poured out her story, the near accident in the highway, the crash into the church parking lot, the dazed walk into the sanctuary, the vision of Jesus, the serenity that followed . . .

"I don't know what it all means, Les, but I feel like I've turned a corner of some kind. I've made an appointment with a minister to talk about what happened. It's like a quiet pool inside me where I can retreat when things get blurred. It's a focus point I've never had. It's hard to explain, but for the first time in my whole life —"

Les, who had listened patiently through the whole story, had heard enough. He cut her off. "Hey, honey, I'm happy for you. But, to be honest, I'm more concerned with John's situation right now. Tell me more about what happened at the police station."

Katherine squeezed the phone and closed her eyes tightly. "I told you John was fine," she said. "There's not a whole lot more I can tell you about it."

"Then I guess I better go," said Les, suddenly irritated with her for a reason he couldn't quite identify.

"Yeah, I suppose you should," agreed Katherine. "Maybe we can talk again soon."

"Yeah, I'll call as soon as I can," said Les, his voice trailing off.

"Yeah, call soon, Les."

He could tell she wanted to say more. But she didn't.

"Bye," said Les.

Both hung up. Les cursed silently. Obviously Katherine had gotten hysterical after he left. Alone, with John missing, scared and anxious, she had fallen prey to a momentary psychological breakdown. She had sounded steady on the phone, though, even if she still clung to the vision she'd had. In a week or so it would pass and she would be normal again. He certainly hoped so. He didn't need anything else to worry about.

Chapter Twenty-six

Clemons hoped to give Les plenty more to worry about. He scrambled furiously the next three days, digging to uncover information about the shooting. He hadn't for an instant bought John's story about finding the gun in an alley on the way home from school. Teenagers always had friends or parents who would drive them home. The chances of John walking home were as slim as Clemons' chances of winning the Missouri Lottery, which he'd played since it first began with absolutely no luck at all.

The confidence that John was lying stoked the resentment Clemons held toward all teenagers like him. John symbolized exactly what Clemons hated. Too much money and not enough appreciation for what he had.

The day school started back after the holidays, Clemons found plenty of people willing to tell what they knew about John. School teachers described him as, "Bright but unmotivated. Still makes good grades though. Getting by on sheer brilliance." His basketball coach offered, "Gifted. Driven to compete. A little angry, even. It comes out on the court. Tossed out of a couple of games in his freshman year." John's fellow students said little. "Righteous dude. Mega bucks. Super ballplayer. A hunk. Party animal."

Clemons deliberately interviewed John's principal last. Doing so gave him time to get a handle on where he stood, how much he still needed before he moved to make an arrest. So far, he'd come up empty. No one connected John to the killing. Stone looked like his last resort.

Clemons strolled unannounced into Stone's office right as school ended on Friday, January 4. Stone was seated, his bulbous bottom nestled in his long-suffering chair. Stone motioned for Clemons to sit also. Clemons pulled his hat off and twirled it three times. The glare of the skylight in the office bounced off his balding head and washed his face in bright light.

Stone shifted in his chair. "How can I help you, officer?" he asked.

"Well, as you can probably guess, I'm here to talk with you about John Tennet. Tell me again everything you know about him."

"But we've already gone through this, officer," protested Stone, obviously not wanting to cause any more trouble for the wealthy Tennet family.

Clemons stared at him. "Humor me, Mr. Stone, I'm slow. I need to hear things more than once."

Stone then launched into a repetition of what everyone else had said. Clemons rubbed his head front to back, front to back, front to back as Stone talked. Then, unceremoniously, he interrupted him. "Look, Stone, I've heard all that. Don't keep regurgitating stale details. Tell me why he kept a gun in his locker. Tell me why he ditched school so much. Tell me why he lied about where he found the gun. Tell me how he's involved with the drive-by shooting. Tell me something you haven't told me or that I can't read in his folder."

Stone leaned forward in his chair and scratched his stomach. "I don't know if I can answer any of those questions," he said. "You know, confidentiality and all."

Clemons gritted his teeth and rubbed his head one more time. "Okay, Stone, you leave me no choice. I haven't said anything yet about the lie you told me when you turned over the .38. You knew Tennet had it from the start. So, you either hand me something to move this investigation ahead or we can talk about obstruction of justice. You get my drift?"

Stone shifted to the side. His chair squeaked. "Well, Lieutenant Clemons, I didn't know exactly what you wanted. I'll do what I can. But, as you should know by now, John's hard to pin down. In some areas, he's outstanding. Athletically and academically. But he picks and chooses those areas. He hates it when someone else tries to make him do anything. Independent, yeah, maybe that's it. John seems independent—cut off from other people. He knows lots of kids—not just at our school—all over town, but I don't know that he's close to any of them."

"Any particular girlfriend?"

Stone hesitated a blink. "Let me see . . . yeah, I can think of one. A cheerleader for the St. Louis High basketball team. I don't know the girl myself, never even seen her, but I talked with her on the phone once when John skipped classes. One of the kids told me John might be with her."

Clemons pulled a notepad from his shirt pocket. "Got a name?"

"First name Tina. Let me check Tennet's folder." Stone lifted himself from the creaky chair and opened his file cabinet. "Here it is—Tina Spicer. A senior at St. Louis. Home address: 801 Citadel Square. Nice neighborhood. Number 555-1998."

Clemons jotted it down. "Thanks, Mr. Stone, if I need anything else, I'll get in touch."

"I'm sure you will."

Clemons pushed his hat over his head and left the campus. Forty minutes later he parked his car and ambled back into the station house. He had a bit of paperwork to clean up; then he would head to Citadel Square. He wanted to talk with Tina Spicer.

Chapter Twenty-seven

About ten miles away from Stone and Clemons, Katherine smoothed her tan skirt over her thighs and sighed. She gazed around the room, admiring the swag drapes over the windows. The navy drapes were open and the dancing rays of the first warm sunshine in two weeks showered the room with warmth. The sunshine blanketed the ceiling-high bookshelves that covered three of the study walls.

Perched on the edge of a leather sofa, Katherine clasped her hands in her lap. She fought the urge to bite her fingernails. She had put her hair in a tight bun for the visit. Somehow that seemed appropriate.

She licked her lips as she waited on the Reverend Doctor Peter Thomas Tebbs, senior minister of St. John's Baptist Church. It had taken her several days to drum up the courage to do it, but the days of isolation before New Year's convinced her she couldn't understand her experience by herself. So, what better place to ask for assistance than from the minister of the church where it happened? She had called the church after finding the number in the yellow pages. The church with the window filled with Jesus over the pulpit. The phone book listed Tebbs' name with the church and she had made an appointment with his secretary.

Now she sat in Tebb's study and wondered how she would

begin. Hearing a shuffle of feet, she turned and watched an elderly gentleman enter the door. He smiled at her and the crinkles around his ancient eyes and the thick mane of silver hair made him look wise and loving; the age spot on his left cheek reminded her of her deceased grandfather. His smile made her want to smile too and suddenly she relaxed and the urge to nibble her nails vanished. She untied her hands from each other.

Still grinning, the diminutive man stepped to her and shook her hand. "Afternoon, Mrs. Tennet, I'm Peter Thomas Tebbs. Good to see you. Would you like a spot of tea?"

His Scottish accent surprised her but she made no comment on it. Instead, she nodded her head.

Tebbs leaned over the table under the window and lifted an ornate silver kettle from a tray that matched it. He poured two cups of tea, then turned and handed her a cup and saucer and settled himself down into a wingback chair beside the sofa. He sipped lightly from his cup. Nodding at her, he placed his cup into its saucer and spoke.

"Mrs. Tennet, I can see you're a smidgen nervous, so why don't you take a deep breath, relax a tad, and start from the beginning. Tell me why you're here today."

Katherine rested her cup on the table by the sofa and rubbed her hands on the lap of her dress. "It's a little weird, Dr. Tebbs, when I actually try to describe it. But, eight days ago, something unusual and, I must say, confusing happened to me in your church." She stopped and waited for encouragement. He offered it to her.

"Call me Peter Thomas," he said. "And don't worry about how weird your experience may sound. I've heard weird things before and I expect I will again. I expect Moses had a hard time describing what happened to him too." His grin looked elfish, playful. Encouraged, Katherine plowed ahead.

"Let me start this way. My husband is in Saudi Arabia. He's a surgeon. I had just taken him to the airport and was on the way home. . . ."

She poured out the story to Peter Thomas Tebbs as she had to Les, describing her actions and trying to describe her feelings. But this time the man who heard her listened, nodding his head with understanding, acknowledging her story, blessing it, embracing it even.

"I don't know what it means, but somehow I believe Jesus touched me and changed me. I've never been what you call religious, not even as a child. My parents never attended religious services, except funerals and weddings and an occasional Christmas service. I never went to the funerals and the Christmas services never made any sense to me, and now this has happened and I don't know what to do about it and—"

Tebbs' smile never left, but he lifted his thin hand and waved it slowly side to side. "Whoa, Mrs. Tennet, whoa, let's slow down just a touch and see where we are." He said it patiently, like a doctor wanting to make sure he heard all the symptoms before offering any diagnosis or prescription.

"You almost wrecked, you walked into our sanctuary, you saw the picture of Jesus, you believe He touched you, and now you're trying to figure out what it all means. Does that sum it up?"

"Yes," nodded Katherine, unsure what Tebbs was thinking. "Did you ever hear anything so crazy?"

Tebbs' grin turned into an out-and-out chuckle and he lifted himself from his chair. "Let me show you something, Mrs. Tennet." He walked to his desk and picked up a Bible. He flipped the pages to Acts 9 and started to read, "As Paul neared Damascus on his journey, suddenly a light from heaven flashed around him. He fell to the ground and heard a voice say to him, 'Saul, why do you persecute Me?' 'Who are You, Lord?' Saul asked. 'I am Jesus. Now, get up and go into the city and you will be told what you are to do.' "

Tebbs laid the Bible on his desk and reseated himself in the wing chair by Katherine. "Would you say that was a little weird?"

Amazed by the story, Katherine nodded. "Absolutely."

"Is it somewhat like what you experienced?"

"Somewhat, yes, the encounter with Jesus in the flash of light is almost identical."

Tebbs lifted his cup and sipped from it. "Religious people call what happened to you a Damascus Road experience."

Katherine whispered the words, almost afraid of the answer. "But is it real, Dr. Tebbs? I mean, did Jesus really appear to Saul? Did He appear to me? Touch me? Does God work that way?"

Tebbs flipped his delicate wrists and shrugged. "Who's to say how God works? If we believe God exists, then I suppose He can pretty much show up when and how He decides, don't you think? If you're THE BOSS, then you're THE BOSS. Right?"

Katherine found herself wanting to laugh with Tebbs, but her anxiety boxed in her humor. "What do you think, Dr. Tebbs? Do *you* think God appeared to me?" she asked. "It seems so insane, so miraculously insane."

Tebbs clinked his cup back into its saucer and stared back at her. "The question, Mrs. Tennet, is not what *I* think, but whether *you* think God appeared to you. What's real and miraculous to me might be entirely insane to someone else. Do *you* think He did?"

Katherine pulled at a strand of hair that had escaped her bun, considering the question. "Y-e-s, I . . . I do, I really think I do. Yes, God did speak to me. God came to me, not in the flesh necessarily, but He touched me."

Tebbs nodded his slender neck. "If you believe it, then it's true. God did appear to you."

"My belief makes God appear?"

"No, I didn't exactly say that. Your belief doesn't make God appear. God's already here, all the time. All around us. You know, 'Every bush is afire with God' as the poet said. But your belief means God's presence can make a difference in your life."

Katherine rolled the strand of hair with her fingers. "Kind of like flying."

"Huh?"

"You know, flying. If you don't believe an airplane can fly, you'll never allow it to take you from one place to another. Your belief makes it possible for it to make a difference in your life, as you put it."

"I hadn't thought of it in those terms, but it makes a certain kind of common sense," agreed Tebbs. "Your belief doesn't make God real, but your belief means you trust God enough to get on board, so to speak."

"That makes sense in my terms," agreed Katherine.

"And in mine," said Tebbs. "But now we face the big question."

"Which is?"

"Has this experience with God made any difference in your life?"

Katherine dropped her hands from her hair and interlocked her fingers in her lap again. "I don't know, Dr., uh, Peter Thomas. It's so new to me I don't know how to let it make a difference. But I sure need something to help." She sighed and lifted her right hand to her mouth as if to chew on a fingernail.

"You're struggling with some problems?" asked Tebbs.

"That's the understatement of the century."

"Want to elaborate?" he coaxed. "If not, it's all right, but I'm here to listen." His voice soothed her and Katherine felt safe.

"I won't go into the gory details, but if my marriage was a cat with nine lives, we would already have used up 8.9 of them."

Tebbs lifted his cup and took another sip of tea. Then he wiped his lips with a white linen napkin. "What else?"

"I have a daughter with a learning disability."

"Severe?"

"Yes. She'll never mature beyond five or six years."

"You blame yourself?"

"Yes." Katherine dropped her eyes to her lap.

"There's more?" asked Tebbs.

"Yes, my son."

"What about him?"

"The police picked him up for questioning in connection with a murder—a drive-by shooting." Katherine's eyes moistened and turned red as she concluded her story. Tebbs pulled a monogrammed handkerchief from his suit pocket and handed it to her. Released by his gentleness, the tears suddenly gushed out, a torrent of water soaking down her face. She sobbed and her body shook and she started rocking herself out and back on the leather sofa.

Without a word, Tebbs eased himself from his chair and tiptoed to her side and leaned over. With pristine care he put his hands on top of her head and his hands were warm and the energy radiated into her body and she exhaled a tentful of air. Tebbs began to whisper—he was talking to God and the prayer washed over Katherine and brought her peace.

"Loving God, we come to You as children seeking to find a place of rest and joy. We get upset at times like children do and we get lost too, and we need someone to help us find our way. Life gets complicated and we don't know where to turn. Thank You, O God, for inviting each of us to turn to You. You've said the weary could find strength in Your arms, the sad could find joy in Your presence, the confused could find wisdom in Your guidance, and the guilty could find cleansing in Your grace. So today I want to pray for this dear child of Yours. I pray for Mrs. Katherine Tennet and for her family, her husband, daughter, and son. You know exactly who they are and precisely what they need in their lives. Meet their needs today, dear Lord, through the grace You promised would be sufficient for us. That's what we're asking, and we ask it in the name of Jesus. Amen."

As he finished his prayer, he eased back into his seat. Katherine continued to cry but the tears weren't anger anymore, and they weren't sadness either; they were joy, and they cut rivulets into her cheeks and chin, and as they dropped onto her lap they washed the toxins of her guilt away and made her clean.

Chapter Twenty-eight

Clemons called the Spicer home at 5:30 P.M.—as quickly as possible after finishing his paperwork. A woman answered his call.

"Mrs. Spicer?"

"Yes."

"This is Lieutenant Tom Clemons from the Kirkwood Police Station. I'm calling to see if I can drop by and talk with your daughter about a Mr. John Tennet."

"John Tennet?"

"Yes, your daughter dates him."

"Not anymore, Mr. Clemons."

"But she did at one time?"

"Briefly, yes."

"Then I'd like to talk with her."

"About what?"

"Nothing serious. I just want to see what she can tell me about John."

"He in trouble?"

"Maybe, I'm not sure. That's why I need to talk with Tina. Try to find out a few things about him."

"Okay, but I don't think she can help you much."

"Maybe not, but anything she can tell me will be helpful. Is it all right if I come by within the hour?"

"That'll be fine."

Clemons hung up, puzzled. Something wasn't right, but he couldn't pinpoint what it was. Almost like the woman had expected him to call about John. And he hadn't told her a thing about the gun or the shooting. Grabbing his hat and jacket, he hopped into the squad car and roared out of the drive and into the swirl of commuter traffic. He'd find out what it was when he talked to Tina Spicer. He was sure of it.

The stream of vehicles closed in on him as taillights and license plates and spinning wheels blurred, and Clemons suddenly found himself surging back, back many years, back to a trip, a trip taken with his family right after he turned seven years old. . . .

In a whirlpool of traffic much like this. On a late Friday afternoon, just as the sun dropped over the dashboard of the car. He sat in the backseat and his mom and dad and four-year-old sister were in the front. They were traveling to his grandmom's for Christmas dinner. He clutched his favorite present, a Bonanza gun and holster set, to his chest. He felt warm and happy and content and then—then it all ended.

Out of the glare of the sunset a car appeared—a bullet fired with his family's name on it. It pierced the hood and the windshield of their car and plowed into the heads and bodies of his mom and dad and sister. The ricochet of the crash propelled him into the back of the front seat and smashed his nose and face. Unfortunately, he thought later, it left him alive. Even today, when he closed his eyes to sleep, he saw the bloody bodies of what had been his family.

But, more than that, he still heard the sounds of rock music pouring from the radio of the car that snuffed out the lives of the people he loved most in the whole world. And, worst of all, he still heard the crazy laughter of the sixteen-year-old rich kid who had piloted the kamikaze Corvette.

The kid was rich and drunk and oblivious to the death he had just visited upon an entire family. For over forty minutes, waiting for the ambulance workers to pull him from the death trap of his family's car, Clemons heard the teenager laughing. He would never forget the sound. . . .

Clemons rolled his neck clockwise, trying to calm down, around and around he rolled his neck on his shoulders as the anger crept down from his head into his heart. He couldn't be angry when he talked to Tina Spicer. He had to stay controlled.

Fifty minutes later he turned off the ignition and peered through the windshield at a two-story, red-brick colonial home. Dormer windows peered back like square eyes and the bare limbs of eight mammoth oaks bowed to him as he stepped out of his car.

He paced up the bricked walk and rang the bell. Waiting, he tugged off his hat and whipped it around on his finger, once, twice, three times. The cold air nipped at his bare ears. The door opened. Clemons almost dropped his hat. Standing in the doorway was the prettiest black girl he'd ever seen in his life. She had eyes like black olives and skin the color of Irish coffee and equally as smooth. Her hair was jet black and soft. He wondered if it fell naturally that way.

Though he didn't see himself as a prejudiced man, it shocked him to think Tennet had dated her. Even in St. Louis, that was rare. Not as rare as it had once been, but still unusual. He didn't particularly care for it, but he wasn't sure why. Oh well, if she could help him tie John to the murder, he would be grateful.

Clearing his throat, he gathered himself, hoping Tina didn't notice his surprise. "Tina Spicer?" he said, extending his hand. "Yes, that's me," she said, shaking it firmly and leading him into a spacious den, warmed by a stone fireplace in the center. "And you're Lieutenant Clemons?" She pointed him to a seat and he took it.

"Yes," he said, as he pulled a yellow notepad from his jacket pocket. "I talked to your mom a little while ago."

"Yes, she said you had called. She's not here now, though;

she had to run some errands."

"Are you comfortable talking to me without her here?"

Tina shrugged, "Yeah, sure, why not? You wanted to talk about John, right?"

"Yeah, John. The principal at John's school, Mr. Stone, said you dated him for a while."

"I don't know how he knew that."

"Well, uh, he had made a note of it in his files for some reason."

"I wonder why," said Tina, arching her eyebrows and letting a tiny smile play on the corners of her mouth.

"You date John long?"

"Thirteen times to be exact. Spaced over a three-month period."

"You're pretty precise about that."

"Sure I am."

"Any reason why?"

"Let's just say the whole experience is etched in my mind."

He caught a tinge of anger in her voice and pursued it.

"Want to expand a little?"

Before Tina could answer, the door adjacent to the den popped open and a broad-shouldered young man entered. Not seeing Clemons, he called to Tina, "Is Mom home?"

Tina jumped from her seat and hustled to him. "No, Jamaal, Mom's not here, but Officer Clemons from the Kirkwood Police is." She indicated Clemons' presence with a twist of her head in his direction. "He's here to ask me about John Tennet."

Jamaal whispered something to her, but Clemons couldn't make it out. Then Tina and Jamaal turned to him. "This is my older brother, Mr. Clemons," said Tina, her voice going up a note.

Clemons scanned Jamaal—a "J" cut into the left side of his short hair; a diamond dangling from the ear on the same side. Clemons guessed his age at eighteen to twenty and his height at five or six inches above six feet.

Jamaal stayed still and Clemons examined him, knowing from the glare on the boy's thick face that he didn't like the scrutiny. Neither man moved to acknowledge the other. Tina broke the silence. "Jamaal's out of school right now—he's looking for a job."

"Good, hope he finds one," said Clemons, switching his gaze to Tina and talking to her as if Jamaal didn't exist. When the kid acknowledged him, then he would return the courtesy.

Jamaal didn't give him a chance. "I'll be upstairs, sis," he said, "if you need anything." Sliding across the room, Jamaal moved slowly, shoulders roll, feet slide, shoulders roll, feet slide, a movement Clement read as pure arrogance. Oh, how the kid worked to impress him. Only one problem—the slide had a slight limp in it. Though barely noticeable, the right leg dragged behind the left, not the severe limp of a born cripple, but the limp of a boy who had once walked perfectly but now knew he never would again.

Clemons, wondering about the limp, watched him leave, then shifted his attention back to Tina. "Where were we?"

Tina licked her lips and reseated herself by the fireplace. "We were talking about my relationship with John."

"Yeah, the experience was, as you said, 'etched' in your mind. You were going to tell me why."

"Oh, use your imagination, Mr. Clemons. A black cheerleader dating the white basketball star of our arch rival. Everyone etched it in their minds."

"Including your parents?"

"Yeah, but they didn't mind too much. My folks were pretty open-minded about it all. Not like some others I know."

"Like Jamaal?"

She answered quickly. "No, Jamaal didn't have a problem with it."

Clemons, intent on getting to John, missed her hurry. "And John's folks?"

"I don't know. He never told them about us."

"He dated you for three months and never told his parents?"

"You got it."

"How did that make you feel?"

Tina pursed her lips and Clemons saw her effort to rein in her emotions. "Let's say I didn't like it too much. Figured he was ashamed of me."

Ah, thought Clemons, *that explains the anger.* He tried to exploit it.

"What caused you to break up?"

"I think that's easy enough to understand. I'm black, he's white, he wouldn't tell his parents about me. So, I broke it off."

"Was he happy about it?"

"Hard to tell with John sometimes, whether he's happy or not about anything."

"So you didn't break up under the best of circumstances?"

"Not hardly."

Clemons rolled the calendar back in his mind. "How long ago did you break it off?"

"About eight weeks ago."

"About the time Trevor Mashburn was shot?"

Tina jerked her hands to her face and covered her mouth. For a second she sat immobile, her eyebrows arched toward the ceiling. When she spoke, her voice fell to a whisper. "Is that why you're asking me about John? Did he have something to do with that shooting?"

Clemons proceeded cautiously. "Maybe—we don't know yet. We're in the questioning phase right now." He paused a beat, then continued. "So you and John broke up about the time Trevor was shot?"

As if fighting to regain her composure, Tina dropped her hands and smoothed her skirt. "Yeah, the same night, in fact."

"Same night?" Her answer surprised him, but he didn't let her see it.

"Yeah, after the football game."

"You broke up after the football game?"

"Yes, and Trevor was shot the same night in the parking lot after the game."

"You knew the boy?"

"Uh, sure, everybody knows everybody in their class just about. You know how that is."

"Were you with John when it happened?"

"The shooting?"

"Yeah."

"No, I wasn't with him. We'd already had our scene and he had left."

"Were you by yourself?"

"No, I wasn't."

"Who were you with?"

Tina gritted her teeth and shook her head. Clemons pressed her. "Who were you with?"

Tina dropped her eyes to her hands in her lap. "I was with Trevor."

"The boy who was shot?"

"Who else?"

"You were with Trevor when he was shot?"

"Yeah, I said that already." Tina's voice notched higher and Clemons eased up.

"Okay, Tina, only a few more questions. Obviously, if you were with him, you've got to tell me what happened. Just take a deep breath and describe what happened."

Tina adjusted her posture and rubbed her palms together. "Well, it, um, it happened like this. John and I had argued. He left me outside the gate of the game and I started to walk back inside to catch a ride. Then Trevor walked out. He saw me alone and offered me a ride, and we were headed to his car when another car flashed by us and almost ran over us. We both stumbled out of the way and I couldn't see because the light from the car blinded me. Then a shot came from the car and the shot hit Trevor in the head. It killed him. I knew he was dead the minute I saw him." Tina stopped talking and her eyes reddened. She rubbed the sleeves of her blouse across her face.

"Why hasn't anyone questioned you before now?" asked

Clemons quietly, milking the compliant girl.

"Because I wasn't there when the cops arrived."

"You ran?"

"Yeah, I ran. Nothing I could tell them anyway. And I couldn't help Trevor, so I ran."

"And John knew Trevor?"

"Yep, they played basketball against each other."

"Were they friends?"

Tina laughed through her red eyes. "Nope, anything but. They hated each other—arch rivals, competitors, star players—you know the scene."

"And you?"

"Whatcha mean?"

"They compete for you?"

Tina shrugged her slender shoulders. "Boys always do that."

"Enough to kill each other?"

Tina tilted her head and said nothing for several beats. Finally, she spoke. "That's a good question, lieutenant, a good question. I hadn't thought of John as a suspect, but it makes a certain kind of sense, doesn't it?"

Clemons put away his notebook, figuring he'd learned all he could for now. "Yeah, in a way it does." He pushed up from the chair. "Look, Miss Spicer, I'll need you to make an official statement, but I think you can wait until tomorrow. That okay with you?"

"No problem," said Tina. "You think John did this?"

Clemons tried to look neutral. "Do you?"

"That's a good question, lieutenant, a good question."

Clemons left her then and strolled back to his car, pleased with his work. With her statement supporting the other evidence he had, he planned to go to the D.A. and ask for a warrant for John's arrest. John had motive and opportunity. That ought to get him before a grand jury at least. And who knew what would turn up in the days to come. He could still do it, thought Clemons. He could punish the kid.

Upstairs in his bedroom, Jamaal Spicer pinched his nose and sucked in the sleeve of cocaine he'd just inhaled. Energized, he scurried to the curtains and watched Clemons pull out of the driveway. He knew why Clemons had visited, but it surprised him Clemons had connected Tina to John. Maybe he should have expected it, though. Salt and pepper still stirred up feelings. Didn't like his sister dating a white boy. Especially this white boy. His sister had no business dating him.

As Clemons' car disappeared around the curve of the street, Jamaal plopped himself down on his bed. Grabbing his right knee, he rubbed it tenderly, as if trying to rub the ache out of it. Then he rubbed it harder and harder and harder, as if trying to rub the limp out of it.

His frustration intensified by the cocaine coursing through his veins, Jamaal dropped his hands off his leg and began to thump his leg up and down against the mattress, pounding it and pounding it, whump, whump, whump, up and down, up and down. Sweat jumped up on his face and curses rolled off his lips. John Tennet had done this to him. John Tennet had crippled him. He hoped Clemons pinned Trevor's death on Tennet. Even though he hated cops, he hated Tennet more.

Chapter Twenty-nine

Two days before Clemons interviewed Tina Spicer, the Gang of Four—Les, Roger, Nelson Reed, and Macy Spencer—flew out of Frankfurt, Germany. After an uneventful flight, they landed in Dhahran, Saudi Arabia and spent two days in transition, including one incredibly uncomfortable night sleeping in a parking garage at the Dhahran Airport.

On January 4, to the relief of everyone in the 804th, the whole group boarded a C-140 transport jet and flew north to their permanent assignment—the King Khalid Military Hospital, a modern facility with the best equipment that Saudi oil money could buy.

Les couldn't believe their good fortune. Instead of suffering in a field hospital, complete with tents and cold showers and distasteful food, they were quartered in a Western-style apartment building. They were only about a 100 miles from the Iraq border, but the proximity to possible danger didn't seem nearly so bothersome when compared to what they might have received.

Colonel Harper described it for them as they fell into formation on the airport tarmac soon after landing at King Khalid.

"Listen up, gang. We've drawn a cushy assignment. Your quarters here are the best in this theater of operations. You'll be in an apartment complex—with hot water, phones you can receive calls on, television sets in the lobby and hot meals three times a day.

"Your hospital duty is equally as good. The Saudis deliberately copied an American military hospital when they constructed the King Khalid. It's a contemporary facility equipped with medical technology as sophisticated as any at an American base.

"The work pattern will also conform to normal hospital routines. We'll begin the day about 7 in the morning and complete it between 6 and 7 at night. Obviously, we'll have shifts when we're on call all night, but that's just like home too."

Harper paused, cleared his throat, and then continued. "Look, I know this sounds easy. But let me remind you why we're here. We're here to fight a war. Some say we won't have to fight, but I wouldn't bet my last dollar on that. I'd bet the opposite, in fact. I'd bet that sometime in the next few weeks we're going to find ourselves ankle deep in wounded men and women."

He stopped again and strolled up and down the rows of troops stretched out on the concrete. "That's where we come in. If we do our jobs right, lots of those wounded will live. They'll make it home from this Myrtle Beach in the Middle East, and they'll kiss their wives again and play softball for their church and watch their kids graduate from high school. That's what happens if we're sharp. If we're not—" He stopped walking and lowered his eyes to the ground.

"Well, we're not even going to talk about that, because we're going to be sharp. Even if it kills us. So pay attention to the training, all of it. It might make the difference between life and death for one of the soldiers you'll be treating in the next few weeks."

Harper concluded his remarks, "Now, get your gear stowed and report to duty stations at 0700 in the morning."

Les shook his head in disbelief as he and the Gang shuffled toward the trucks that would take them to their quarters. "Seems wrong, man," he said to no one in particular.

"Whatcha mean?" asked Roger.

"Well, you saw those troops shoved into tents all over the sand in Dhahran. No comforts, no benefits, no nothing. But we get the Hilton. Doesn't seem right, somehow."

"You want to trade places with them?"

"No, not exactly, but this wasn't my idea of what we'd be doing over here."

"Look, Les," chided Roger. "If your conscience is bothering you, sleep on the floor. And don't eat the hot meals, eat your MRE's. Take cold showers too, if that makes you feel more noble. But don't bother me with it. I'm happy as a hog in summer slop. So, let's count our blessings and leave it at that."

Les nodded and dropped the subject. They were loading up for the ride to their quarters. It didn't take long to get there, or to unpack. Within two hours they had stowed their gear— Les, Tills, and Reed in one apartment as in Frankfurt, and Macy one hall over with another female officer.

With everything in place, Roger and Reed headed downstairs in search of food. Les stayed behind. Alone for what seemed like the first time since he had left St. Louis, he stretched out on his cot, found pen and paper, and scratched out a letter.

Dear Katherine, Sherry, and John,

I hope this letter finds you all doing well. I'm okay myself, but I have to tell you, I've lost seven pounds since I left home. I'm almost back to my college weight. I don't know if it's bad food or more exercise. Anyway, I'm surviving.

The last few days have zipped by like a blur. They've kept us extremely busy. For the most part, I'm glad they have. It's kept me from having too much time to think. In spite of the rush, though, I've been doing a lot of that since I left—thinking about all of you.

When the phones were out and I couldn't reach you and didn't know what was happening, I about went over the wall. Colonel Harper refused to let me come home, even though I pushed him over and over to do so. He kept telling me to wait and see what happened. In hindsight, it appears he was right.

I want you to know I wish I was home. I miss all of you.

Sherry, are you swimming every day? I expect you'll be a lot better swimmer when I get home. I'll look forward to your showing me all that you've learned.

And John—well, let me be honest—I'm not sure what to say to you. But I want to make this admission. I know I'm not perfect. Never made any claims to be. But, and you've got to believe me, I do try. Maybe not hard enough to suit you, but I do try. When I get back, I hope I can make up for some of my past mistakes.

Katherine, I know you have a lot on you right now. As we discussed before we left, with my income cut, you'll have to be more careful with the household expenses. But, with the savings we have, we should be all right. Hopefully, this won't last long.

It looks more and more though like war is coming. The President's deadline is fast approaching, and neither he nor Saddam His Insane (that's Roger Tills' name for Hussein) seems willing to back off.

You may be surprised to hear this, but for a war zone, my situation here is excellent. I'm in a normal kind of apartment complex and at a modern hospital. If this is as bad as it gets, then I'm going to be fine. Just hope that's the case.

I don't know when I can call home again. I'll try soon. You'll be able to call me as soon as they get our phones in place in our rooms. The system in this complex is strange. People can call in but not out.

Anyway, I wanted you to know I'm alive and well. Take care of yourselves and know that I love you. Even if I don't always show it too well, I do love you.

Les

He folded the paper, shoved it into an envelope, licked the seal, and closed it up. Tomorrow morning he would mail it.

Chapter Thirty

Clemons tried not to smile but failed. So he squeezed his smile into a grimace and punched the doorbell of the Tennet home. After the interview with Tina Spicer, he had spent the weekend gathering corroborating testimony. Students who had seen John and Trevor exchange words and threats. Others who were with John at the football game the night Trevor was shot, but who were not with him when the game ended. By Sunday evening he thought he had enough, and on Monday morning the D.A. agreed—they had enough evidence to arrest John Tennet for murder.

Now, just before 10 A.M., Clemons stood on the stoop of the house he hated and patted his jacket pocket to make sure it was still there . . . the warrant that gave him power over John Tennet.

Waiting, he turned to the officer sitting in the squad car in the driveway. Clemons nodded to him. He had left him there on purpose—he wanted to enjoy this moment privately.

The door opened and Katherine's eyes widened when she saw Clemons.

"Morning, ma'am," gleamed Clemons, taking off his hat. "Can I come in a minute?"

Katherine stepped back and both walked into the living room. "What can I do for you, officer?" she asked.

"Is John home?"

"Yes, he's upstairs."

"You sure?" Clemons arched his eyebrows, not so subtly reminding her of the last time she'd said that.

"I'm sure," Katherine said, her voice terse.

"Good. I need to see him for a moment."

"Can I ask why?"

Clemons desperately wanted to laugh. He twirled his hat instead. "Absolutely, you can ask. But I suspect you know already. It's about the shooting. Seems your boy and the deceased disliked each other intensely. Several kids heard them threatening each other on the night of the murder. I'm afraid I've got to take your boy in on murder charges." He twirled his hat again.

Katherine stood still for a moment. Clemons waited. Good. By stretching it out, she gave him more time to relish the feeling. "I'll get John," she said, turning to leave.

Katherine found him in his room, headphones over his ears. He pulled them off when she entered. "I knocked," she said.

"No problem," he said, gesturing for her to come closer. "I couldn't hear you, the music and all."

She nodded, then sat down beside him on the bed. For several beats, she just stared at him. He furrowed his brow.

"What's up, Mom?" he asked.

"I've got bad news, John," she said. "Clemons, the cop from Kirkwood Station, is back. He's downstairs. Says he needs to take you downtown."

Now it was John's turn to hesitate. His hands squeezed the earphones he'd taken off his head. "The gun they found in my locker?"

"Yeah, he said you and the boy who was shot had a bad history. Is that true?"

John gritted his teeth. "Yeah, but so what? Who doesn't have a few enemies? The fact that I didn't get along with the guy doesn't mean I shot him. What kind of evidence is that?"

Katherine laid her hands on his. His fingers had turned white from clenching the earphones. "Not much, sweetheart, but Clemons says you had motive and opportunity. That's all he needs to take you in for questioning. I guess we better get back down there."

Shaking his head, John pulled his hands from Katherine, twisted his earphones into a pretzel, then whipped the tangled pieces against the wall across from his bed. As the earphones slid to the floor, he jerked his long frame off the bed and poised himself beside it, looking uncertain what to do next. Katherine thought for a moment he was about to run.

But she wouldn't let that happen. Not again. Moving with him, she stood up, wrapped her arms around his chest, and squeezed him as tightly as she could. For almost a minute, they stood there, John quivering against her. Gradually, his breathing slowed. He sucked in big draughts of air. He sighed and nodded.

"Okay, Mom, I'm all right, now." As if to prove it, he bent over and kissed her on the top of her head. "Okay, Mom, if this is the way it has to be. I halfway expected it anyway. Trouble seems to follow me. Maybe it's my fault, maybe it's not, but it doesn't seem to matter. With no other suspects, the cops had to move to me. They've got to nail somebody and with my connection to the gun, I'm the logical guy. Let's go get this over with."

Pulling away from her, he grabbed a leather jacket from his closet, slipped it over his shoulders, and led Katherine down the stairs into the living room.

Clemons watched them walk down.

"I thought I'd see you again," John said, his lip curling upward in obvious derision.

"You thought right," said Clemons. "I just needed a few days to put a couple of things in place. You know why I'm here."

"Sure I do. Is this where you read me my rights?"

"You got it, kid. It goes like this. You have the right to remain silent. If you give up the right to remain silent, anything you say can and will—"

"I know the rest."

Clemons felt himself about to explode with joy. He smirked. "Then you know the lawyer part. Can you afford a lawyer?"

John turned to his mother. "Can I afford a lawyer, Mom?"

Katherine, who had stood like a sphinx while her boy and Clemons sparred, roused herself from her catatonic trance.

"A lawyer, uh, sure, John, I'll call Dad immediately." She turned to Clemons. "What happens now?"

John stuck his arms straight out. "Officer Clemons arrests me now, Mom. He pops handcuffs on my wrists, gives me a ride downtown, fingerprints me, takes my mug shot from front and side, and sticks me behind bars."

She looked at Clemons for confirmation. "John's about said it, Mrs. Tennet."

"He actually goes to jail?"

"Yeah, that's what happens. We're talking about a murder charge here. We've got no choice but to arrest him and book him. He had motive and opportunity." He turned to John. "You ready?"

"I can't wait," said John.

Clemons snorted and pulled a set of handcuffs from his back pocket and snapped them onto John's wrists. "Let's find out how ready you are," he said, grabbing John by the elbow and leading him toward the door.

Katherine followed them like a whipped dog trailing after an abusive owner. Clemons opened the door and a slap of cold air blasted them.

"Hold it a minute," Katherine commanded. Clemons sighed, but then obeyed.

Katherine ran past him and grabbed John around the shoulders. She leaned her head against his chest and listened to his heartbeat. Raising her chin, she looked up into her son's brown eyes. "I'll have Granddad at the station when you get there, John. You won't be there long. We'll get bail and you'll be home. You'll never spend a night in jail."

Clemons stepped toward them and touched John's elbow. John jerked it away and whispered to Katherine. "Don't let this guy see you lose your cool, Mom. That's what he wants to do — scare us, make us whine. Don't let that happen. I love you and I'm scared, but I'm not going to cry and I don't want you to either. Don't give this clown the pleasure. Now hug me tight and then step back." She nodded and followed his orders.

Clemons touched his elbow again and this time John didn't flinch. Nodding to his mother, he turned and let Clemons lead him to the squad car.

Behind them, Katherine turned away, closed the door, and sagged down to the floor, spent by the effort of holding back her tears. She decided to let them loose. But, amazingly, when she relaxed her hands and slumped her shoulders to cry, no tears fell. Instead, a warm energy engulfed her and, though it was cloudy outside, she thought the room suddenly brightened. For a long minute she rested there on the floor, letting the intensity of the moment wash over her body. Then, comforted by the glow she felt, she stood up, hugged herself, and headed to the kitchen to make a phone call. She would get through this horrible moment and so would John. The tears that didn't fall told her so.

Chapter Thirty-one

The day started out routinely enough. After breakfast, the Gang of Four split up—Roger and Les trooped out with seventeen other doctors to a seminar on battlefield surgical procedures; Reed and Macy headed to two other buildings for specialty training in their spheres of operations.

After two hours in the conference room listening to the lecture, Les and Roger and their group watched a film describing Middle Eastern diseases. A mock Scud missile attack followed the film—everyone shoved their gas masks onto their faces and buried their heads under their hands on the floor. Then, the morning over, they broke for lunch.

It wasn't much worth it. A dry piece of ham, cold candied yams, green beans, and canned peaches. Les and Roger stuffed the meal away with little conversation except for their complaints about the food. Finished, they shuffled back to the lecture hall for another three hours. But then the classwork stopped. At least for Les and Roger it did.

A voice from the intercom paged them: "Doctors Les Tennet and Roger Tills, please report to the surgical ward. Doctors Les Tennet and Roger Tills, please report to the surgical ward."

Instantly excited, Les grabbed his notepad, nodded to the others in his group, and steamed from the room. Maybe now, he thought, rushing down the corridor beside Roger, he could use his training to help someone.

"Whatcha think we got?" asked Tills, as they boarded the elevator.

"Don't know, no battle action yet. Probably a training accident or a car wreck."

"I bet on the second. It's amazing how reckless these Saudi drivers are."

Les knew how true that was. They had been warned about it. Never use a left-hand turn signal. The Saudis took it as a sign the car behind should pass. And they had no speed limits on the roads outside the cities. Traffic accidents were the most hazardous danger the troops faced so far.

But this call wasn't because of a car wreck. It was worse, much worse.

Les and Tills saw the bodies simultaneously. Three soldiers, two men and one woman, draped in white sheets up to their necks. The sheets on all three were blood-soaked.

A coterie of medical personnel surrounded the three victims, preparing them for surgery. A nurse handed Les a clipboard with the preliminary medical information on it. Scanning it quickly, he moved from patient to patient, checking the wounds. Someone touched him on the shoulder. He turned around. Macy Spencer was standing by the injured woman.

"You bring them in?" he asked, looking back at his chart.

"Yeah, me and a couple of medics."

"What happened?"

"They were in a live ammo drill. Fifteen miles from here. Mortar fire. Just one problem—someone behind them entered the wrong coordinates into the computer. They caught a round. Eight were wounded but only these three are serious."

"How long ago?"

"Less than an hour."

He flicked his eyes up to Macy, noticed a swath of blood on her face.

"You okay?" He pointed to the blood.

Macy looked puzzled. "Sure, what's the problem?"

Les reached out and touched her cheek. "You've got blood on you." His fingers stroked her face, checking it for an injury. Finding none, he held his fingers on her cheek for a beat, then dropped them.

Macy rubbed her hand over the area Les had just touched. Then she pointed to the blonde woman stretched out on the table. "The blood is hers. She tried to talk when we brought her in. I bent over to listen—"

Harper's booming voice cut Macy short. "Tennet, you get Williams. Tills, take Lackey. I'll work on Smith. Let's move."

Les shifted into high gear, hurrying from the emergency room into the scrub area. Within minutes he had scrubbed, donned his gown, mask, hat and shoes, and rushed into the surgical area. Williams was a private with the Big Red One, an army grunt with nothing to distinguish him except the fact that he now found himself fighting for his life due to friendly fire.

Les bit his lower lip as he checked the chart. No one here knew his superstition about names, so he had no way to make up a pseudonym for the guy on the table in front of him. His surgical team wouldn't understand.

The people working with him were practically strangers. Yeah, they'd trained together at Ft. Ben Harrison and had seen each other on airplanes and in mess halls for the last two weeks, but that meant little to a surgeon who depended so completely on his team.

Les read the name on the chart. Ben Williams. Sweat broke out above his mask, on his nose and forehead, even though the room was cool.

His hands trembled as he scanned the body with his eyes. No one seemed to notice his shaking. They were too busy with their own duties to watch him.

Ben Williams had lacerations on his left cheek and above the right eye. Nothing overly serious there. A few stitches would fix those. He also had a broken ankle, but a doctor in the field had splinted it.

Les moved immediately to the source of Ben Williams' main problem—a gaping hole in his stomach. A slice of smoking shrapnel from the mortar fire had cut a divot into his flesh; although the medic had pulled the shrapnel out, he couldn't fix the gash it left behind. Les and his crew had to do that.

The hole seemed to grin at Les as he focused on it. As it grinned, it revealed its insides—the intestines and stomach of Ben Williams. The intestines and stomach were chopped up and tangled together, and sand mixed in with the blood and body fluids flowing out of them and produced a quagmire of human gruel.

Les went to work separating the stomach and intestines from the foreign matter clinging to them. He cleaned out the wound first, flushing the stomach and intestines with saline solution, swabbing the sand from the oily surfaces, lifting out globs of blood and flesh.

For the next three hours Les and his crew meshed their skills. He cut out the worst section of severed intestine and tossed it into the refuse can by the operating table. Then, he connected the ends of the bowels.

The stomach called for a similar procedure . . . remove the ripped portion and stitch together the rest. Fortunately for Ben Williams, he had a lot more stomach and intestine left than Les had to cut out. He would. make it.

Les breathed a sigh of relief when he realized Ben Williams was out of the war, but not out of time. Snowball hadn't been so fortunate.

Almost finished, Les turned to the nurse at his side. "Looks like Mr. Williams will make it home for Valentine's Day."

The nurse nodded. "Good work, Dr. Tennet."

Twenty minutes later, Les pranced from the room, happy about his work and relieved it had gone well. A couple of belts from Roger's forbidden liquor stash would do him just fine. Pleased, he checked the surgical unit looking for Roger. Not there. He headed to their apartment. Not there either. Only one other place to search.

He found Tills in the mess hall, slouched at a table with Reed and Macy. Though unusual for Les, he couldn't keep himself from bragging a little.

"I haven't lost my touch," he crowed, pulling a chair from the table and straddling it backwards. "Too bad you guys didn't see it. Ben Williams is as good as—"

It dawned on him in a heartbeat. Tills and Macy and Reed weren't smiling. His heart dropped to his ankles.

"What happened, guys?"

Tills' eyes rolled downward and his words croaked out. "She died, Les. Barbara Lackey, a communications officer and second lieutenant from Macon, Georgia, died about forty minutes ago." Tills stopped talking and lifted his hands from the table. He turned his palms upward and stared accusingly at them.

Reed picked up the account for Tills. "She had chest wounds, but most of that seemed manageable. Worse, though, she also had a damaged aorta. Unfortunately, Roger didn't know it until it was too late. It burst during the surgery and she died. Nothing anyone could do."

Les' hands started shaking and he gripped the back of his chair to keep anyone from seeing. Tills rose up in his chair and turned to Macy.

"What did the woman say to you?" Tills asked her.

Macy stared back at him, apparently not comprehending. "Huh?"

"You know," he pointed at her. "When you brought her in, you said you leaned over to talk to her. What did she say?"

Macy blinked her green eyes. "I don't see how that matters—"

"I didn't say it matters, Mace. I just want to know," groaned Tills, gritting the words out through clenched teeth.

"Okay, Roger," said Macy tenderly. "She said, well, she said . . . 'Tell my daughter I love her.'"

Tills sagged back down, as if shot by a sniper.

Wanting to comfort him, Les searched through his mind for the right words, but he found none. He should have known—

no one had words sufficient to comfort him when Snowball had died. Now Les knew why. Words like that didn't exist.

Les leaned over the table to his friend and placed his hand on Roger's shoulder. There they sat, the Gang of Four, in complete silence as the clock toward war ticked and ticked.

Chapter Thirty-two

John stared at the clock hanging above the top bunk on the left side of the green wall in cell block four at the Kirkwood Precinct. The only decoration in the square room, the clock stared back at him like a cyclops and seemed to ignore the other four inmates stuffed into the cubicle. John both hated and loved the one-eyed clock—loved it because it assured him time was moving, but hated it because it showed him time was moving far too slowly.

Only eight hours had passed since they'd booked him on suspicion of murder and shoved him behind the bars, but it seemed like days. It had gone like John expected. The glare of flashbulbs in his eyes. Turn left. Flash. Turn right. Flash. Straight ahead. Flash.

They printed him. One finger, two fingers, three fingers. . . . They strip-searched him. Take off your clothes. Turn around against the wall. Bend over. Stand up. Turn back around. Open your mouth. Get dressed.

John was in the holding area when his granddad arrived. That's when John learned the first hard lesson of incarceration—things don't happen when and how you expect them to happen. John had believed his mom's promise—that he wouldn't have to spend a night in jail. He had trusted in Granddad Walter Tillman's clout and money to get him out of this hole in hurry. Not so, on either count.

Granddad Tillman eased himself into a chair beside him and explained the particulars.

"You'll see a magistrate judge in the morning. He'll set your bail."

"You mean I have to spend the night in jail?"

"I'm afraid so."

"But Mom said—"

"I'm sorry, John, but she was wrong. Nothing she nor I nor anybody else can do. Until they set bail, you're here."

John heard a knock on the door and looked up. He saw Clemons stick his head inside. "Time's up, Walter," said Clemons.

Walter patted John on the shoulder. "It's going to be okay, son. We'll get you out in the morning." Then he was gone. Just like that. Nothing left to do.

Now John had to wait. So far, waiting hadn't been pleasant.

Clemons had personally escorted him to his cell. There the fear hit him for the first time. Clemons had pushed open the door of the cell and tossed him to the floor.

John, deciding to hold his fire, didn't resist the treatment. Like a crumpled rag, he lay on the floor while Clemons cackled at the other prisoners. "Fresh meat, boys. But, be gentle with him. He's a rich kid with powerful friends." Rubbing his head, Clemons strolled out.

Unsure if the horror stories about jails were true, John lay on the floor for a moment trying to decide what tack to take. Whatever it took to survive the night, that's what he wanted. Tomorrow he would go before a judge for a bail hearing. Then out of jail. *If* he made it through the night.

The four other inmates, two blacks and two whites, waited until Clemons left, and then they stood up from their bunks and stepped toward John. For another second he stayed still. The quartet moved closer, their faces near to his. The tallest of the four, a young black man with a Cardinals' baseball hat perched sideways on his head, poked John in the ribs with a bony finger. John decided that cowardice wouldn't play well. Better to act tough and get abused than to meekly submit to it without a fight. He raised his head and glowered at the four one at a time, focusing his eyes on theirs to show his courage. They glowered back, a circle of smoldering eyes staring at him. They looked about his age. At least Clemons hadn't thrown him in with older prisoners.

The man who poked him suddenly grinned. A gold tooth flashed from the center of his top teeth. The gold tooth bent over closer and closer to John until he could smell the fetid breath of the mouth that housed the gold tooth. Then, suddenly the gold tooth disappeared as its owner spoke.

"Rich kid, are you scared?" asked the man, his voice a deep bass that rocked the walls of the cell.

John didn't know what to say, so he said nothing. Instead, he pushed himself off the concrete floor and stretched himself to his full height in the center of the circle. The gold tooth moved away from him as he raised up. With his six feet, four inches and well-muscled body, John was bigger than any one in the room, including the owner of the gold tooth.

"Yeah, I'm scared," agreed John, "and you'd know I was lying if I said I wasn't. But the fact that I'm scared doesn't change the situation."

"And just what is the situation, scared rich kid?" asked the owner of the tooth.

"The situation is this. I'm in for murder. A drive-by shooting. Whether I did it or not is immaterial to you. What you need to know is my dad is rich and my granddad is richer, and if you guys will let me get through tonight with no hassle, I'll make it worth your while in the morning."

"You trying to buy us off, scared rich kid?"

John forced himself to grin, trying to keep up his courage. "Yeah, that's about the way of it. I'm trying to buy you off. A hundred bucks apiece. In the morning, after I know I've made it through the night."

"And what if we don't agree to this arrange-m-e-n-t?"

John shrugged and inhaled, trying to fill up more of the space he'd carved out for himself in the center of the circle, trying to make himself look bigger. "Well, I don't know about that. I don't know who you guys are or why you're here. But, if you make my life miserable tonight, I promise my family will make yours miserable starting tomorrow."

Gold Tooth turned to the other guys in the circle. "What about it, do we leave the scared rich kid alone and pick up a hundred bucks, or do we have our way with him and pick up a bit more trouble in the morning?"

The circle turned on itself, each one in it nonchalantly rolling his shoulders to the one beside him. "Don't matter to me." "Either way." "Whatever."

Gold Tooth grinned again as he stared back at John. "Okay, rich kid. You win. Take the top bunk and stay quiet. If we don't change our minds, you'll make it till morning."

John didn't argue. He quickly climbed to the bunk in the corner, fastened his eyes on the clock, and wished it through the minutes. They passed slowly, but they did pass.

Chapter Thirty-three

Les sat on the edge of a cot in the doctor's lounge and swung his legs over the side of it, like a small boy playing on a bridge. But he didn't feel playful. Images of Roger Tills and Barbara Lackey and Snowball and Ben Williams danced about in his thoughts—a pinball machine full of faces ricocheting off each other and pounding the sides of his brain.

He wondered if *he* could have saved Lackey, if he could have patched her up and sent her home to her infant daughter. Two months ago, he would have had no doubts. Les the Blest could save anyone back then.

But today he wasn't so sure. He felt glad he hadn't drawn Barbara Lackey as his assignment. If she had to die, better under Roger's care than under his.

Deep in thought, he didn't hear the door open. Neither did he hear Nelson Reed enter the room. Then, like an apparition, Reed appeared at his elbow.

"How you doing, Les?" Nelson asked, his voice soft.

Les tried to fake it. "Hey, I'm good, man. A long day, but, hey, we expected that, didn't we?"

"Long days go with the territory," agreed Reed.

The two said nothing for a second.

"Too bad about the woman," suggested Reed.

"Yeah, too bad," said Les, with a tad of a shrug. "But hey,

in wars, death happens. We expected that too, didn't we?"

"Yeah, we did, Les, but not so—"

The intercom cut Reed off. "Dr. Les Tennet, please report to Colonel Harper's office."

Les welcomed the interruption, grateful its summons severed the conversation with Reed. He didn't want to talk about Barbara Lackey. Not even to Nelson Reed.

"Sorry, Nellie," he said, "but I better scoot. Harper doesn't like to wait."

Nelson smiled and waved his hand, dismissing him.

Three minutes later, Les clicked open the door to Harper's office and stepped inside. Harper glanced up at him, tossed a sheaf of folders from his hands onto the top of his desk, and pointed Les to a seat opposite his. "Take a chair, Les." Les complied.

Harper rocked back and forth in his seat, once, twice, three times. Then he stopped.

"I've got bad news for you, Les."

Les knew immediately. "John?"

"Yep, afraid so. He's been arrested. For murder."

Les pushed his hands through his hair, trying to digest what this meant, trying to figure out his feelings. Not anger anymore, not really. More like resignation and sadness. And hurt too.

"When did you find out?"

"A few minutes ago. Katherine called, said it was an emergency, said she had to talk to you. Dispatcher asked her the nature of the emergency. She told him. Dispatcher told her we'd page you and get you to call her right back."

Les stared at Harper and noticed the concern etched in his commander's face. "Can I call her from here?"

"You bet," said Harper. "That's why I brought you in. Call on my phone and take as long as you like. I'll be outside when you're finished."

Harper left and Les dialed his home number. He focused his eyes on the numbers on the phone as he waited. One ring.

Two rings. On the third one, Katherine picked it up.

"Hello."

"Hello, Katherine, this is Les."

He heard an intake of breath. Then Katherine's voice, hurried, but strong. She poured out the story. "Les, it's not good. This morning Lieutenant Clemons came to the house and arrested John. He's up for bail in the morning and Dad says they'll probably ask for a figure between $500,000 and $1 million and we've got to get him out of there. He's already—"

"Shuush, Kath," he broke in. "Slow down a minute so I can get this straight. First of all, where is John right now?"

"He's in jail at Kirkwood Precinct."

"Has your dad seen him?"

"Yeah, right after Clemons arrested him."

"How long will he stay in jail?"

"Probably only overnight. Dad says until the magistrate judge sets bail."

"And that's tomorrow?"

"Yes, in the morning, about 10:30 Dad said."

"And bail will be between one-half to $1 million?"

"Probably, and we'll need about 10 percent of that for the bondsman."

Les sucked in a potful of air and squeezed his forehead with his hand.

"Kath, we may have a problem finding that much money."

She paused, then said, "You've got to be kidding, Les. With your salary? What about our savings?"

"Not much there," Les said, his face reddening and the scar on his forehead turning purple. "Don't forget—the house we built two years ago took most of it for a down payment. Our savings are pretty thin right now."

"What about investments, Les? Can we sell some stock?"

Les almost chuckled. "We've got about $20,000 left in the market. Remember, I sold another batch to buy the Mercedes and John's jeep. The twenty grand is a start, but we're still short."

"What about my parents? I can get the money from them."

A hardened edge crept into Les' words, even though he tried to keep his voice even. But he couldn't hide his objection. "No, Katherine, absolutely not. We won't borrow the money from them. If we do, your mother will never stop interfering. She'll think we're obligated to her for the rest of our lives and she'll use her leverage to control you and to try and control me. I can't—"

"You'd let your son rot in jail rather than accept help from my parents?" Katherine interrupted.

"That's not the point, Katherine."

"I think it is, Les, it's precisely the point. You care more about your pride than you do your son. Or me either, for that matter."

Les gripped the phone tighter. "Look, Kath, this isn't the time to discuss my pride. It's time to think."

"Well, I have thought and if we don't have the money, then I'm going to get it from my folks."

Katherine spewed the words out and the fury in them surprised him. Instead of changing Les' mind, though, her anger served to set it further. His response sounded clipped and cold.

"You borrow money from them, Katherine, and—"

"And what?" she challenged him.

"And I'll never forgive you. And you better believe me when I say that."

Katherine paused. Les waited. She said, "Look, Les, I don't like what I'm about to say. It doesn't sit well with me, but I've got to say it anyway. If John spends more than one night in jail because you won't let me borrow money from my parents, I'll never forgive you. And you better believe me when I say that."

Separated by half a world of geography and more than half a world of rage, Les decided to back off. No use escalating this thing any more than it already was. "Kath, listen to me for a second," he said. "This isn't how we need to handle this.

Now's a time to support each other, not issue ultimatums."

Katherine edged off too. "I know, Les," she soothed, "but I'm scared and I don't know where to turn."

Les leaned forward in his seat and propped his elbows on the desk, an idea forming. "Look, Kath, I just had a thought. Call the bank first thing in the morning. We've got over $100,000 in the house. Take out an equity loan for whatever amount you need. That should cover it. If not, call me again and we'll try something else. That sound okay to you?"

Katherine nodded. "Yes, that should work. I don't care where we get the money, just so John gets out tomorrow."

"All right," said Les. "Call me as soon as bail is made."

"I'll call immediately," said Katherine.

Tenderly, Les lowered his voice and concluded the call. "I'm sorry I'm not there for you, Katherine. When I get home I'll be different."

Katherine paused and he heard her breathing.

"Don't you believe me?" he asked.

"I want to believe you," she said. "But I don't know if I can."

"Then I'll have to prove it to you, won't I?"

"Yeah, Les, maybe we can both be different then. I'll call when I can."

"Bye," said Les.

"Bye," said Katherine.

He put down the phone and walked out into the hallway.

Chapter Thirty-four

At 9:01 the next morning, Katherine followed Les' orders. She took Sherry and marched into the MidState Bank of Missouri and opened a home equity line of credit for $100,000.

Comforted by the immediate cash, she drove to her parents' home and picked Walter up for the drive to the courthouse. Beatrice would keep Sherry. John was scheduled for a bail hearing on the second docket at 10:30 A.M.

"I called the Kirkwood Precinct first thing this morning," said Walter, as she turned onto the freeway and headed the car downtown. "Sarge there said he'd seen John at breakfast. Said he looked tired but fine."

Katherine tightened her fingers on the steering wheel. "Can we bring him home immediately after bail is set?"

"Yeah, pretty much so. After processing him at the police station, we're finished and he's out." Katherine nodded and fell silent. Walter followed her lead. For several miles they were quiet, absorbed in their thoughts. The white stripes of the highway darted by them and Katherine threaded her way through the midmorning traffic. Pulling off the interstate, Katherine asked, "When will he go to trial and all that?"

Walter straightened his tie. "It all depends. The judge will set a date for a preliminary hearing. That should be within a month or so."

They stopped for a red light. Katherine wanted more details. "What next?"

"Well, we get ready for trial, investigate, interview witnesses, see if John's got an alibi—you know, the typical preparation."

Trying to stay calm, Katherine took one hand off the wheel and patted her dad on the leg. "Dad, this isn't any old trial. It's John we're talking about, my son, your grandson. We've got to find a way to get him free from all this. I don't want this hanging over his head a single minute longer than necessary."

The light changed and they pulled through it. Walter gazed out the window. "Look, Katherine, no one wants it to last a minute longer than necessary. If we end up going to trial, it'll probably be scheduled three to four months after the prelim. And there's not much we can do about that."

"Half a year," moaned Katherine, slowly losing her struggle to stay even-tempered. "It'll take five to six months to get this settled?"

Walter shrugged. "At least, and that's assuming it goes to trial the first time it's set and he's found innocent during the actual trial."

Katherine pulled into the courthouse parking lot and they unloaded. She glanced at her watch—10:20. Walter patted her on the back as they hustled to the courtroom. "This is all routine, Kath. We should be in and out within an hour."

"With John?"

"Without a doubt."

Clicking up the stone steps, they pushed open the double-paneled oak doors and stepped into the St. Louis County Courthouse. Within five minutes, they left the elevator on the third floor and entered the third door. Inside, the court session had already begun. A bald man with a brown birthmark the shape of Florida on his forehead and a black robe draped over his rounded shoulders, perched on the bench.

"Judge Harold Bayslip," said Walter in a whisper. Katherine nodded and stared down at her hands for a beat—her fingernail polish had chipped.

The slap of a folder on a desk snapped her attention back to Judge Bayslip. He had tossed down the file in his hands. Now he intoned in a heavy voice. "Call the next one, bailiff."

The bailiff recited — "Case 1067-493. Bail hearing." At the sound of his voice, two uniformed officers walked into the courtroom escorting a prisoner. Katherine stared at the tall, dark man between the policemen. Her heart picked up its pace. She recognized John, but he appeared different somehow, not in a way she could identify exactly, but changed.

His hair popped out in all directions and he wore the stubble of two days of inky beard. More than his physical appearance, Katherine searched for signs of his emotional state. How was he? What happened during the night?

She watched him scan the room with his eyes, and then, spotting her and Walter, he nodded ever so slightly. She wished he would smile, but then she realized how arrogant that would seem.

Gradually, as if waking slowly, Katherine sensed a set of eyes inspecting her and she swiveled around to check. She should have known — Clemons. He grinned and tipped his hat to her, and for the first time she read his grin correctly. He enjoyed this spectacle of John trapped between police, this murder drama he now investigated. Katherine met his eyes, unwilling to glance away and give him the satisfaction of knowing he scared her. She forced herself to smile back at him, and the anger in her faked pleasantness matched his, tooth by visible tooth.

Disgusted by Clemons, she turned back around. The cops escorted John to a chair in front of the bench. He sagged into it.

Walter, resplendent with his silver hair and pin-striped blue suit, took his place beside John, then leaned over and whispered to him. John nodded.

Bayslip stared down at the printout of the day's cases. Then, shifting his gaze to the crowd in the courtroom, he raised a pair of glasses off his bench and perched them on his nose.

"So," he boomed, his voice shaking the stone walls of the chambers. "What does the State have?"

The D.A., a pencil of a man with a pointy head and a haircut right off a Marine recruiting poster, stood. When he spoke his voice had a nasal twang to it, like someone had stapled his nostrils together. He summarized the case against John. "The defendant had the murder weapon, had a history of bad relations with the deceased, was identified in the vicinity near the time of the shooting, has no alibi, and disappeared when the arresting officer tried to apprehend him. That about sums it up."

Bayslip shifted his eyes to Walter. "Good to see you in harness again, Walter. How long's it been?"

Walter cleared his throat. "About eleven years, judge, since I worked any criminal."

"You got anything to add here before I set bail?"

Walter adjusted his suspenders. "Yes, your honor, a word or two. First, this young man has no previous record. He's a strong student at Archway Academy and an outstanding athlete. He and his family have strong ties to the community. Plus, we have no witness who actually saw the unfortunate shooting; and, though I know in a murder case he can be tried as an adult, he is still a juvenile. He poses no risk to the community, has no risk of flight, and his parents are willing to assume all responsibility for assuring he will be available for trial when it begins."

Bayslip flipped off his glasses and glanced down at the file again. Then he rolled his eyes toward the prosecutor. "Any final word before I set bail?"

The skinny prosecutor squeezed out the words. "The State suggests a bail of no less than $1 million, your honor."

Katherine sucked in her stomach and stuck her index finger into her mouth to chew on the nail. If bail went that high, she would barely have the 10 percent for the bondsman. John might end up in jail again. She wanted to jump out of her seat and scream at Bayslip, but the prosecutor continued to twang and she needed to listen. . . .

"And I don't have to remind you that a spate of drive-by shootings have plagued our community over the last two years, and it's possible that if the defendant is responsible for one, then he might be responsible for others. He has already resisted arrest by flight once, and we have no reason to assume he won't resist by flight again. For these reasons, the State requests the higher bail."

The prosecutor stopped talking and folded his frame into his chair.

Walter held a pen into the air and waved it toward Bayslip. "Yes, Walter?" asked the judge.

"One final note, your honor. I can personally guarantee you this young man will not resist trial by flight."

Bayslip popped his glasses on again. "That's a big risk, Walter. Tell me why you'd do that?"

Walter straightened his spine up so he measured his full and regal height. "I do it because he's my grandson."

Bayslip rocked back into his chair and steepled his fingers together. Seconds slipped by. He rocked forward again. "Okay, bail is set at $435,000, with a 15 percent minimum cash deposit. Preliminary hearing is set for February 16 in my court at 11 A.M."

Bayslip swiveled his seat to the left and barked, "Bailiff, call the next case."

As Katherine let out the air she'd stuffed into her chest for the last two minutes, it felt like a tire deflating. She had enough money. John could get out. She thrust her fist into the air and twisted around to smirk at Clemons. He wasn't there. Just as well.

She bounced up and floated to John who stood now with Walter in the center of the room. Both were beaming. With relief, she flung her arms around John's neck and whispered into his ear, "You'll be home tonight, John, you'll be home."

He leaned down and let his head rest on her shoulder. After all, he was still only a boy.

Chapter Thirty-five

Tired and tense, Les slipped out of his white coat, hung it on a hanger, and laid the charts he held on the counter at the nurse's station. He rubbed his eyes, wondering why they were constantly streaked with red. The lack of sleep, obviously. He knew he didn't look too good these days. Dark half-moons wrapped under his eyes, and the scar on his forehead seemed larger since he'd landed in Saudi. Not a happy man.

Eight days had passed since Katherine called him with the good news about John's bail. Les had celebrated with her over the phone, but his joy proved short-lived. In fact, almost immediately after the call ended, his euphoria turned sour. The money for the bail meant they were carrying a double mortgage on their home.

Les had tried to push away his worries over that. After all, he had far greater reasons for anxiety than the financial problems his military stint caused. How would John prove his innocence? He knew murder cases were usually dependent on eyewitnesses, but he also knew people were convicted on strong circumstantial evidence. And they definitely had that on John. Besides, once a D.A. had a preliminary trial assured, he poured more and more energy into making the case. No telling what would turn up under the sway of the extra manpower—maybe an eyewitness out there would decide to come forward.

Since the mortar fire tragedy, he hadn't faced any more emergencies at the hospital. No more splintered bodies to fix, no more sheets pulled over waxen figures for the last time, no more fellow doctors to console.

After the death of Private Barbara Lackey, the days sagged into a kind of uneasy routine—uneasy because a sense of imminent catastrophe pushed down on him a little harder each day, uneasy because mocking doubts pointed fingers at him and laughed, uneasy because the doubts scared him. He suspected he couldn't long survive in his work without confidence, without the sense of personal pride that had driven him out of his tortured childhood, and intense feelings of inferiority.

His doubts about himself and his fears about John's trial added to his anxiety about the deadline for war, and the three together spawned a foul mood. The mood wrapped its fingers tighter and tighter around his throat and he found it tougher to sleep and difficult to plug along with his work at the hospital.

Now it was January 15—President Bush's line in the sand for Saddam His Insane to withdraw from Kuwait. Activity at the hospital had picked up substantially over the last three days. The rumors swirled faster than Saudi sand in a windstorm. The latest one said the air war would kickoff on the 16th.

Leaving the charts on the counter, Les shuffled down the hall to the chaplain's office. He spotted Reed through the open door. He was sitting and staring out the small window by his desk.

When Les knocked, Reed twisted away from the window and nodded. A swirl of sand popped against the glass, pushed by the winds picking up outside.

"Les, come on in," Nelson said. He motioned to a seat.

"You finished for the day?" asked Nelson.

"Yep, all done."

"Things pretty quiet?"

"Yeah, a lot of sound and fury, but so far not signifying much."

"No emergencies lately?"

"Nope, not a one. I just finished my shift. On my way back to the apartment."

Nelson leaned back in his chair and picked a deck of cards off the table beside him. He fingered the cards as he looked at Les. Nelson wouldn't push—that wasn't his style. He would wait for Les to speak, to talk out what was on his mind.

Nelson nodded and flipped a card over to him. A deuce. Les sighed. He wanted to talk, but didn't know how much to say. He had told the Gang about John's arrest, but he hadn't said anything about the circumstances that led to it. He didn't know if he could. He edged forward in his chair as if about to leave. He hesitated, hoping Nelson would take the first step for him, would read his mind and open the gate and give him room to come clean with all the hurt clogged up in him. The wind snapped sand against the window.

Nelson flipped a seven onto the desk. "Sit back and relax a minute, Les," he said, his eyes never leaving the card. "You look a mite tired."

Les blinked and obeyed. "You're right about the tired part, Nellie. I can't seem to sleep enough these days."

"Yeah, our cots aren't exactly posturepedic, are they?"

They both laughed, but only for a beat. Then Les bit his lower lip, knowing it was now or never. Why not? He trusted Reed.

"I wish the cots were the only thing keeping me awake, Nellie," he started. "But I suspect they're not. Fact is, they're the least of my worries right now." Les stopped and stared back at his friend, pleading with his eyes for understanding.

Reed flipped up another card from the deck—a jack of diamonds. He showed it to Les. "When we first met, you asked me why I became a minister," he said. "You wanted to know what part I thought God had in it. Do you remember that?"

"Sure, it was not too long ago."

"Well, let me answer your question for you. I became a minister for the same reason I like to play poker."

Confused, Les shook his head. "I don't follow."

"Think of it this way. In ministry and in poker the most important thing you do is read people's faces. How confident are they? Do they like the cards they're holding? Are they about to throw in the hand? Do they have enough to call you, to keep playing? Well, that happens in the ministry and in a poker game. I like to read faces. In fact, I think the good Lord gave me a gift for it. I read the face and then I act based on what I see."

"Yeah, in poker you act like a thief," grinned Les.

"And in ministry I try to act like a friend."

Les glanced past Reed, past the window and toward the increasingly dark sky outside. The wind whipped faster and faster and gritty particles of dust cracked like microscopic firecrackers against the walls of the hospital. For a skip, both men sat waiting, knowing Les stood at a crossroads.

Slowly, Les asked, "What do you read in my face, Nellie?"

Nelson laid the cards down and leaned up in his seat. He squinted his eyes and clasped his hands across his chest.

"I'm only one opinion," he warned, "and I could be wrong."

"I'm willing to chance it," said Les.

"Okay, here's what I think. I read loneliness in your face. You've been lonely for a long time. For some reason, I suspect you've been lonely since you were a boy. You've been trying to fight your way out of your loneliness since then, trying to find a way to make friends. But that hasn't happened. So, without friends, you've settled for admirers, for people who think you're wonderful for what you do, rather than for who you are. But, inside it all, I see a scared boy who wants someone to like him—no, to love him—to love him no matter what he is and no matter what he has or hasn't done."

Nelson took a breath. Les' face showed no reaction.

"You want me to say more?" asked Nelson. Les nodded.

"I see a man who's scared of who he is. Insecure. Not sure he's worth loving. Not sure he loves himself. So, he's not sure anyone else can love him either, not if they really know him. That makes him hide, cover up, wear masks. So, he has problems with relationships. With his son, and probably his wife too."

Les' body stiffened and he jerked his eyes away from the window and back to Nelson. But he wasn't angry. Stunned was more like it—stunned that Nelson had seen through him. And grateful that he had.

Relieved that someone understood him, he invited Reed to continue. "Anything else you want to say, Nellie?"

Nelson picked up his cards again and grinned his high-voltage smile. "Yeah, Les, there is. I want to say this. I read in your face that you care deeply about people. You want to help them. You hate to see people hurt. You want, more than anything else, to make the people around you happy. And, I think, if you'll ease up on yourself and let those closest to you know that, you'll find the love you're seeking. You'll find the peace you want."

Without a word, Les pushed out of his chair, nodded at Nelson, and shuffled out. Reed turned up a card from his deck. A king of hearts. He said a quiet prayer that it would be so.

Chapter Thirty-six

The smell of steamed cabbage and country ham sifted through the kitchen and into the den where John was lying on the sofa, remote control in his hand. He flipped through the channels, not really interested in anything but searching to see what he could find to watch. Sherry sat at his feet on the end of the couch, combing through a doll's hair.

"Wash up, you two," yelled Katherine from the kitchen. "I don't want it to get cold."

John didn't move and Sherry mirrored his inaction. He had stopped flicking the channels and his eyes were now transfixed toward the television screen.

"Come on, you guys," insisted Katherine. "If I go to the trouble of cooking, you can at least do me the courtesy of eating it while it's hot."

Though he turned his head to the sound of her voice, John kept his eyes trained on the television. Silver streaks zigzagged across the monitor; booms and thuds and ack-acks roared through the speakers. It hit John then, with a sudden dawning of revelation. Anti-aircraft fire over Baghdad! Bombs dropping over the Iraqi capital! The war had started.

"Mom, get in here!" he screeched. "We're at war."

Dropping her serving spoon into the sink, Katherine skidded into the den, then stopped and watched as the cameras piped the images of a distant war into her home. She edged her way to the sofa, wedged herself between John and Sherry and grabbed both of them by the hand.

Sherry's tiny voice quivered. "Mommy, are we in a war?"

Katherine lifted her index finger to her mouth as if to quiet her, to tell her to ask no questions, but then apparently thought better of it. With one eye on the screen and one shifted to Sherry, she tried to answer. "Yes, sweetheart, we are. We're at war."

"Is Daddy in the war?"

Katherine pried her attention away from the television and faced Sherry directly. Tears dotted Sherry's pink cheeks and she cuddled Elmer under her chin, rubbing his fuzzy body against her face. Katherine reached over and wiped away the wet streaks rolling down her face. "Yes, sweetheart, Daddy's in the war."

"Does Daddy carry a gun?" Sherry asked.

"I think so, for protection, just in case he should need it."

Sherry's thin shoulders sagged. "Will Daddy get dead in the war?"

Katherine shook her head. "No, sweetheart, we don't think he will get dead in the war. Daddy's a doctor; he doesn't fight in the worst part of the war."

Sherry gritted her teeth. "But Daddy has a gun."

"Yes."

"Because somebody might hurt him."

"Yes, that's true."

"Then Daddy might get dead in the war."

Katherine's eyes filled with tears. "You're right, sweetheart, I don't like to think it, but Daddy might get dead in the war."

She squeezed their hands tighter. "Would it be okay if we said a prayer for Daddy?" she asked.

John, engrossed in the scene from Baghdad, shrugged. Sherry, though, warmed to the idea. "Yeah, Mommy, let's say a prayer. Do you want me to say it?"

"Sure, sweetheart, why don't you say it?" Katherine nudged

John to pay attention. He muted the sound of the commentator on the news. Sherry closed her eyes and said, "Dear God, my daddy is in a war. We want him to stay safe. Would you make sure he stays safe? Don't let Daddy get dead in the war. And God, help the cabbage taste good 'cause I think I smell it burning. Amen."

John snickered and turned up the television sound, Sherry started combing her doll's hair again, and Katherine scooted back to the kitchen to rescue the burning cabbage. But that part of Sherry's prayer went unanswered.

Chapter Thirty-seven

Everyone in Saudi expected the daily routine to change drastically once the air war started. For the first couple of days, they were right. Fighters and bombers and reconnaissance jets and helicopters zipped through the air like autumn leaves in a windstorm, and Les and the rest of the medical staff at King Khalid Hospital went on instant alert. They kept their ears perked, listening for the first wail of the siren, warning them of incoming Scuds. They slept fewer hours, expecting a call to the operating room at any minute. They laughed less but talked more, and waited for the parade of casualties to begin.

But it didn't. To everyone's surprise, nothing substantial happened in their theater of operations—not on the first day and not for the next several days. Though 1,500 aircraft dropped thousands of tons of bombs each day, almost all the jets returned safely to base. No bombers crashed and casualties were minimal. The few who were hurt were shipped to hospitals other than King Khalid.

The days passed with a bland sameness. Shifts at the hospital, poker games at night, shifts at the hospital, poker games at night. It didn't take long for the numbing inactivity to become downright boring—for Les and everyone else in the 804th. Except for the gas mask he carried everywhere with him and the horizon of sand as far as the eye could see, the war seemed no closer to him than to millions of Americans stateside.

It wasn't that he wanted casualties. No sane person wanted that. But casualties gave him and his buddies their purpose for being in Saudi. Without casualties, they might as well go home. But they couldn't—despite the lack of action.

Slowly, the days passed, one dull blur after another. Les thought of approaching Harper again about going home, but sensed it was useless. He would have to wait it out like everyone else.

Thankfully, things at home had improved. The pressure there had eased off. John, though awaiting trial, had returned to school. Katherine stayed calm when Les talked to her on the phone. He sensed a quiet strength in her, one he hadn't noticed in previous years. And Sherry, well, Sherry always stayed the same—simple, sweet, and loving. He missed them all and wished he could catch the next transport back to St. Louis.

But he couldn't. So, like his family in the States, he waited— waited while Saddam His Insane played "rope-a-dope" with the U.S. military, trying to draw the troops into a war on the ground; waited while people in the U.S. marched, a few against, but most in support of the war to free Kuwait; waited while Scud missiles hit Tel Aviv and Haifa in Israel, hoping to draw the Jews into the fray. Through it all, Les watched and waited, worked and waited, worried and waited.

On January 26, his waiting unexpectedly and suddenly ended. He was leaning against a countertop in an examination room, writing a prescription for a soldier with a diarrhea problem. No wonder, Les told the man. MREs would do it to anybody. The soldier, weak from his affliction, didn't appreciate the stab at humor.

With no response from his patient, Les heard a set of heavy feet hurrying down the hallway. The feet entered the examination room. They belonged to Colonel Harper. "You finished here, Les?" he asked.

Finished scribbling, Les looked up. "Yeah, colonel, all done. What's shakin'?"

Harper motioned for him to step outside. In the hallway, Harper filled him in. "I've just received orders to put together a temporary assignment team for transport to Jerusalem. The brass is shipping in some training personnel to teach the Israelis how to use the Patriot missiles, and they need a medical support group to go along in case of injuries or casualties. They've assigned us to the detail. It won't take long, probably a week at most."

Les rubbed his palms together and his eyes lit up. "That makes sense. The Jews have taken the worst pounding of all in this thing. What is it now, six or seven Scud attacks on them already?"

"Yeah, something like that. His Insane is determined to bring them into the war. That way it becomes a Jew versus Arab conflict and splits the coalition forces."

"And the Patriots are the best defense against the Scuds."

"No doubt about it, a heck of a kill rate so far."

"So we give the Israelis the Patriots to protect themselves and they stay out of the war."

"So far that's the plan."

"Great. When do we move?"

"Tomorrow morning."

"Who else is with us?"

"Well, I thought you and me and Roger Tills. They said three doctors should do it. Plus, we'll bring nurses, technicians, you know, the regular support personnel."

"Any particular gear I'll need?"

"No, just a regular pack. And don't forget your gas mask. Intelligence says His Insane will probably drop chemicals on the Jews."

Harper turned to leave. Les nodded. "Thanks for taking me," he said.

Harper grinned. "See you in the morning, 0700."

Les sprinted back to his quarters where Roger was already packing. He saw Reed packing too. Les patted him on the back.

"You're going with us?"

"Wouldn't miss it," said Reed, tossing several pairs of socks into his bag. "I've always wanted to go to Jerusalem — every preacher's dream, you know."

Les moved away, to his bunk. "I'm glad Harper assigned you. If someone goes down, it'll be good to have a soul doctor on our side."

Nelson shoved a pair of khakis after his socks and laughed. "Harper didn't exactly assign me, Les."

"He didn't? Then how are you going?"

Nelson stopped packing. "Well, let me say this carefully. Harper owed me a little cash from a previous game of chance. So, I cut the deck with him — the cash he owed me against the trip to Jerusalem."

"And he obviously lost."

"Was there ever any doubt he would?"

"Not against you, there wasn't."

The three men laughed in unison then, happy to move, to do something.

At supper, they received one final surprise. Macy eased into a seat at their table and showed them her orders for Jerusalem. Not because she piloted a helicopter, she said, but because her father wore two stars on his helmet and he happened to be in Jerusalem for ten days and hadn't seen his little girl in almost eight months.

Through the meal and the poker game and the late night news reports of the war, the Gang of Four teased and laughed and reveled as they celebrated the joy of having friends in a war zone so far away from life at home.

Chapter Thirty-eight

Les flipped a book into Nelson's lap and eased into the seat on the C-5 beside him. "It's full of information about Jerusalem."

Nelson picked up the book, *The Modern Middle East,* and thumbed through its pages.

"Thought you might find a saloon with a poker game listed in it," said Les.

"Thanks, Les," said Nelson, obviously pleased. "I've always wanted to go to Jerusalem, to see the Wailing Wall, the Garden of Gethsemane, to walk the streets where Jesus lived and taught."

"Seems to me you'd be a little more critical," said Les, strapping on his seat belt and turning more serious.

"How so?"

"Well, according to your faith, Jerusalem is the place where Jesus died. The place of the crucifixion and all that." The plane roared off the ground and pointed its nose west.

Reed laid the book down. "Yeah, that's true, Les, but it's also the place where He was resurrected. Plus, if you think His death had purpose, then you can even forgive the death."

Les furrowed his brow. "I don't get it, Nellie. You're an intelligent guy. How can you hold to ideas like that, a purposeful death, an actual resurrection? Your whole faith rests on the premise of a resurrection. If that fails, it kicks your entire belief system right in the stomach. Am I right?"

"Sure, you're right. But let me ask you this—do you know what happens after death?"

"Well, no, nobody can know exactly."

"So, if you don't know, you have to reach a best guess, right?"

"Right."

"Then let's consider the possibilities. One, complete annihilation—we simply cease to exist and no one knows the difference. I take it that's your position?"

"More or less."

"What do you mean 'more or less'?"

"Well, I've never really thought about it that much."

Reed grunted out a choked laugh. "You never really thought about it? As much death as you see? How could you not have thought about it?"

The tone in Reed's voice was accusing and Les turned defensive. "Hey, man, I don't need to think about death to keep people alive. I think about how to keep them alive."

"I concede the point," agreed Reed. "You don't have to think about death just because you work around it. But let's think about it now. What do you think happens after death?"

Les unsnapped his seat belt. "Well, why don't you list those possibilities you mentioned and let me see if any of them fit."

"Multiple choice, huh?"

"Yeah, multiple choice."

"Okay. First, as I said, complete destruction—no consciousness of any kind. You die and bingo, you're dead as a dog in the middle of the road. Number two, you die and you get reincarnated, over and over again; you move up or down in the scheme of things until you get good enough to dissolve into Nirvana."

"The old 'You might be a cockroach or a king in your next life' routine, huh?"

"Precisely. Number three, you die and end up in purgatory. You wait your turn until someone who loves you either prays or pays your way out and then you go to heaven."

"Not a bad option," teased Les.

"Unless you're poor or not very lovable."

"Unfortunately, I'm short on both money and lovability."

"Then that one's not for you."

"What else is there?"

"The view I accept."

"Which is?"

"That death opens a door to another dimension. We can't imagine what it'll be like. It's a mystery to us—like this life is to a fetus in the womb. We're in a womb in this life and we're being formed every day and one day, when we die, we'll go through another birth process. When we pass through that birth canal, we'll find ourselves in a realm of beauty and love and wonder beyond our capacity to fathom."

Les wiped his tongue over his front top teeth, out and back, out and back, out and back. Then he spoke. "So how does this fit with the idea of Jesus' resurrection?"

"Well, it's simple really."

"Hey, don't tell me that anything about resurrection and eternal life is simple. The terms contradict each other."

Reed laughed. "Maybe you're right. But think of it this way. God wanted to get a message to us. He wanted to tell us a truth we couldn't receive any other way. He wanted us to know not to fear death. So God—"

"So God sent one ahead to explore it for us and then came back with a report. Kind of like a recon patrol." Les finished the sentence for him.

"I don't know if I would've said it that way, but yes, now that you mention it, that fits pretty well. Jesus stepped into the darkness of the room and flipped on the light for us so we wouldn't be so scared when we entered. Then, He came back to tell us the light was on. In fact, the first thing Jesus said after the Resurrection was precisely that, 'Don't be afraid.' "

Les remained unconvinced. "Your story tells me *why*, Nellie, but it doesn't tell me *how*. How could God resurrect Jesus?"

Nelson chewed on his lip for a skip, then said, "Look at it this way. If God exists, couldn't He do whatever He wanted in the world He created?"

"Sure, Nellie, sure, but I haven't conceded yet that God exists."

Reed sighed deeply and his voice dropped a notch. "I know, Les, and nobody can argue you into that belief. And I won't even try. Ultimately, it's not only a matter of the mind anyway. It's also a matter of the heart."

"Explain yourself, my friend," coaxed Les, genuinely interested.

"Let me say it this way," said Nelson, turning sideways in the seat so he faced Les directly. "You depend on what you can see and touch and measure and smell. You're logical, left-brained—all that jazz. That's good. That's the way God made you. God put some of that in all of us. But God also gave us intuition, emotion, imagination, heart. And we can't discount that part of our personalities. Faith in God comes when we get the two together. The head and the heart, the logical we can prove and the intuitive we can only imagine. We know God where the two intersect."

"So I can't know God by deducing God."

"Neither can you know God only by feeling Him. It's an experience of both. When you believe in God with your mind and trust in Him with your heart, then you'll have an experience with God."

"That's a tall order," said Les, honestly saddened by the commitment it demanded.

"Yep, it is," agreed Nelson. "But nobody ever said Christian faith was for wimps."

Les leaned his head back against the seat and closed his eyes. He sensed a dead end in the conversation and that bothered him. But, with no more questions to ask, he accepted the stalemate.

"It's too much for me right now," he said, his voice little more than a whisper.

Reed didn't push him. "No problem. Give it time. Think about it. Will you do that for me?"

Les nodded. Nelson opened the book and started reading.

The C-5 bulled ahead, cutting through the blue sky. Both men were quiet for the rest of the flight, Les dozing fitfully and Nelson soaking up the words from the book. Two hours later, the plane circled past the Dead Sea and descended over the Jordan River, making its approach into the Jerusalem airport. It touched its wheels onto the earth — sacred earth to many, earth that had shifted under the sandals worn by the Carpenter.

Chapter Thirty-nine

The size-fourteen feet inside John's black Nikes squeaked as they pushed off the hardwood floor and kicked him into the air. Almost eleven feet above his basketball shoes, his vise-like fingers gripped the rebound. Holding it firmly, John settled back to ground and pivoted to turn upcourt. He looked for a passing lane to start a fast break but spotted no one ahead of him.

Like a giant waterbug he spurted out of the pack of sweaty bodies, dribbling the basketball through the human traffic, up the court, past the midline to the foul line, and to the glass. Soaring over the last defender, he jammed the ball through the rim for two more points. John clenched both fists and thrust them into the air as he headed back to play defense.

With a 19-point lead over St. Louis High and only four minutes left, they were guaranteed the number one seed in the state tournament.

Standing on the opposite side of the court beside her team's bench, Tina Spicer hung her head. It wasn't only that her school trailed so badly with the game almost over. The worst part was John had scored 32 points and had rubbed it into the St. Louis cheering section all night long. The clenched fists after the slam dunk simply capped his night of scoring and gloating.

In the stands several rows above Tina, Jamaal held his head high. Standing with his pack of friends—students and former students of St. Louis High—he stomped his feet in chaotic rhythm with them and waved his arms and slapped palms and hooted his disgust. In chorus, his mob of buddies pointed down at John and his teammates. In chorus they screamed and shouted obscenities. If the roar of the rest of the crowd hadn't drowned out the worst of their language, someone would have taken offense. But no one, except those in the middle of the herd, could make out any single voice. All they could hear was an erratic bellowing which they chalked up to youthful exuberance.

Jamaal, though, couldn't ignore John's actions on the court. He kept shaking his head, almost violently, in exaggerated motions. No, No, No way should John Tennet get away with the trash he talked and the game he played on the court. Someone ought to take him down. He was showing no respect to the brothers on the St. Louis team. Tennet had shot over them and driven past them and slammed between them, and somebody ought to take him down.

Jamaal hated John for all of his friends. He hated the styling, the finger-pointing, the fists in the air, the woofing, and the showboating. He hated it because he wasn't doing it—not anymore. Not like three years ago when he led his team in scoring, when he had college scouts panting after his signature, when he read his name in the paper almost every morning. No, all that had ended during a sandlot game. . . .

Jamaal had taken a rebound just like John did. He had hustled it up the asphalt court, slithering past two defenders. Then he broke free with no one in front of him. With practiced ease he lifted off his feet and twisted his body—a reverse jam on the way.

Never one to stand and watch, John had raced down the court after Jamaal. Then, when Jamaal left his feet, John followed him—inch by towering inch—his hand reaching up

from behind to block the shot. In mid-air the two bodies
tangled together, a violent thud of hands and knees and ankles.

As if moving through an exotic dance, the two boys crashed
back to the asphalt, John landing safely on both feet and
Jamaal landing with his right knee rolled backward under his
thigh. The two heard the sound together—cartilage and liga-
ment and bone stretching, stretching, and then separating and
tearing.

An accident—the kind that happens every day. But it was
fourteen months and two surgeries later before Jamaal finally
hung up his hightops. No more basketball for him.

But putting up his hightops didn't mean the end of his
battle with John Tennet. Not by a long shot. And then John
had added insult to injury when he began to date Tina.

Thankfully, that at least had ended. But Jamaal's anger
hadn't. As long as John Tennet played ball, the anger would
continue. . . .

Yeah, thought Jamaal, as John checked out of the game to
let the subs mop up the victory, *somebody ought to take him
down a notch or two.*

Suddenly, a smile the size of a frisbee broke out on Jamaal's
scowling face. The newspaper had printed the story and he
suddenly remembered. John faced a preliminary hearing in
only a few days. If all went well, the boy might go on trial
during the state playoffs. No way could John play ball if he
was on trial for murder.

Jamaal doubled over with laughter. He wrapped his thick
arms around his stomach and howled and swayed side to side.
John Tennet on trial for a drive-by shooting!

Chapter Forty

The contingent from the 804th had a simple assignment—to provide medical care in case the troops setting up the Patriot missiles had need of it. Harper had warned them the duty might bring no action at all. His words were prophetic.

Each day, Les and his crew drove in from their quarters at an American hotel on the outskirts of the city and stationed themselves in the medical wing of a hospital the Israelis had provided for them. But, as in King Khalid, nothing happened. As in zero, no action at all. To make it worse, they didn't even have the usual contingent of soldierly complaints to check out. Their days passed in total boredom, the clock hands moving as slowly as frozen molasses.

Les pulled the pages off the calendar each morning at the hospital. They received orders to go back on the seventh day. Another contingent would relieve them while the Patriot batteries finished up their work.

Colonel Harper relieved the Gang of Four. "Go see the city," he said, "and prepare to fly back to King Khalid in the morning." Relieved at least to be moving, the Gang left the hospital and drove back to the hotel.

"What's on the agenda for the afternoon and evening?" asked Roger, as they trooped to their rooms.

"I don't know what we will do, but I know what I *won't*

do—I won't play any more poker," said Les. "I've lost everything to Reed but my last pair of good socks."

"Be a good sport now," teased Roger. "You know how badly he needs the money. What about a meal, a little exercise on the machines downstairs, then a movie?" No one answered Roger's suggestion.

Reed plopped down on the bed and stared up at the ceiling. "Look, guys, we've been in the one city I've wanted to visit all my adult life and we've not had a single free moment to see anything in it. I say we hire a cab and explore Jerusalem. And I don't mean modern Jerusalem, either. Let's see the Old City. Anybody with a better idea?"

No one said anything. "Better tell Macy," said Les.

Nelson got up and buzzed her room. "Yeah, Mace, we're going to get a bite to eat and go see the sights. You up for it?" He nodded. "Meet us downstairs in ten minutes."

The meal passed quickly. An hour later, they piled out of a cab and stepped onto the streets of Old Jerusalem.

Nelson directed them, his book on the Middle East open to the chapter describing Jerusalem. "We'll enter through St. Stephen's Gate, the site of the first Christian martyrdom." None of the group objected. A hush settled over them as they passed through the ancient archway, each of them sensing the drama of the centuries that had unfolded within these stone walls.

"Look at the lions," whispered Macy, pointing at the images of the majestic beasts carved into the rock wall as they passed under the arch.

Les felt like tiptoeing along the streets. It wasn't because of Jesus, he told himself stubbornly, but because he appreciated the historical significance of what they were seeing. This place awed him. The walls had watched a succession of armies scale them, the streets had supported horses and soldiers and housewives on pilgrimage and holy men on divine assignments.

The Gang inched their way through the Old City, Nelson giving them information as they walked. They explored the Dome of the Rock—three different temple structures were built here, said Nelson, the first by Solomon, the second by a king named Zerubbabel, and the third by Herod the Great in 20 B.C. Herod's structure stood in place when Jesus lived. The Moslems built the present mosque in the seventh century. It's their third holiest shrine after Mecca and Medina.

"And the Jews own it now," said Les.

"Yep, since the 1967 war," piped in Macy.

"No wonder the Arabs and Jews don't get along," suggested Roger.

The Gang walked on, softly talking, staring, reflecting, pointing. They found themselves at the foot of a towering sandstone wall—over sixty feet high, Nelson informed them, as high as ten men, and thirteen feet wide in some places.

"The Wailing Wall," said Macy, reflecting a knowledge of the city that surprised Les. "Where the Jews come to weep over the destruction of their temple."

"And where orthodox Jews come to pray for the restoration of their glory under David," added Nelson.

"And where they ask their God to send their awaited Messiah," concluded Macy. The group stopped and stared at her.

"Didn't know you were such a Bible scholar," teased Les.

"I'm not, not really," said Macy. "But my time in the Middle East hasn't been completely wasted. I've always enjoyed history and I simply tried to educate myself while I was here, that's all. Don't make such a big deal of it." She said the last sentence like a command rather than a request, and the Gang knew better than to argue. They backed off and stood gazing up at the Wall.

A light breeze blowing in from the west picked up and Les suddenly felt chilled. He wrapped his arms around his chest and rubbed his shoulders with his hands. "Hey, let's keep moving," he suggested, and the Gang complied. They shuffled their feet over the stone pathway—slap, thud, slap, thud, slap, thud, lost in their own thoughts.

After a few minutes, Nelson raised his hand like a scout on a wagon train and halted them.

"Here's where it starts," he said, his voice a whisper.

"Where what starts?" asked Les.

"It's where the path Jesus walked to the cross starts."

"It's called the Via Dolorosa," added Macy.

With a wave of his hand, Nelson described it in more detail. "Soldiers and leaders of the Jewish religious establishment escorted Jesus as He left Herod. He trudged along this route, through the archway there." He pointed toward a stone arch that spanned the top of the narrow street and connected two buildings. "Jesus probably had the twin beams of wood they would use for His cross on His shoulders by this time, though scholars don't know for sure."

Les trailed behind the Gang as Nelson moved ahead, detailing the fateful steps Jesus had taken. "Jesus fell here, too injured from the beatings the Romans gave Him to continue. A man named Simon picked up His cross and carried it for Him."

"These buildings and streets are obviously refurbished editions of the old structures," Nelson explained. "And they are several feet above the originals. Jerusalem has been destroyed and rebuilt several times."

Les marveled at the wonder Nelson expressed as he offered them his tour. They walked on, slap, thud, slap, thud, slap, thud.

Suddenly, Nelson stopped and raised his eyes from the book. Without a word, he dropped to his knees and lowered his forehead to the ground. As he knelt for several minutes, no one said anything. Everyone froze, watching him with reverence, not necessarily for the God he worshiped, but for the sincerity with which he worshiped that God.

Breathing heavily, Nelson stood to his feet and pointed to the building in front of them. "There it is, Gang," he whispered.

Les asked, "What is it, Nellie?"

"It's the Church of the Holy Sepulchre," said Nelson, "The church standing over what is believed to be the site of Jesus' crucifixion and the tomb where Jesus was buried. If you're a believer, it's the most important piece of real estate in the universe."

Sobered, Les and the Gang followed Nelson inside. They entered on the right and climbed two steep flights of steps, going upward to the Hill of Calvary, the Hill where Jesus died. They waited in silence at the top of the steps as Nelson bowed again, this time for a shorter prayer, but one equally as intense.

When he finished there, they followed him back down the steps and into the inner room of the Holy Sepulchre. There they saw the rock, covered with marble, which God supposedly removed from the front of Jesus' burial cave on the morning of the Resurrection. When Nelson didn't bow in front of the rock, Les remarked on it. "Not bowing, Nellie?"

Nelson turned to him and grinned. "Nope, not here, my friend. Jesus told the women who saw Him first, "go and tell." The Resurrection calls us out of our worship and out to our work. It tells us it's time to be going."

"I'm for that," broke in Roger. "All this walking has made me tired."

The Gang laughed then and the laughter echoed through the hallowed room, breaking the spell of somber thought and tying them together. They linked their arms around each others' waists and trooped out of the room, past the arched doors of the building, and back into the light outside.

Leaving the Old City, they found a restaurant a few blocks away and squeezed into a booth and ordered a meal to satisfy their growling stomachs. But then a bomb exploded three doors down from them, reminding them again that Jerusalem, the city whose name means Peace, hadn't even come close to finding it.

Section Four

As peace is of all goodness,
so war is an emblem,
a hieroglyphic,
of all misery.

John Donne

Chapter Forty-one

Les jumped first as the quaking of the detonation shook their table. A glass of water fell off onto the floor. Macy grabbed the table as if to hold it in place, and Roger cursed loudly. Nelson's eyes widened.

A Scud, thought Les, jerking up from his chair. But no siren had sounded. The sound seemed to have risen from the ground up, not fallen from the sky down.

The smell of smoke punched into his nostrils and he heard screams. He sprinted to the door of the restaurant, the Gang hanging close behind him. Within seconds, he stood on the pavement outside. He scanned left and right, then saw the source of the smoke. The Jerusalem City Bank. An international business specializing in service to foreigners.

Les heard sirens — ambulances and fire trucks, he guessed — but they were distant wails, obviously streets away. The sound of screaming intensified and rose into the air with the smoke of the bombed bank. Running now, Les followed the screaming through scores of startled bystanders, followed it until he skidded to a halt in front of the destroyed building.

For one brief instant he paused. Smoke belched into his face. He heard a loud scream. Without looking back, he barged through the crowd and shouldered himself to the gaping hole in the front of the bank that marked the ground zero of the bomb. There he joined the throng, lifting and pulling and dragging away pieces of smoking debris—frantically searching for the people buried underneath.

Nelson, Macy, and Roger followed his lead and together they worked, picking through the fire and the smoke and the water falling from the sprinkler system in what was left of the ceiling. They tore away plaster and steel and glass and wood, desperate to uncover the trapped.

Les heard multiple screams and moans—the roar of human voices notching higher and higher, more and more desperate as strength gave out and blood seeped from savage slashes and smoke filled up burning lungs.

He coughed as the smoke turned blacker and thicker and bellowed out of the cavernous hole. Heat followed the smoke, surging upward from the fire inside the building's belly. To his left, a rescue worker collapsed and a second one pulled him out of the wreckage.

Les' shirt caught on fire. The flames singed into his left arm and he hugged it to his body and snuffed out the orange death.

To his right two men shook their heads and backed up, unwilling to go any deeper into the bowels of the inferno. Les stopped and tried to breathe. The smoke filled his lungs and he thought he was about to pass out. From behind him, he heard someone calling his name. For a second, he thought it was Katherine, then realized it wasn't. It was Macy, calling to him to give it up, to get out.

A light fixture from the ceiling thudded to his left and fire rose up off the floor and licked toward his shoes. He stared at the flames for a beat, then looked around. He was alone.

Les heard a scream. Louder than any of the rest. And higher too. The scream of a child, directly in front of him. A child buried under concrete and plaster, a child choking on smoke and maybe burning in flames. The child screamed again.

Les took a step forward. A ceiling beam—a shredded piece of steel and concrete—blocked his way. It lay like a diagonal roadblock, one side connected to the ceiling and the other collapsed into the floor. He reached for the bottom of the beam with both hands, bracing his feet against a stack of rubble on the floor. He pulled with every ounce of strength in his weary body. The scar on his forehead stood up, purple, as blood flowed into it.

His feet slipped. Losing his balance, Les grabbed upward, trying to right himself. His hands clutched and slid, backward, backward, no way to stay up.

A slice of pain cut through him. His right hand had raked over the jagged edge of the steel beam and the edge had clawed into his skin and taken out a chunk of it. Les released the beam and thumped to the floor, his back hitting first, then his shoulders, and finally his head. He jerked his hand up so he could see it and the depth of the cut surprised him. But it didn't hurt, not really. Only a dull throb.

He twitched the fingers on the cut hand. All of them worked. Good. No nerve damage.

The child shrieked again. This time, though, the shriek had less edge to it, less energy, and Les knew that meant the life was ebbing, growing quieter, less resistant to the thief who stole life and put it in a black vault where it couldn't escape.

With rising panic, he yanked a shoestring out of his left boot and tied it tightly around his wrist to stop the bleeding in his hand. The shrieks of the child stopped. Les paused to listen. Nothing. For a second, he thought the worst, then gritted his teeth, not allowing himself to believe it.

Kneeling, he lowered his shoulders until they were directly under the steel girder that trapped the child. He arched his broad back and grunted. Then, he screamed himself, screamed in agony, hoping the beam would move. His scream bounced through the blackness of the smoke and at the height of the scream, he raised himself up. The beam moved.

Loose pieces of plaster fell off as it crawled upward, upward off the child. The beam heaved and then it let go completely and debris crashed down off of it and then, then he stood there, a shattered beam on his back and a crying child at his feet.

His eyes burning from the smoke and his face soaked from sweat and streaked with dirt, Les braced himself and heaved one final time and this time he tossed the beam off his back and instantly, he dropped back to his knees.

For a beat, he rested, sucking in mouthfuls of soot-filled air. From behind, from the front of the building, from the light that he could barely see through the smoke, he heard voices pleading with him to get out. He ignored them.

Moving again, he pushed aside several pieces of wall and ceiling. He spotted the child. A boy.

He reached for him and pulled the youngster from the debris. About five, from all he could tell. Brown eyes that stared back at him. A black bruise the size of a baseball covering his left eye. Les grabbed the boy and stood up with him and cradled him in his arms. Then he turned and ran, ran toward the light of the street outside the fiery cauldron, ran into the arms of Macy Spencer who was yelling for him, ran toward Roger who was loading the injured into the ambulances that had arrived, ran toward Nelson who was praying for him.

Handing the boy to Macy, Les twisted around to go back inside. But Macy grabbed his arm and held him tightly and wouldn't let him go. "That's all, Les, that's all you can do," she yelled above the roar of the street.

At first he resisted, tried to pull away, tried to go back into the building, but then he nodded his head. He could see it. The black smoke billowing from the bank made it clear. The thief had captured the rest of those trapped there. He heard no more screams.

Chapter Forty-two

FOURTEEN DEAD IN BANK BOMB EXPLOSION

Les read the headline the next day as he sat in the hotel cafeteria munching a blueberry muffin. The article beneath the headline detailed the story. Eleven others injured, two seriously. The seriously injured were expected to live.

He searched the story for the name of the boy, but couldn't tell from the list of survivors which one he was. Les wished he knew. But that the boy had survived was what counted.

After getting eleven stitches in his hand, Les had spent the night and morning undergoing tests in the hospital. They showed no lasting damage from the smoke he had inhaled.

Now he was out and getting ready to deploy back to King Khalid Military Hospital. His group was scheduled to leave at 7 that evening.

Staring down at the paper, he didn't hear the door of the café swing open and he didn't see Reed approaching him from the back. Only when Reed tossed a set of keys onto the table did Les glance up.

Nelson flashed his toothy grin. "You're alive and well, I see, after your heroics yesterday."

Les waved him off. "Nothing most people wouldn't do. I just reacted, that's all, wanted to help if I could."

"Well, you certainly did that."

"Everyone there did."

Les munched another bite from his muffin. "We shipping out at 7?"

"Yeah, back to King Khalid."

"Where's the rest of the Gang?"

"Tills is writing letters and Macy went shopping for souvenirs. Looks like it's me and you."

"You packed?"

"Yeah, pretty much so. You?"

"Yep, ready and waiting."

"Good, because I've got one more sight I want to see."

Les groaned and tossed his muffin onto his plate. "No, Nellie, I refuse to go. Your trip yesterday almost got me killed."

Nelson patted him on the back. "Yep, but my trip yesterday also got a boy saved, because you were there. Almost like it was providential, huh?"

"Hey, no way, Nellie," Les said. "No way are you going to get away with that. Nothing providential about my being near that bank. That was sheer coincidence."

He kept talking even when Nellie turned and walked away. Unwilling to leave the comment uncontested, Les stood up and followed him out the door of the hotel. Followed him into the parking lot. Followed him as Nellie hopped into a Humvee and they roared away from the hotel, headed north out of Jerusalem.

Chapter Forty-three

Sherry licked her lips sleepily and clutched Elmer close to her chest. It was cold outside, and for a couple of minutes she snuggled deeper into her warm bed covers. Then a ray of sunlight peeped through the shutters of the window across from her bed and bathed her face. She opened her eyes and smiled at the sun and sat up in bed.

Without putting Elmer down, she rolled sideways and dropped her feet to the floor. She completed her morning routine—push hair out of eyes, wash face, brush teeth, slip on swimming suit, pull night coat around body, pad down the hall, peek into Mom's room to see if she was up yet, no not yet today, clump down the stairs through the den, Elmer still at her chest, edge over to the pool, lay her night coat aside with Elmer, push toes into chilly water and then, finally, plunge full body into the slick liquid.

Sherry loved the water and gradually had improved as a swimmer. Not that she was good at it yet, but lately she had grown more and more confident. Especially since Daddy had gone away.

She thought about him today as she always did, missing him, wanting him with her as she enjoyed the water. It seemed so long since he had splashed and jumped and played with her. But he had told her she could swim by herself. And she'd been doing so almost every morning since he disappeared.

Where was he now? She couldn't remember exactly. A war? Yeah, that was it, Daddy was away at war. Being brave. Protecting their country, protecting her.

Well, she could be brave too. She could make Daddy proud of her. She could swim all by herself. That would make Daddy proud. She couldn't wait to tell him when he came home.

Chapter Forty-four

Nelson pulled to the side of the road and skidded the Humvee to a stop. "Here we are," he said dramatically, hopping down from the vehicle.

"Here we are where?"

"Follow me and you'll see."

Without waiting for Les to say yes or no, Nelson loped across the craggy rocks and sand. Like an obedient puppy, Les tagged along, his curiosity getting the best of him.

Within five minutes Les could see the sliver of bluish water cutting through the brown of the rocky ground. Within five more, he and Nelson were standing beside the river.

"It's the Jordan River," beamed Nelson, slightly out of breath.

"Not much to it," grunted Les, not wanting to appear impressed. "Less than twenty feet wide it looks to me."

Nelson kept beaming. "Doesn't matter how big it is, Les. It's what it represents."

"And what's that?"

"It all started here, Les, here in the water, the public ministry of Jesus. A prophet named John baptized Jesus here and from that point He started teaching and preaching."

Nelson bent down and shoved both hands into the clear water. Cupping them, he lifted the liquid to his face. Then, with a flourish, he splashed it over his head.

Les shook his head, amazed at the joy Nelson found in the tiny river. Suddenly, Nelson yanked himself up, ripped off his jacket, unbuttoned and pulled off his shirt. "Come on, man," he urged. "Let's go in."

"You're crazy, Nellie," said Les. "Not only do I bet that water is as cold as an Eskimo's nose, but the Israeli army keeps patrols all along this river. I don't think I want to get shot for taking a swim."

Nelson laughed and kicked off his boots and socks. "I only want to go in for a minute." He eased his feet into the water. "Get moving, Les. You're right about the water and the patrols. But I won't leave until you get in."

"No way, Nellie. You're around the bend on this one, if you think I'm stripping down to get in that water with you."

Nelson stopped his gradual movement into the stream. He stared back at Les. "Les, you've got to come in."

"Give me one good reason why I've got to come in."

" 'Cause if you don't, who's going to baptize me?"

"Baptize you?" groused Les. "I'm not exactly qualified."

"I can't argue with that," said Nelson. "But John wasn't qualified to baptize Jesus either. But Jesus insisted that he do it."

"So you're insisting that I baptize you?"

"Exactly."

"But you're not Jesus."

"No, and you're not John, so that makes it about even. Now get in here before we both get shot."

With no defense against Nelson's arguments, Les began to undress, muttering to himself all the while. When he was naked except for his pants, he dipped his toes into the water. Then, still grumbling, he pushed himself out waist deep into the river where Nelson waited for him.

Chapter Forty-five

Sherry pushed herself off the side of the pool and into the center of the water. She dimly remembered a promise she'd made to Daddy not to get away from the sides, but that was so long ago, and she was a much better swimmer than she'd been when she made the promise. Besides, she was still in the shallow end. She could swim easy here.

She ducked her head into the clear liquid and opened her eyes. She always did that. Yeah, it made her eyes a little red, but she loved to see the shimmering sights under the surface.

The water shut out all sound from above. Sherry liked that too. The quiet calmed her.

She loved the underwater world. Everything slowed down underwater and words muffled and bubbles flowed like magic in a faraway kingdom.

Kicking her legs, Sherry raised her head for a breath, then submerged her face again, edging further into the pool, toward the diving board, toward the deep end. Not too far, not far enough to be dangerous. She could still reach the side easily enough.

She stared through the sunlight that danced in the bubbles ahead of her. She loved the brightness of the sun's rays as they hit the surface and slipped downward. The rays warmed the water and made her goosebumps go away.

Through the sunlit water, she saw the edge of the pool under the diving board. She turned her mouth sideways, gulped in air from above and ducked underwater again. She glanced down the side of the pool, toward the bottom. She had never swum this far into the deep end by herself and she felt free, big, strong.

Her eyes scanned all the way down, down to the drain. What was that on the bottom of the pool ahead of her? An animal? What kind of animal was in her pool? Elmer?

It is Elmer! On the bottom of the pool! How did he get there? Must have dropped him when I jumped in. He must have sunk to the bottom. Elmer on the bottom of the pool . . . Elmer drowning on the bottom of the pool . . . Save Elmer . . . Have to save Elmer.

But Elmer's on the bottom of the pool! But I'm a good swimmer. Daddy told me I was. I can do it. I can save Elmer.

Thrashing through the water, Sherry dove toward the stuffed toy. She clutched handfuls of water and shoved it behind her, shoved it behind her as she reached lower and lower and lower into the bubbling wet. She grabbed another handful of water and pushed her body to the bottom of the pool. Elmer was almost within her grasp.

Chapter Forty-six

"Here's what you do," instructed Nelson. "You put one hand under my back, and you put the other one over my chest. You lean me backwards while I bend my knees. You say, 'I baptize you in the name of the Father, and of the Son, and of the Holy Spirit.' Then you plunge me down, hold me for a second, and then lift me back up. When I'm up, you say 'Amen.'"

Les shook his head over and over. "I feel like holding you down for good, man. This is crazy. I mean, isn't it sacrilegious or something?"

"Not to me it isn't. You can do it. Don't sweat it."

"No way to sweat it in this water."

"Okay, get on with it. The sooner we do it, the sooner we can get out of here."

"I'm all for that," agreed Les.

"Good, let's do it."

Les sucked in a potful of air. "Okay, here goes nothing." He placed his right hand on Nelson's back and his left hand on Nelson's chest. Nelson took Les' left hand with both of his. Les looked down in his friend's gray eyes, and the sight lifted his heart. The eyes were glowing with a light Les didn't recognize. Didn't recognize because he'd never experienced it. But, in that moment, he wished he had.

He spoke reverently. "I baptize you in the name of the

Father, and of the Son, and of the Holy Spirit."

He laid his friend horizontally into the current. He watched the water wash over Nelson's face and he sensed power in it. But it was a power outside his grasp, a power he suddenly recognized he couldn't attain on his own. It was a power as natural as a river and equally as free.

He lifted Nelson out of the water and whispered into his friend's face, "Amen."

Nelson, sopping wet and shivering from the cold, reached up and hugged Les around the neck. Instead of griping and pulling away, as he typically would, Les accepted the embrace.

Letting go, Nelson stepped away and said, "Now, I have to baptize you."

Les sputtered, "Uh, Nelson, no way, I don't—what sense would it make to baptize me? I don't believe in—well, I don't think I believe in God like you do, so no, you can't baptize me."

Nelson dipped his hands back into the stream. "Hey, relax man, I'm not trying to force you to do anything. Just a suggestion. I'm a minister, and I've always wanted to baptize someone in this river. It's every minister's dream, and I might never get another chance. I know you don't believe like I do, but I think you do believe and just haven't admitted it yet. Besides, this water won't make you something you're not." Nelson looked disappointed and that caused Les to reconsider.

"Look, Nellie, wouldn't it be wrong?"

"Not if you don't pretend to believe when you don't. I know where you stand and so does God. You're not trying to fool anyone. You'd just be doing a friend a favor, that's all. No big deal." He grinned big and wide. "Hey, it's really something, you know."

"What's that?"

"Well, think about it, a man who doesn't believe in God concerned about doing something sacrilegious."

Les chuckled. "Rather ironic, huh?" He paused a beat. "Look Nellie, if it means so much to you, I don't guess it's my place to say it's wrong. If you want to baptize me, well, then, I'm game."

"You mean it?"

"Yeah, why not? But, let's do it fast. A patrol is probably due by here any minute."

A huge crease cut through Nelson's cheeks, the biggest smile Les had ever seen on him. "Okay, man." Quickly, he situated his hands, one on Les' back and one on his chest.

He braced his feet and spoke softly. "I baptize you in the name of the Father, and of the Son, and of the Holy Spirit." Les leaned over backwards and Nelson dipped him into the moving stream. As the water coursed over Les' head, he opened his eyes and peered through the water into his friend's face. The sun behind Nelson beamed downward and danced off his golden hair, making him look angelic. Then Les closed his eyes, because he felt himself wanting to believe; but he was scared of it and so he shut off the sunlight on Nelson's face and looked into the darkness again.

Chapter Forty-seven

Sherry plunged deeper into the belly of the pool, toward the drain where Elmer lay facedown. She had sucked in at least three mouthfuls of water. Most of it she had gagged out, but the gagging had slowed her progress toward Elmer. It had also turned her around so she wasn't sure about the quickest way to the side of the pool anymore.

At this second, though, that didn't matter to her, didn't matter at all. Nothing would matter until she saved Elmer.

With a final thrust, she lunged through the bubbles and grabbed for her friend. She grabbed him by the leg just as her lungs gave up and churned out the last of her oxygen. She gulped in water and wished it was air, but it wasn't. But she had Elmer. She clutched him to her chest and twisted side to side, like an alligator fighting against a net, trying to find a way of escape. But the water wasn't air and she kept sucking it in through her nose and mouth and it filled her lungs and gradually, gulp by weaker gulp, she stopped fighting it. She thrashed easier and easier and finally stopped fighting altogether and rolled over on her back and closed her eyes and let the darkness claim her as she floated to the surface of the pool, with Elmer against her now relaxed chest.

Chapter Forty-eight

Les and Nelson pulled the Humvee into the parking lot and hustled into the hotel lobby. Though they were already packed, they were still rushed for time. The military bus that would carry their group back to the airport was parked at the entrance. Les glanced at his watch — he and Nelson had about twenty minutes to get their gear downstairs. They would make it. No problem.

Nelson veered off as Les walked to the elevator. "Need to stop by the desk a second," he said.

Les nodded and walked away. He stepped into the elevator and the door began to close. He heard someone calling his name. Twisting about and shoving the door back open, he saw Macy rushing down the hall, a worried frown on her face.

"Les," she yelled, "hang on a second." She covered the last few feet separating them and stopped, as if uncertain what to do.

"What's up?" Les asked, somewhat impatiently.

Macy seemed shell-shocked. "Well, Les, you might need to sit down a minute."

He stepped back into the elevator. "Come on then, I've got to get my stuff. Tell me in the room while I pick it up."

She nodded and stood silently beside him as the elevator climbed to the third floor. The door opened and they walked to the fifth room. Les unlocked the door.

"I think you need to sit down," said Macy.

Les shrugged and obeyed. "Okay," he said, taking a seat in a chair by his bed. "Spit it out. What's up?"

Macy placed herself on the bed, stared down at the floor for a brief instant, then looked back at him. "Les, I don't know how to tell you this except to say it straight out."

He nodded.

"You got a call from home a few minutes ago. It's—"

"It's my son, John. You don't have to tell—" he interrupted.

This time Macy cut him off. She grabbed him by both forearms and shushed him. "Noooo, Les, listen to me, it's not about John. Fact is, John's the one who called. It's Sherry."

"Sherry?" Les jerked back, trying to separate himself from Macy, but she held onto his arms. "Sherry's fine," he insisted. "We never had any trouble with Sherry. What's wrong?"

Macy let go of his forearms and grabbed his hands. She squeezed them and gently told him the story. "She's in the hospital. Katherine found her in the pool, unconscious. She's alive, but the outlook is not good."

Macy kept talking, but he only vaguely listened. Harper was cutting through the red tape, she said, sending him home, not for good probably, but long enough to get things in order, long enough to see what happened with Sherry.

"In the pool?" he asked, still in a daze.

"Yeah, she was swimming, like she did with you every day."

"In the pool?" Les asked again, the truth still not dawning.

"Yeah, in the pool," repeated Macy.

Then it hit him. Sherry had drowned in the pool. Without standing, he jerked his hands from Macy's hold and slammed his injured fist into the palm of his left hand. "I did it!" he grunted through clenched teeth. "I put the pool in so I could swim. I taught her to swim. I told her she could use the pool all by herself. I did it. I drowned Sherry. I drowned my own daughter!" He slammed his hands together again.

Macy reached out and took his hands into hers again. Her touch warmed him and her smooth voice soothed his anger.

"She's still alive, Les, don't forget that," she said. "She's still alive and as long as there's life, there's hope."

Les blinked and stared into Macy's green eyes. With Sherry dead, he had nothing left. Not Katherine. He'd failed her too many times. Like now. Not there, not there while Sherry died. She'd never forgive him. And she shouldn't.

And John? Well, John and he had always struggled. He'd never known how to love his son. He was too much like his drunken father to love John. Not drunk with alcohol, but drunk with ambition, self-absorption. His addiction had destroyed lives as completely as his father's had.

Macy rubbed his hands. He furrowed his brow. Macy? Yeah, Macy. Here with him.

As if testing a theory, Les slowly leaned his chair toward her. She didn't move. He touched his lips to hers and moved his hands around to her back. Then he stood up from his chair, pushed it away and pulled her to him. She didn't resist.

For several long seconds, the two embraced, the warmth of his body against hers, the loneliness of war pulling them together, the loneliness of life keeping them that way.

He leaned Macy down, easing her toward the bed. Everything gone. Nothing for him at home. Why not wrap himself in Macy's arms. She cared for him. No one else did.

No one else, except Sherry. Sherry cared for him. His daughter. His lovely daughter. Still alive. Sherry hadn't died yet. Where there was life, there was hope. Sherry needed him.

As if waking from a dream, he broke off the kiss with Macy and stepped away from her.

"I'm sorry, Mace, I shouldn't have done that," he said, his face turning red with embarrassment.

She dropped her hands to her sides. "Maybe not, Les, and maybe I shouldn't have let you."

He rubbed his teeth with his tongue. "I just don't know what's happening to me right now, what's going to happen in the future."

"I know, Les, I know. None of us do."

"I do know this, though."

"What's that, what do you know?"

"I know I have to go home to Sherry. I have to find out where Katherine and I are headed."

Macy turned away from him and walked for the door. Then she twisted back. "Look, Les, I'm not sure why I let you kiss me. Maybe to comfort you, maybe to see what would happen, maybe to see if what I feel for you is only friendship or something more. I don't know."

Les waited for her to finish. "But I do know I don't want to come between you and your wife. That's not my way. Go home to your family. They need you. Sherry needs you. We can talk about this later."

He nodded and she left him then, and less than an hour later Nelson drove him to the Jerusalem airport. The fog of shock that enveloped him grew thicker as they drove; and though Nelson tried to get him to talk, he said almost nothing. The shock stayed with him as Nelson said goodbye and as he boarded a flight to New York and then a second one to St. Louis.

Through the two flights, his shock-drugged mind revisited much of his life. It all squeezed in on him again . . . his loneliness as a boy, his drive for perfection as a student and doctor, his isolation as a husband and father. Most of all, he felt his guilt. Guilt for losing Snowball, guilt for losing John and Katherine. And now, worst of all, guilt for losing Sherry. She would die. He knew she would. Like his mother, she would die. And if she died, so would any hope he ever had for happiness.

Through the fog of his guilt, Les stared out the window of the jet at the lights of St. Louis. He had made it home.

The plane touched the ground. Walter picked him up at the gate. Still numbed, Les barely spoke as they gathered his baggage and headed to the hospital. Sitting beside Walter in the car, he hoped the shock would stay with him. He much preferred it to the pain that was sure to come when he allowed himself to face reality.

Chapter Forty-nine

Walter drove Les straight from the airport to the St. Louis Medical Center. He filled him in on the way. "Katherine found her in the pool when she came down to the kitchen for breakfast. Don't know how long Sherry stayed in the water. She wasn't breathing and had no pulse when Katherine got to her, but she gave her mouth-to-mouth and her heart started beating again. An ambulance arrived within minutes and they've been working on her ever since. Her lungs are in bad shape, her blood gases are fouled up, and there's cranial swelling from the trauma to the brain. Don't know how long she went without oxygen."

Les listened, but he knew the dangers better than Walter. If she lived, and that was a major if, she might suffer irreparable brain damage, and be left with no motor function at all. With no more mind than a lump of coal. A fleshy existence, but no life.

Though he hated to think it, Les knew he preferred death to that. And he believed Sherry would too. At certain times, death was not an enemy, but a friend.

Arriving at the hospital, Walter let him out and drove away to park the car. Les rushed through the hallways, caught the elevator and hopped off on the third floor. He spotted John immediately and hurried to him with his arms open. He hugged his son almost violently and the two stood in the middle of the intensive care waiting room and drew strength from each other.

"Are you okay, John?" he asked gently, easing off the embrace.

"Yeah, Dad, I'm making it, but I'm really worried. The doctors—"

Les shushed him. "I know, John, the doctors aren't exactly optimistic. But they never are. They paint it as bad as possible, so if the worst happens they don't get blamed for raising false hopes."

John nodded. "Mom's in the room with Sherry," he said. "Room 23. She's been praying you'd get here."

"Praying?"

"Yeah, Dad. Since her experience at the church, she's been doing a lot of that."

Les started to probe John about Katherine's religious change, then thought better of it. Time for that later. "I think I'll go on in. You want to come?"

"No, I just came out. You go ahead, I expect Mom will want to see you alone anyway."

"Maybe so," agreed Les. "Back in a little while." He punched the automatic opener and the double doors leading into the intensive care unit swung wide and he stepped inside.

Room 23 was the second one on the left. Outside it, Les paused and wiped his hands on the legs of his pants. An egg-sized lump rose in his throat and he choked hard to get it down. He swallowed and eased into the room.

Katherine sat in a chair with her back facing him and she apparently didn't hear him enter. He stood there for a beat, silently watching. Katherine held Sherry's left hand in both of hers and she rubbed it over and over, not stopping for even a second. And she was singing to her, a song Les didn't recognize, a low lullaby.

Switching his attention from Katherine to Sherry, he saw exactly what he expected. Tubes running into his baby's nose and mouth, an IV stuck into her arm, heart monitors taped to her pale, bony chest. Her eyes were closed and circles the color of charcoal ringed them. Someone had pushed her long, blonde hair back from her face and it lay like strings on her pillow. Her cheeks were hollow.

"Katherine," he whispered.

She turned to him instantly and, still holding Sherry with one hand, pushed herself up and reached for him with the other. He stepped to her and hugged her and began to cry, and the tears rolled down his cheeks like rain off a windshield. The tears puddled around the corners of his mouth and made the kiss he gave Katherine salty and sad.

He stood that way, clinging to Katherine and crying for a long time, but then, finally, the wracking in his shoulders stopped and the clouds supplying his tears dried up.

"I got here as soon as I could," he said, letting go of her and turning his eyes to Sherry.

"I know," said Katherine. "I know."

Without another word, he stepped over to the bed, leaned down, and kissed Sherry on both cheeks. "Daddy's here, sweetheart," he murmured. "You don't have to be afraid."

Katherine pulled up a chair for him and he took it, and there the two of them sat. He wanted to talk with Katherine, to tell her he didn't blame her, to tell her he was a different man, and that if they made it through this, their marriage would get better. But he wasn't completely sure if any of that was true, so he said little and Katherine joined him in the silence.

Together they waited as the clock ticked off the time. Nurses moved in and out, checking periodically on Sherry. John joined them and took a chair in the corner. The Reverend Dr. Peter Thomas Tebbs stopped by and visited for a few moments and offered to pray with them. Katherine nodded yes and John and Les shrugged okay and the minister prayed and left. They drank coffee and stared at Sherry and sighed a lot and listened to the clock tick, tick, tick. The vigil continued and the hours rolled by as Sherry pitted her slender frame against the giant of death and fought for her life.

Chapter Fifty

At 5 A.M. Les shifted in his seat. "Need to find a men's room," he explained to Katherine. She nodded, "I'll go after you do."

Five minutes later he washed his hands and left the bathroom, heading back to the room. He arched his back as he walked, trying to stretch out the kinks of a day in the air and a night in the ICU. Turning the corner of the hallway, right outside the waiting room, he almost ran over Clara Wilson.

"Lester, Lester," she said, as she opened her round black arms to greet him. "I've been waiting for you to get here."

For several seconds they embraced each other, patting and holding and relishing the warmth of friendship. Finally, Les whispered, "Well, I'm here, Clara. But I feel so helpless. Ever since I—"

The doors to the intensive care unit burst open and John sprinted past them. Seeing Les, he slid to a stop and yelled, "Dad, get in here. Sherry has her eyes open!"

Leaving Clara behind, Les rushed through the doors behind John and into the room. He hurried over to the bed where Katherine leaned over Sherry.

Sherry's eyes were open—wide open like half-dollars—open and staring at the ceiling. No, Les decided, she wasn't staring at the ceiling, she was staring past the ceiling, at something none of them could see. She wasn't moving, but her blue eyes gleamed with a spark he had seen in only one other person's eyes in his whole life. Like the spark in Nelson Reed's eyes as he baptized him in the Jordan River.

Circling Sherry's bed, John and Katherine squeezed her hands while Les stroked her forehead. "Sherry," he whispered, "we're all here, Mama and John and Daddy. We're all here around you. We love you, Sherry, we'll always love you. Remember what Daddy always told you—nothing you could do could ever make Daddy stop loving you. That's true, baby, we all love you and—"

"T-h-e w-a-t-e-r." Sherry whispered the words, and Les wasn't sure he understood.

He bent lower to her. "We're here, baby, we're here. What did you say?"

"T-h-e w-a-t-e-r," she repeated, barely loud enough to make out.

"Yes, baby, the water, but it's okay that you were in the water. Daddy said you could be in the water. You didn't do anything wrong, sweetheart. You did what Daddy said you could do."

Sherry moved her head as if trying to shake it "no."

"The w-a-t-e-r," she whispered again. "In . . . the water."

"Yes, baby, Daddy gets in the water with you. We do it all the time and I can't wait to get in the water with you again when you're better and back home. We'll—"

Sherry did shake her head "no" this time. "In . . . w-a-. . . She didn't finish the words.

Les turned to Katherine, confused. "What does she mean Katherine, 'in the water'?"

Katherine shrugged, "I don't know, Les, I really don't. She's talking—"

Without warning, Sherry arched her back. In surprised terror, Les and Katherine and John watched as she raised her arms from the side of the bed, raised them up, up into the air, reaching for something above her head. Her eyes widened even further. Blue frisbees were spinning through the air, spinning higher and higher, up and up and up.

In the blink of a second, her face changed color. As if radiating heat from a source foreign to them all, her cheeks shifted from ash white to sunlight gold.

Then, in the heartbeat of another second, her blue eyes relaxed and shrunk back to normal size. And she smiled. As simply and as innocently as always, she smiled. The glow from her smile burned the shadows from the corners of the bleak room. Then her eyelids dropped and closed and the glow dimmed and disappeared and Sherry died. But the smile still played on her tiny cheeks.

Staring at her from above, Les wondered at the joy the smile wrote across her face. For no reason he could imagine, Les smiled too.

Chapter Fifty-one

No smile crossed his face three days later, the day they buried her, the day they followed her casket from the back of a black hearse to a six-foot hole carved out of the soggy ground. Walking behind the casket, Les hugged Katherine to his side. John followed right behind them.

They buried Sherry in a white wedding gown — the gown Les brought from his trunk in the attic. They buried her in the wedding gown with Elmer clutched to her chest and the smile still playing on her cherubic face. They buried her under a dripping gray rain that forced them to carry umbrellas, a rain that teased them with a mix of ice. The grainy liquid of ice and rain ran over the frozen earth and made frost puddles under their feet.

Scores of people had gathered at the funeral home to mourn her. All her friends came — her preschool buddies who rode with her most mornings on their cucumber green bus; her "Y" pals who swam with her during her weekly lesson; her neighborhood playmates who enjoyed her swing set in her backyard.

Clara Wilson came — her black face turned blacker with grief. Ned List came too and Les' surgical staff. Walter and Beatrice, of course, and countless others, good friends and casual acquaintances — all of them gathered to whisper their condolences. "How tragic . . . So sad . . . We love you all. . . .

She was such a sweet girl ... It's better she didn't survive if she couldn't get better ... She's gone to be with God now ... It's God's will ... We're here for you ... If there's anything we can do to help. ... "

Les listened to them all as they spouted their particular philosophies through tired clichés, but none of it made any sense to him; and, of course, no one could help the stabbing ache that sliced through him. No matter where he went—the hospital, the funeral home, the mall, a restaurant to eat—the ache cut through him.

At home, the ache throbbed most intensely. With its cursed pool, the house vibrated with Sherry's presence. In the days after her death, Les walked in and out of her room countless times, in and out, in and out, somehow hoping he would see her with Elmer. But he knew he wouldn't and his knowledge drove him to fury. He wanted to burn the place down, to raze it to cinders and ashes, to consign it to the hell he now endured. But he didn't do that. Even that wouldn't purge him. No, burning down the house wouldn't consume the rage building in him. Nothing could.

At first he didn't recognize the rage. But today, walking behind the casket, he acknowledged it—a nuclear rage radiating through his pores. Anger was too weak a term for it. He was furious, furious to the point of insanity, furious at Katherine for not watching Sherry better, furious at the U.S. government for sending him to the Middle East and letting this happen, furious at a God he didn't accept for allowing blue-eyed girls to burst their lungs with water. But mostly he was furious at himself and for all the obvious reasons.

His fury hidden for the moment, Les held Katherine and John by the hand as they waited beside the hole in the ground that would mark the burial place for his baby girl. The Reverend Dr. Tebbs spread his feet as if to establish a balance for his slight body against the flapping wind.

Watching the Reverend Tebbs, Les shook his head. Faith seemed so flimsy here beside the grave of a child. What sense did it make to speak of a God of love, when tragedy cut such a huge swath through the life of the innocent?

Tebbs began to speak, reading from the Bible. His voice rang out surprisingly robust for a man his age. "The Lord is my shepherd . . ."

Les had to admit he liked what he knew of Reverend Tebbs. He appreciated the man's visits at the hospital and at their home after Sherry's death. To please Katherine, Les had even agreed to meet with Tebbs sometime after the funeral. He wondered how Tebbs would explain Sherry's death. As if anyone could. Sighing, he turned his thoughts back to the funeral.

Tebbs finished the psalm, closed the Bible, and said, "We come now to the final human resting place for Sherry Louise Tennet. As we do so, some of you here will find yourself facing a temptation—the temptation to blame yourself or someone else for this tragic event. I want to ask you this one question—is that what your Sherry would have wanted? I think not.

"From talking with you in the last three days, I think I have come to know Sherry a little. I know she had limitations, but she also had wisdom, the wisdom of the innocent child. And today, in her childish wisdom, she would tell us this—'Do not compound the pain of my untimely death with the pain of an accusing life.'

"No, Sherry would want you to do what she did so well. She would want you to embrace life, to embrace each other, and to embrace God. She did all three. Can't we all become as a little child today and follow her example?"

Tebbs paused now and opened his Bible again. "Hear these words from Paul's letter to the church of Corinth, 'Behold, I tell you a mystery. We shall not all sleep, but we shall all be changed. In an instant, in the twinkling of an eye, at the last trumpet. For the trumpet will sound, the dead will be raised imperishable and we will be changed. For the perishable must put on immortality and the mortal must put on immortality.'

"I leave us now with this thought. Today, Sherry returns to

the dust from which she was physically birthed. But, I would remind you, she also returns to the God from whom she was spiritually created. The God who created her in this life can certainly create her in a new life, in which she has none of her former limitations. A life where her body is strong, her mind is sharp, and her spirit is forever. A life with Jesus. Comfort one another with these words. Amen."

Tebbs closed his Bible, bent his knees to the ground, and lifted a clod of muddy earth from the mound stacked by the casket. He nodded and Les and Katherine and John knelt with him, taking a handful of the soggy clay themselves. They rose as one and stepped to the brown coffin. Tebbs dropped the dirt onto the lid and turned to Les.

Following Tebbs' lead, Les and Katherine and John opened their fingers and let the soil fall onto the box. Hearing it clump, they stopped moving. A drip of melted ice fell from the top of the canopy, dropped onto Les' head, and slid down onto his forehead. He still didn't move. Katherine nudged him. He turned toward Reverend Tebbs who handed him three yellow roses. Les gave one to John, one to Katherine, and kept one for himself. He held it for a second, then laid it on Sherry's coffin. Katherine and John followed his lead. As a bell tolled from a church two blocks away, Les turned to Katherine. She nodded. He understood.

He touched Sherry's coffin one final time, then lifted his umbrella over his head and walked away. With head bowed, he led Katherine and John over the soggy graveyard and back to the black limousine. With the umbrella covering his face, no one saw the mud that smeared on his cheeks when he wiped away his tears.

Chapter Fifty-two

Katherine lifted her head off the pillow and squinted her eyes at the clock—5:30 A.M. She reached over for Les, then realized he wasn't there. For an instant she lay immobile, trying to quiet her pounding head and to remember what had jarred her awake.

TWANG! The sound erupted from downstairs and crawled up the walls into her ankles and then through her body up to her head. TWANG. TWANG. TWANG. What in the world?

She rolled out of the covers and slipped on a robe. TWANG. TWANG. The noise reverberated through the house again.

In the hallway, she almost ran over John. "What's going on, Mom?" he asked, rubbing his eyes.

She shrugged her shoulders. "I have no idea."

Together, they rushed down the stairs, past the den and toward the source of the sound. Flinging open the door, they saw him. Les, clad in gym shorts, was standing in the middle of an empty swimming pool.

As they watched, he raised a shovel over his head. Like a lumberjack attacking the trunk of a redwood, he jerked the shovel downward. TWANG. The shovel bounced off the concrete bottom of the pool. Les jerked the shovel over his head again and repeated the movement. TWANG.

Apparently oblivious to their presence, he slammed the metal against the pool floor over and over and over again. TWANG. TWANG. TWANG.

Sweat dripped down his nose and his hair was wet with it. Time and time again he lifted and slammed, lifted and slammed, lifted and slammed.

As if energized by a hidden switch, his actions accelerated faster and faster and faster, lift, slam, lift, slam. Out of nowhere, he suddenly changed direction. He lifted the shovel again, but instead of slamming it to the bottom of the pool, he dashed to the side where Katherine and John waited and smashed the metal against the side now, smashing it and smashing it until his hands and arms shook from weariness and his chest glistened with perspiration.

He stopped suddenly, his sides heaving, like a tornado expended of its energy. He glanced up at Katherine and John but didn't seem to notice them.

After several long seconds, Katherine spoke. "Les?" He didn't answer. "Les, we're here, John and I. We're here with you."

His shoulders quivered as if cold. "No," he said. "No, you're not here with me. No one is here with me."

Katherine pushed back her own anger. "Yes, we are, Les, we're here with you. We're together, trying to get through this. That's the only way we'll make it out of this—together, with each other and with God."

Les grunted. "Don't say anything to me about God, Kath, no matter what happened to you. I'm not going to accept any God who lets innocent little girls die. Don't talk to me about God. I don't want to hear it."

Katherine decided not to press. "Okay, Les, I won't talk to you about God. Not now. I don't know the answers to the questions you have anyway. But let me tell you this—I know that God can help us through this."

"How do you know that?" asked Les, his mouth twisted in derision.

"Because God is helping me through it."

Les dropped his eyes to his hands. The right one, the one injured in Jerusalem, bled through its bandage. "I'm glad God is helping you, Kath, but I don't need that kind of help."

As if finished with a task, he picked up the shovel, tossed it over the side of the pool, and then followed it himself. Without another word, he picked up the weapon, hoisted it over his shoulder, and headed toward the garage.

Katherine and John stood and watched him go. Nothing they could do. Behind them, the pool seemed to smile. It was empty but anyone could fill it back up easily enough.

Chapter Fifty-three

After patting John's shoulder one final time, Les leaned back and took his seat behind the defendant's table. With a deep breath, he grabbed Katherine's hand and squeezed it. Thirty feet in front of them, Clemons sucked in his stomach and perched himself on the witness stand. A few feet in front of Clemons, the St. Louis County prosecutor, the man who looked like a sixteen-penny nail, leaned over on his desk and questioned the lieutenant.

Already aware of the facts, Les tuned out the rehash the prosecutor repeated with Clemons. Instead of listening, he studied the back of John's neck. The days since the funeral hadn't been easy.

He had spent a couple of afternoons with Ned List discussing the impending malpractice suit. "Still in the initial stages," Ned told him, "but it looks as if Snowball's wife plans to press ahead with it. She's filed it with the courts and her brother-in-law wants $1.5 million to make it go away. Your surgical staff supports you, and neither the hospital board nor your insurance company wants to settle at this point. We want to see how it develops. They might come down on their demands. If not, we'll give a trial a shot. We think we've got a good chance to beat it."

Though Ned didn't seem too confident as he said this, Les

didn't have energy to worry about it. Right now, the suit seemed relatively insignificant compared to the degeneration of his family. He and John had talked a little, but it was mostly about nothing—John's basketball, Les' time in Saudi, the lingering cold that gripped the area.

Yeah, they'd talked some about the facts of the trial, but nothing about the circumstances that brought John to it. John kept assuring him that he had nothing to do with the shooting, that Clemons simply needed a suspect, and he was the logical candidate, and Les believed him. But that didn't change the distance between them.

Les felt as if he and John were tap-dancing with each other, each afraid they would say something to offend. Out of their desire to be connected, they stayed superficial and so lost their opportunity to communicate. They said almost nothing about Sherry and absolutely nothing about their relationship.

It was the same story with Katherine. A word or two about the funeral, but nothing about their mutual grief. A scrap of conversation about Reverend Tebbs, but nothing about the God Katherine now trusted.

Les rubbed his tongue across his front top teeth. He accepted the blame. His anger, so visible the day after the funeral, scared them off. He knew it and regretted it, but he could do nothing about it. And day after tomorrow he left to return to Saudi. Well, at least he was here for John's preliminary hearing. . . . The nasal voice of the prosecutor pulled Les back to the courtroom. "So Mr. Stone told you he found the murder weapon in John Tennet's locker?" he asked, summing up the facts one last time for Judge Bayslip.

"Yes," said Clemons.

"And Tina Spicer confirmed the dislike that John Tennet had for Trevor Mashburn?"

"Yes."

"And she also confirmed that right after an argument between herself and John Tennet, he left her?"

"Yes."

"And then Trevor Mashburn walked out from the game and offered her a ride home?"

"Yes."

"And then, a few moments later, a car almost ran over them?"

"Yes, sir."

"And someone in that car shot Trevor Mashburn as it went by?"

"Yes."

"And a classmate confirmed that John Tennet had the gun the day prior to the shooting?"

"Yes."

"And when you went to question John Tennet about the gun, he had fled his home?"

"Yes."

The prosecutor faced Bayslip. "No further questions, your honor," he said, hooking his hands in the lapels of his jacket and retreating to his chair.

Les turned his attention to Walter Tillman. Good old Walter. Not practicing criminal law anymore, but still a bright, capable man. Les felt confident with Walter at this stage of the game. If it went to a jury trial, he might call in another attorney, but for now, Walter would do.

Dropping his notepad onto the table, Walter pushed his gnarled fingers through his hair. He faced Clemons.

Clemons smirked at him.

"Lieutenant Clemons, when you received the gun from Mr. Stone, did you have it checked for fingerprints?"

"Sure we did. That's routine."

"And were John Tennet's fingerprints found on it?"

"No, they weren't, but I suspect he knew enough to clean—"

Walter threw up his hand and signaled Clemons to stop his answer. He turned to the judge. "Your honor, would you instruct the witness to answer the question with a simple yes or no and spare us his speculative comment?"

Bayslip nodded and glared at Clemons. "Lieutenant, you

know this process. Don't make it more difficult than it is. Just answer the questions. No editorializing."

Obviously pleased, Walter shifted his attention back to Clemons.

"So, John Tennet's fingerprints were not on the murder weapon?"

Clemons scowled. "No, they weren't."

"Thank you. Now, you say a car almost ran over Tina Spicer right before the shot was fired. Is that right?"

"Sure, and you can ask her yourself."

"I plan to, in a few minutes," said Walter, turning to Tina and smiling at her. "But for now, I'm asking you. A *car* flashed by, then a shot. Right?"

"Absolutely."

"Good. Now, lieutenant, were you aware that John Tennet drives a Jeep Cherokee, and not a car at all?"

"Well, I, uh," Clemons stammered for a beat but quickly found his composure. "Yes, I know that, but with the glare of the headlights on her, I expect a car or a jeep looked pretty much the same. Wouldn't you?"

"Well, we'll see, we'll see," said Walter, a slight smirk on his face now as he turned to Les and winked at him.

The old guy's not too bad, thought Les. Walter continued.

"One more question, lieutenant. Do you have any eyewitness who actually *saw* this murderer, you know, face to face?"

"No," grunted Clemons.

"And no one picked John Tennet out of a lineup?"

"No," Clemons said, visibly angry now.

Walter turned to Judge Bayslip. "No further questions, your honor."

Clemons stepped down and Walter eased back into his chair. The prosecutor called his next witness. Tina Spicer. After her, Bill Stone. Then classmates who verified the bad blood between John and Trevor. He called them all, building through their testimony the two necessities for a conviction—motive and opportunity.

Following him, Walter cross-examined them all, counter-punching here and there, tweaking their answers, testing their conclusions. But, as Les knew, this wasn't the time to put on a full-court defense. The preliminary served but one purpose—to give the judge the opportunity to evaluate the prosecution's evidence, to see if enough existed to hold a full trial. Walter had told him to expect a trial. Judges almost never threw cases out based on a preliminary.

The whole thing took less than three hours. The prosecutor finished questioning his last witness, made a short summation to Bayslip, and dropped into his seat. Walter waived the presentation of evidence and faced Bayslip. "Judge, I want to say one thing before you make your determination. Without an eyewitness, all we have is circumstantial evidence. And, in almost any murder case, the lack of an eyewitness can lead the average juror to a reasonable doubt. Your honor, I suggest you not find probable cause and save the taxpayers their money until the real murderer is found. Then our able prosecutor can try a legitimate suspect. Mr. John Tennet certainly isn't a legitimate suspect. Thank you."

Walter slipped his fingers through his hair and snuggled into his seat beside John. Les leaned forward and patted him on the back. "Good job, Walter."

"Not good enough, I bet," Walter murmured under his breath.

Bayslip dropped his glasses off his nose. They hung suspended on a rope around his neck as he flipped through his file for several beats. He glanced up at the group below his bench and announced his decision.

"Though the lack of an eyewitness to the shooting disturbs me, these facts remain—a teenage boy is dead, murdered brutally. Mr. John Tennet had the murder weapon; witnesses place it in his hand the day prior to the shooting; he fled the authorities when they came to pick him up for questioning—an inference of guilt; and he and the deceased were known to have ill will between them; he had made threats against his person. I don't see any choice but to find probable cause and set this case for a jury trial. Trial date is set for May 15. Defendant's bond continues from his arraignment."

Bayslip rapped his gavel. "Next case."

As if on signal, everyone connected with John's case rose to leave. Les shook Walter's hand. "Look, Walter, I didn't expect it to end here. You did the best you could. I've got confidence you'll handle it when it goes to trial."

Walter nodded. "Thanks, Les, but I think we should get another lawyer. I know a couple of guys I can recommend. I would hate—"

Les interrupted him. "Let's not worry about that right now, Walter. We'll take your advice, whatever you suggest, but you did as much as anyone could have done. Let's think about it for a day or so, then make a decision. Okay?"

Walter nodded. "Thanks for your faith in me."

"It's justified," said Les, trying to convince himself. "You'll know what to do."

Following Katherine and John, Les and Walter walked out of the courthouse and into the sunlight. Three months until trial. And only two short days until he went back to Saudi.

Chapter Fifty-four

After the funeral, Les had fulfilled his promise to Katherine as he drove to St. John's Baptist Church to meet with the Reverend Tebbs. Parking under a cluster of oak trees and climbing out of the car, he admitted a certain curiosity to himself. Between Katherine's newfound faith and the friendship of Nelson Reed, he didn't want to dismiss out of hand the possibility of God. But, given Sherry's death, the only God he could imagine was either too weak or too callous to stop tragedy. In either case, Les couldn't accept such a God. No, the God who allowed or caused his daughter to die didn't deserve reverence. That God deserved rage, and Les had plenty of that.

As he stepped into the outer office of the church, a secretary smiled at him. "May I help you?" she asked.

"I'm here to see Reverend Tebbs," Les said.

"It'll be just a second." She smiled again, picked up the phone and buzzed the pastor.

A couple of seconds later, Reverend Tebbs stepped out of his office and beckoned Les inside. Les followed and took a seat on a sofa under a window.

"A spot of tea?" asked Tebbs.

Les shook his head no.

Tebbs poured a cup and sat down in a wingback chair across from Les. He sipped from the tea cup and then smiled.

"I'm glad you came by," he said. "And I know you don't have much time. They're sending you back to the Persian Gulf, I understand."

Les sighed. "Yes, afraid so. Apparently the ground war will start soon and they can't spare guys like me."

"Seems rather harsh, don't you think?" asked Tebbs.

"Well, it seems like *harsh* is my fate lately," said Les, staring down at his hands.

Tebbs set his cup in the saucer. "Yes, I suppose it does."

For several seconds, neither man spoke. Les squeezed his hands together. Then he said, "I appreciated your words at the funeral, Dr. Tebbs, but you need to know I don't really accept them."

Tebbs nodded and steepled his fingers in front of his face. "I can see why you wouldn't," he said. "When death hits us we all wonder about God. Does He exist? Does He love us? Why doesn't He stop the pain? The suffering? The death? None of it makes sense from behind our tears."

"It's not just Sherry's death," said Les. "I didn't believe even before this."

Tebbs picked up his cup, stood, and stepped to the window. He looked outside. "Had you ever considered God before this?" he asked.

Les tilted his head, considering the question. "Not really, no. Sure, like most people, I thought about God from time to time. As a boy primarily. Attended church with friends as a teenager. Made fun of a few television preachers. But I never gave God much serious thought."

Tebbs turned back and sat down again. "But you're considering God now?"

Les almost smiled. "Well, in a way, yes, I am."

"Why is that?"

Les sighed. He didn't know how much he wanted to tell this man. Didn't know if he should trust him. But, he thought sadly, tomorrow he flew back to Saudi. And his daughter was dead. And his marriage was about to end. And his son faced a

murder trial. And a malpractice suit hung over his head. And
his rage threatened to consume him. He realized if he had any
chance at all, he had to trust someone. He said, "I don't know,
Reverend Tebbs. Several reasons really. I'm headed toward forty, middle age and all that. Plus, for the first time in my adult
life, I seem to have lost control of things. I'm facing problems
at the hospital, think I might have screwed up an operation.
Plus, as Katherine might have told you, we're struggling as a
family. John's problems, heaped on top of mine and Katherine's, and we're a divorce looking for a time to happen. And
Sherry, well, you know about her. . . ." Les' voice trailed off.
Tebbs leaned in nearer to him.

"Tell me about Sherry, Les. You had a close relationship
with her, didn't you?"

Les nodded. "Yeah, we connected somehow. We gave each
other something the other needed. We communicated in ways
I don't understand. She—" He stopped in mid-sentence and
his eyes widened.

"What is it?" whispered Tebbs.

Les furrowed his brow. "I don't know, Dr. Tebbs, but
something just hit me. The day Sherry drowned something
happened that I don't understand."

"Tell me about it."

"You'll think I'm crazy."

"Let me be the judge of that."

Les nodded. "Well, the day Sherry drowned, a friend of
mine, Nelson Reed, a chaplain in Saudi . . ."

Les related the story to him, the story of going to the
Jordan River, the story of his baptism, the story of the light in
Reed's eyes, the story of finding out about Sherry's drowning.
"She must have been in the pool the same time I was in the
water in the Jordan," he said, his voice rising. "In fact, she
must have been drowning the same minute I was being baptized. Then at the hospital, she tried to tell me something
about being in the water, as if she knew something about
water I didn't know."

For a second, he stopped. Then he said. "Does that make any sense, Dr. Tebbs? Could she somehow have known what I was doing? Did she see or feel something beyond our comprehension?"

Tebbs lifted his tea cup and touched it to his lips. After taking a sip, he answered. "I understand she had her stuffed rabbit in her arms when Katherine found her."

"Yes."

"And her last words at the hospital were 'in the water'?"

"Yes."

"Well, I don't know, I suppose the simple explanation is that she was talking about her favorite toy. You know, Elmer's 'in the water.' Maybe she remembered going into the water to save him. Is that possible?"

Les thought a moment. "Yes, that's possible. But I don't know. In the hospital . . . her face reflected something else, something peaceful, a glow in her eyes, as if she saw beyond the room, as if she saw . . ." His voice trailed off and he stopped talking and stared down at his hands.

"It's ironic, isn't it?" asked Tebbs, a tiny smile playing at his lips.

"What's that?" asked Les, glancing up.

"Well, you're searching for something mystical, spiritual, otherworldly in Sherry's last words, and I am offering you the rational possibility. I thought it was supposed to be the other way around."

Les grunted. "Kind of amazing, isn't it?"

For several moments, the men fell silent. Then Les said, "Is it possible, Dr. Tebbs?"

"What's that, Les?"

"Is it possible something miraculous happened in the water that day? When I was baptized? As Sherry drowned? Did we connect somehow? Chaplain Reed says that's where it all started, the public ministry of Jesus, all of it began with His baptism in the Jordan."

"Would it make a difference if you did connect, Les? If

Sherry did know?" asked Tebbs.

Les considered the question. "I don't know," he answered. "Could the water be the point? Could the water change things?"

Tebbs sighed and eased back in his chair. "You're asking a highly theological question, Les. My particular brand of faith doesn't believe the water itself does anything miraculous. It's simply water, warm or cold, polluted or clean. It's water and that's all. We see the water as a sign; the church uses the word *symbol.* We see it as that, nothing more, and I might add, nothing less. It doesn't make us better in and of itself. It doesn't redeem us, to use church language. But, it is significant precisely as you have said. At the baptism of Jesus, His divine work started. So, our denomination, and many others, offers baptism to believers as they begin their life of faith. It demonstrates a desire to follow the Lord."

"So you don't think anything miraculous happened there?"

"I didn't say that. I said I don't believe the water itself caused anything to happen. No, I would say it this way. Maybe something happened in you. Maybe something happened in Sherry. But if so, God caused it, not the water. What God does, we can never fully fathom. God works in mystery, in ways we don't understand. That's why Christianity requires faith. If we had it all spelled out for us in plain English, we wouldn't need faith. Does that make sense?"

Les sighed. "It does if you believe in God."

Tebbs nodded. "Aye, we do seem to keep coming back to that, don't we?"

"Yes, we do."

"And you're now asking yourself if you believe or not?"

Les patted his knees and leaned up in his seat. "Well, I think I am. But, with Sherry's death . . . well, right now I don't know if I am or not. Maybe I should say, I don't know if I *can* or not. But, I do know that my life can't go on like it is now. Something has to change."

"If it's not faith you're considering, then can you tell me what it is?"

Les shook his head. "I'm afraid that will have to wait until another day." He stood up. Tebbs followed his example and extended his hand.

"I hope that day will come soon," he said.

"We'll see," said Les. "Thank you."

Tebbs nodded and Les walked out.

Through the rest of the day, the anger churning in his chest abated a little. He felt calmer, more at ease. Maybe the talk with Tebbs had helped some.

But that night he dreamed about Sherry. He dreamed about her drowning and he saw her glazed eyes and those eyes seemed to accuse him. Facing the accusation caused the anger to well up again, and by the time he climbed aboard a jet the next morning, popped a sleeping pill down his throat, and leaned back in his seat for the flight back to the Middle East, the anger held him in its grip again and refused to let go.

Section Five

The care of God for us is a great thing.
If a man believe it at heart,
it plucks the burden of sorrow from him.

Euripides

Chapter Fifty-five

The hospital in King Khalid hadn't changed since he left, but he knew he had. Sherry's death had changed him irreparably. His anger, boiling and bubbling like lava far below the ground, now inched its way closer and closer to the surface. He found himself battling to keep the hot rage banked up. If it escaped, he knew it would destroy him.

He sensed he was losing the battle. At any moment he felt something would trigger the eruption and he would splatter out of control.

Les bumped into the Gang one at a time the day he returned to Saudi. Roger Tills as he dumped his gear on the bed in his room. Nelson Reed in the hallway as he made his rounds at the hospital. Macy Spencer as he finished his lunch.

There was no opportunity to talk, and Les felt grateful for that. Yet, he knew he needed to talk with all of them. With Roger to thank him for his friendship and support. With Reed concerning his questions about God. With Macy about the kiss they had shared the day she told him about Sherry.

But he didn't know how to say any of it. How would he begin? Maybe—"Look, my angel of a daughter did what I told her she could do and took a swim by herself, but she swam too far into the middle and she drowned. So, she's dead. Case closed."

No, he had nothing to say to them, and so he was thankful for the silence. It muffled the fury bubbling up higher and higher inside.

The day passed in slow motion, one dutiful action after another, one foot in front of another, one hour behind another, one day down and no one knew how many to go.

Somehow, he finished the day. He slipped out of his white coat, laid down his hospital charts, and left the doctor's lounge. Within fifteen minutes, he reached his room. Neither Nelson nor Roger was there. Good.

Les leaned against the wall beside his cot and began to sort out his gear, putting everything back in place. Toiletries in the bathroom. Clothes arranged neatly in a stack under the bed. A stack of mail he'd picked up that morning. The mail that had arrived in King Khalid after he flew out from Jerusalem back to St. Louis.

Les plopped onto the bed to sort through the mail. A letter from Ned List — the charges of malpractice were pending, waiting on him to return to the U.S. Old news.

A note from Clara Wilson. "Miss you, Les, hope you're okay. I'm keeping an eye on John and Katherine and Sherry for you."

Several magazines, outdated now. A pre-approved credit card. A brown manila folder. His return address. Katherine's handwriting. A package from home. Postmarked the day before Katherine found Sherry in the pool.

Les ripped open the paper. A letter inside. And a videotape. He read the letter.

Dear Dad,

(This first part is from me, John). It's 6:30 P.M. here and we've been watching the news reports about the war. We're glad you're not in immediate danger, even though we know you're not completely safe, what with Scuds and chemicals and all. But so far it looks like the Iraqis don't have much chance against the forces we've put together against them.

I'm doing great in basketball, averaging 26 points and 8 assists per game. And my grades are good. I'm trying to help Mom around the house. My preliminary trial is coming soon and, to be honest, I'm nervous about it. And mad too. It just seems like this Clemons guy has it in for me. I don't know why. But Dad, I want you to know this—I wasn't involved in that shooting. I wasn't. You have to believe me. Anyway, I hope you get home soon.

DAD, Mom is helping me write this. I love you. And miss you. Hope you come home soon. Love, Sherry.

Les, Katherine now. The kids are doing all right. We've enclosed a videotape for you to see when you get a chance. I'm doing fine too. In fact, better than I can ever remember. I know you probably don't want to hear this, but what happened to me in the church several weeks ago was real. Somehow, God touched my life and made me a new person. Not a perfect person (not even close to it) but a different person. I'm calmer now, more able to understand things and people too. I feel stable for the first time in my life, like I'm standing on a rock that nothing can shake. I don't feel so confused, so indecisive, so . . . I don't know . . . maybe *insecure* is the word, as I once did.

I know we've had our problems in the past and I don't know if my new faith can change any of that. But I want you to know I'm willing to try. I hope you are too. Please know that I pray for you daily. And I've asked the members of the church I've been attending to do so too. I hope that's okay. Remember, we all love you and look forward to the end of the war. Hope you enjoy the video. Love, Kath.

His hands shaking, Les laid aside the letter and picked up the video. He rubbed his fingers over it, laid it on the bed, stared at it for several minutes, and picked it up again. He clutched it to his chest, then held it up to the light and stared at it. He wanted to see it, but it scared him. He shoved the video under his arm and rubbed his palms together. Sweat broke out between his eyes and rolled down his nose.

Like a man walking to the electric chair, he trudged downstairs to the lecture room and flicked on the television sitting in the corner. He inserted the videotape, punched on the TV screen, switched it to channel 3, and punched play on the tape player. The images from the video flickered, then stabilized.

Katherine, John, and Sherry were waving at him. "Hi, Dad, Hey, Les, Hello, Daddy." They were dressed in warmly knit sweaters—John's navy, Katherine's kelly green and Sherry's pink.

"Grandmom is taking the pictures, Dad," said John.

"Hi, Les, this is Beatrice. It's Sunday afternoon. Hope you're doing well."

"Dad, we're undefeated right now," John again. "No doubt we'll make the playoffs, I think we'll win the state championship." John lifted his right hand into the air as he talked about his team and their season and his exploits with them. He jumped slightly off his feet, as if shooting a basketball. "Don't guess you're getting to shoot much hoop over there, are you?"

"Les, we're all well," said Katherine, her face replacing John's in the frame of the camera. "I'm keeping an eye on the budget these days. So far, we're making it fine. Don't want you to worry about that. Everybody is healthy too. I saw Clara the other day. She sends her love."

Katherine filled him in on home details, gave him news about St. Louis, told him the date of John's preliminary hearing.

"We're okay about the hearing..." It was Walter's voice now, first from behind the camera and then as he stepped in front of it. "I don't think we can get the charges dismissed before trial, Les, but all they've got is circumstantial evidence. I think I can convince a jury of reasonable doubt." Walter disappeared beyond the edge of the camera again and then

Sherry's light voice filtered through the screen.

"Mom, I want to talk too. It's my turn to talk to Daddy."

"All right, Sherry, go ahead."

John stuck his face nearer the camera, hamming it up.

"Move, John, my turn to talk," insisted Sherry. Les watched as she grabbed John by the back of the pants and pulled him away. John pretended to fight her but then he let her win, and she stood alone in the picture and looked at Les.

"Hey, Daddy, I miss you and love you. I go swimmin' every day, like we used to, but I miss you not bein' with me, but Elmer is and he watches me swim. When you coming home? We all want you home. I hope you're safe in the war, Daddy. Don't want anything to happen to you in the war 'cause who would swim with me then? So come home soon, but until you do remember who loves you and who will love you forever and no matter what you do will love you forever, that's me and Mom and John. See you soon, I hope."

Sherry waved her hands at him and smiled hugely and then Katherine's face filled up the screen again, but Les barely noticed because his eyes had frosted over and he was staring past what the camera saw, past the room in which he sat. He was staring into the eyes of his rage. His rage stared back at him and grinned a savage grin. The yellowed teeth of his rage were bared and the fetid breath of mockery poured through the bared teeth. Les smelled the foul aroma and decided then and there that he would kill his rage. One way or the other, he would kill his rage.

Chapter Fifty-six

Right after breakfast the next morning it dawned on him. He knew how to kill his rage. But not yet. Not until he was sure it would work. Until he knew he could get away with it.

He took a deep breath as he headed down the hallway to begin his daily rounds at the hospital. With a plan in mind, he felt relieved. If he did this right, no one would ever know. No one but him and Rage. And that was enough.

Focused on his thoughts, Les almost ran over Colonel Harper as he turned the corner two doors up from the doctors' lounge.

"Hey, Les," said Harper, reaching out his hand to shake. "I was coming down to talk to you. Look man, we, uh, we've all been thinking about you. So sorry about your little girl. A tragedy, a real tragedy. I didn't know if they would send you back here or not. Guess we really need doctors, huh?"

Les shrugged. "Seems so."

"Anything we can do to help?"

Les shook his head.

"Well, let me know if there is," Harper said. "I can't imagine what you're going through." Harper stopped as if waiting for Les to describe it to him; but when Les said nothing, Harper continued. "Well, anyway, here's what I wanted to talk to you about. I'm sending you down to Dhahran for a couple of days, to do some lecturing relating to battlefield trauma. Word is the ground war is about to shove off and the high brass want to pull all the best teachers together for some last-minute review. It shouldn't last too long, and I thought a change of scene might do you some good. Get your mind on something other than this boring routine. Besides, you're the best I've got." Harper laughed. "But don't tell Roger I said that."

Les remained quiet. Harper again waited for a response. Les said nothing.

"That okay with you?" Harper asked.

Les nodded.

"Good," said Harper. "Be ready to go in the morning. You'll go by C-5 transport at 0800."

Harper pivoted to leave, then swirled back around. "Les, I really am sorry about your girl." Les nodded and shuffled on down the hallway. It didn't matter to him where he was when he did it. One place was as good as another.

Chapter Fifty-seven

Les spent the three days before the beginning of the liberation of Kuwait lecturing a group of medical personnel gathered in Dhahran from scores of duty points in Saudi. He gave his lectures woodenly, sharing information like a computer spewing out charts and graphs. Except for his lectures, he talked little, glad he didn't know anyone in the group. Each day and night, he stayed on guard for the right moment, for the killing time, the time to cut the head off his Rage.

So far it hadn't come. Part of the problem was his housing. He didn't have as much privacy as he did in King Khalid. He was quartered in a four-story housing compound, three miles outside the city—a barracks sheltering hundreds of soldiers from a number of reserve and guard units. He shared his room with four other doctors and so far, he hadn't found enough time alone to carry out his plan. So, he waited, waited for the war to start and for his chance to come.

At 4 P.M. on February 22, he finished his last lecture and folded up his briefcase. The doctors who had listened to him scattered quickly, many of them leaving that instant to get back to duty stations. An air of expectancy hung over the city. Everyone knew the time had come. The ground war would start soon, within hours, many said. They were right.

At about 4 A.M. Saudi time on February 23, the mother of

all battles began. The curtain on the stage of war lifted. Over 600,000 allied soldiers marched into action. The 1st and 2nd Marine Divisions pushed into Kuwait from the southeast, while the 82nd and 101st Airborne Units struck hard from the far west, directly into Iraq. All across the underbelly of southern Iraq, Armored Divisions of U.S. and Coalition Forces rushed ahead in the desert sand.

Les listened to the reports in the early hours of the morning like everyone else, huddled beside a radio or catching an occasional glimpse on CNN as he ate breakfast in the mess hall.

From the beginning, the Allies punished the Iraqis on every front. Thousands of the enemy waved white flags the minute they saw American troops and surrendered without a fight. Casualties were few. To their surprise, Les and his fellow doctors found themselves practically idle as the war moved from the first day to the second. Though he didn't sleep much, Les spent the night relieved. Given his state of mind, he didn't know if he could perform surgery or not.

On the morning of February 25, he climbed out of bed and headed down to breakfast. Scrunched over a bowl of cereal he hardly noticed when Colonel Harper pulled up a chair beside him.

Harper cleared his throat. Les looked up.

"Morning," said Harper.

"What's up, colonel?" asked Les.

"Tomorrow we go back to King Khalid," said Harper. "They'll need us there when the bloodshed starts."

Les swallowed a bite of bran. "You think we'll get casualties soon?"

"If we don't, it'll be the first war we ever fought without some."

"So far it's not been much," said Les.

"So far we've been unbelievably lucky. I don't expect it to hold. See you at 0600 in the morning." Harper swung his leg over the chair and walked out.

Les finished his breakfast and followed him. Harper's orders told him the time had arrived. He needed to murder Rage before he went back to the Gang. Someone there might talk him out of it, and he couldn't have that. Yes, it was time. He could do it. He *would* do it.

He shuffled through the day, musing to himself. *How? And when? A gun?* He had his Army issue .45 Colt. *No, too messy.* And his insurance might not pay off. Had to be a better way — a way the insurance company wouldn't detect. *Ah, that's it. Subtle.* If he was careful, no one would ever know.

Tonight. The night before going back to King Khalid. *After supper.* Three of the doctors bunked with him had already shipped out to other stations. The fourth one spent most of his spare time in the mess hall watching television. *I can do it tonight.*

Gradually, the sun dropped into the west and darkness ate into the sand. The day ended. Les gathered the materials he would need and carried them to his quarters. Laying them under his bed, he walked downstairs and finished the motions of supper, swallowing tiny bits of food, making it seen normal. He chatted aimlessly with his companions at the table. He dumped his tray and headed back to his room. No note. Had to protect the insurance.

A letter would do better. No one would read it but his family and he would tell them not to reveal what had happened.

He lay down on the bed and wrote Katherine a letter on yellow legal pad, explaining everything to her.

> Don't blame yourself. Not your fault. Nobody's fault but mine. I failed, made the wrong choices at the wrong times. I said the wrong words and broke too many promises. You'll be better off this way. A million in insurance, plus insurance on the house to pay it off. You can start over. With your new faith and John—you can start over. I know it will hurt at first, but remember, it's not your fault. My fault.
>
> Love,
> Les.

He scratched a similar note to John, then added,

And, remember this too, John, I believe you when you say you didn't have any part in the shooting. I'm sorry I didn't get to say that to your face. I failed you too. Just like I did your mom. And Sherry. I failed everybody. But this way I can help. I can get out of the way so I won't foul up your life anymore. Remember, it's not your fault, it's mine. Remember, I love you.
P.S. Take care of your mom.
Love,
Dad.

Finished with John and Katherine, he wrote one final note to Nelson Reed.

Nelson, I hate to ask you to do this, but I know what I say to you will be kept confidential. So you're the one who has to do this. I'm about to discover if you're right about the final hand. But I need your help in making sure the authorities don't find out what happened. Insurance and all, you know. Take the letters you find in this envelope to my wife and son. Then, dispose of the rest of these materials. You'll help my family if you do. And that way, you'll help me.
And Nelson, thanks for trying. You almost persuaded me. Take care.
Les.

He stuffed the letters to John and Katherine into an envelope and sealed it up. He addressed a larger envelope to Nelson, but left it open. Then, with increasing energy, he stuck the letters to John and Katherine into the big one and laid it, still open, on the bed.

Relieved, he wiped his palms together and squatted. Carefully, he pulled his briefcase from under the bed and laid it on the cot beside the envelope. With steady hands, he opened the briefcase and lifted the 22-gauge spinal needle out of it. Laying down the needle, he took out a vial of potassium chloride. Nodding his head, glad to get near the finish, he picked up the needle, pushed it into the top of the vial, and drew out the liquid. The needle filled up. He placed the empty vial into the envelope addressed to Nelson.

As if in slow motion, Les lifted the needle into the air and stared at it. It perched in the air, a pointed dagger to the sky, the answer to Rage, his revenge against it, the sweet finish to his pain.

An injection of potassium chloride would do it. It would create a heart attack. Les almost grinned. So appropriate. A heart attack like his mom had. Like so many he'd seen. Like so many he'd saved. Heart attacks had always fascinated him. Now, he would find out what happened when the heartbeat fled. Where it went. What room it entered. The potassium would stop his heart.

If he did it right, he would have just enough time from the moment he punctured his skin until he passed out to shove the needle into the envelope to Nelson, seal it, and drop it back into his briefcase. When the authorities went through his effects, they would send this to the chaplain. They had to— confidentiality and all. Then Nelson would take care of the rest.

Pleased with his plan, Les turned the needle toward his body, but not toward one of his wrists or his forearms. No, this injection wouldn't go there. The doctors would find a puncture wound there.

Les pointed the needle at his chest—at his heart to be exact. Under the fourth rib on his left side. He almost laughed again as he unbuttoned two buttons on his shirt. With the thick thatch of hair that matted his chest, no one would see the sliver of a hole the needle would make. His plan was foolproof.

He sucked in a mouthful of air. Let it out slowly. Another

breath. Out slowly. A third one. In. O-u-t. In. O-u-t. Calm
now. Eyes closed. Floating. Spinning out of Dhahran. Back
home. With Katherine. In their good times. Wedding day. At
the beach in the Bahamas. The early years. High hopes. A
whole life ahead of them. Joy.

John's birth. John so much like him. Tall and dark and
graceful. John the boy who had it all. Then, later, John the
troubled boy.

No, don't think of the troubles. Think of Sherry. Gentle
Sherry. Loving, loyal, wonderful Sherry. Sherry in the water
with him. Sherry hugging him. Sherry loving him no matter
what.

Les breathed slower. I-n and o-u-t. Sherry and Katherine
and John. The images flowed through him and over him and
he pushed back his shirt with his left hand and pointed the
needle toward his heart with the right and the thin point of the
needle pressed into his skin and pricked it and a drop of blood
the size of a black-eyed pea popped out on his chest and the
needle bit deeper.

Chapter Fifty-eight

The words from the page blinked up at her and Katherine, poring over them, pushed her bangs out of her eyes. She cuddled herself with her arms across her chest, basking in the warmth of the sun driving through the glass of the window. Though she sat in the same position as she had months ago, Katherine didn't have her crystal in front of her, and she wasn't channeling. Not in the way most people meant it, anyway.

She studied the words, trying to understand them. She'd followed this routine every day since her encounter with Jesus, reading the Bible, trying to fathom its meaning. It wasn't always easy.

Unlike her past turns of interest, this one hadn't abated. Instead, it had intensified, and the mysteries of the ancient words in the Bible hadn't deterred her focus. Not yet anyway, and she remained certain that wouldn't change.

She closed her eyes and peered into the blackness of her eyelids. She prayed, asking for strength. Strength so she could deal with the black grief caused by the wrenching death of Sherry. She still blamed herself. Only natural. Anyone would.

She prayed for John. His trial coming so soon. At least he was home. "Give him courage to face his daily struggles, O Lord," she asked.

And Les, what about him? How to pray for him? "Relieve his guilt, dear God. Take away his anger. Yes, his anger, Lord. That's what scares me so. His anger. Like he wants to kill someone. Like he wants to destroy—"

With a jerk, Katherine opened her eyes and stared past the window into the bare arms of the trees in her backyard. She saw it as clearly as she saw the sunshine cutting through the sky. She knew who Les wanted to destroy! Though the sun beat down on her face and shoulders, she shivered. Her stomach flip-flopped under her ribs and her skin stood up in even-rowed bumps the size of tack heads. She felt nauseated and sucked the back of the knuckles on her right hand to push down the remains of her breakfast.

He was doing it. Somehow, she sensed it. Les was destroying the anger. Trouble was, that meant he was also destroying himself.

Katherine bowed her head again and tried to pray. But no words formed. Her tongue felt paralyzed. Muted by the terror of what she saw, she doubled over at the waist as if someone had knocked her breath away. She groaned and the groan bounced off the empty walls of the house, and the echo of the groan made God, who a moment ago seemed so close, seem very far away indeed.

Chapter Fifty-nine

In the black sky above the barracks that housed Les Tennet, a Scud missile, randomly fired by the desperate Iraqis, broke apart and fell in big chunks toward the sandy ground. Unfortunately for Les and the other soldiers housed in the barracks, the troops manning the Patriot Scud Killers watched the breakup of the missile and decided no defense was necessary. They were wrong.

The largest piece of the missile tumbled and twisted its way downward through the darkness, carrying death in its pointed nose.

The soldiers in the barracks had almost no warning—a short burst of a siren shrieked through the night for what seemed like an instant—and then the chaos fell. The jagged edge of the wayward Scud hit the top of the barracks and sliced through it into the living quarters below.

Inside the barracks, Les heard the brief blast of the siren, but paid it no attention. He'd heard them over and over during the war and nothing had ever happened. Besides, for all practical purposes, the war with Hussein had ended. Fact is, it had never really begun. For him, it was certainly over. All his wars were over. The war with his guilt. The war with himself.

He pressed the needle a touch deeper into his skin. Though it took only a split second to insert the needle, time seemed to slow down almost to the point of stopping. He marveled at the detachment he felt as the deadly potassium edged closer and closer to his heart. What would it feel like to die? To feel the heart quake and shiver? To hear it thump, thump, thump ... and then thump no more?

The Scud punctured the ceiling. The split second ended and the blast of the explosion above him wrenched Les' attention away from his heart. The roof of the barracks caved in on him and he instinctively threw his arms over his head to protect himself and the needle he'd been guiding to his heart dropped to the floor and rolled away. A ceiling beam crashed across his back and split in two and settled on the floor under tons of plaster and concrete and dust that followed its downward flight.

Buried facedown under the rubble, Les tried to push up but couldn't. His legs seemed glued to the floor and his back had no feeling in it. He twitched his hands—his fingers still worked. He wrinkled his nose. Hot, bitter air slithered through the cracks of the wreckage around him—the first warning of a silent death—the smell of smoke.

With what little strength he still had, Les lifted his arms and pushed out at the sides, trying to move the heavy pile of refuse lying on and around him. Nothing budged. The acrid aroma of black smoke pushed faster into his buried grave. Les pushed at the rubble again and failed to move anything. He put his hands over his nose and mouth, but the smoke slid between the cracks of his fingers and into his nostrils. The smoke wrapped its arms around him and laid its blanket of darkness over his body, and its fingers touched his eyelids and closed them. As he gave up and prepared to die, Les suddenly realized that he very much wanted to live.

Chapter Sixty

Though she tried to shake the nagging fear, Katherine fretted and worried through the rest of the morning and into the afternoon. She tried to call Colonel Harper at King Khalid, but was told he wasn't there. Not due back until the next day. She knew she couldn't reach Les at Dhahran. No phones in his quarters there.

She glanced at her watch. Almost 1. She thought about calling John at school but knew that made no sense. What would she tell him? That she had received a word from God? That his dad would try to kill himself? No, she couldn't do that. John couldn't handle it. Didn't need to handle it. Not until she had something more than her intuition to report.

As the afternoon marched away, she became more and more stressed. Unable to concentrate on anything else, she paced out and back through the house, from the bedroom to the kitchen to the empty pool, out and back, over and over. Finally, frantically, she forced herself to sit down.

With a cup of coffee for comfort, she hunched up in a chair by the television in the breakfast nook and switched it on. The news on CNN didn't surprise her. She almost expected it. The war had gone too smoothly. At some point, tragedy had to strike. It wouldn't be war without death.

The reporter identified the location of the mayhem. Dhahran, Saudi Arabia. Katherine almost dropped her coffee cup. Les was in Dhahran! The reporter gave more specifics. A Scud hit a barracks in El-Khobar—a barracks housing American troops.

Katherine began chewing her fingernails. She wondered where Les was stationed. She stared at the charred wreckage, heard the blaring sirens of the rescue vehicles, watched frantic rescue workers do their duty, listened to the eager journalists describe the scene.

The reporter from CNN filled in the details known so far. "Just after supper, Saudi time, an orange fireball, the warhead end of a Scud missile, plunged into a two-story barracks in El-Khobar, Saudi Arabia, located a couple of miles from Dhahran. The barracks, a converted warehouse, was filled with American soldiers.

"The missile that hit the barracks crumpled the building's girders and buried at least 100 troops inside. Casualties are certain, but how many is unknown at this time. As you can see from this picture of carnage behind me, the rescue effort is continuing."

The reporter paused and Katherine took a deep breath. Then the correspondent continued.

"A convoy of ambulances and helicopters has already carried nearly 200 people, many of them seriously injured, to a nearby hospital. Tragically, though, scores of other soldiers remain buried underneath the rubble you see behind me. These men and women, if they're still alive, await rescue from this, the worst disaster of the Persian Gulf War."

The reporter signed off, but Katherine hardly noticed. She was already dialing a number on the phone.

Chapter Sixty-one

Sometime, in the wee hours of the night, Les woke up. He sniffed the air. Smelled the remains of smoke.

Unable to see anything he checked his body for injuries. The only thing that hurt a lot was his chest. He wondered how much damage the smoke did. Other than that, nothing hurt, not really. But he knew shock could account for that—or a spinal injury that cut off feeling below.

He tried to shift his feet in the wreckage but couldn't. He raised his hands to his face, took a deep breath, and recognized the smell of blood. He touched his fingers to his lips. Tasted the blood on his hands. He was losing a lot of it. He suddenly felt dizzy. What had happened to him? He felt so confused. The blood on his hands . . . the blood was his life and he was losing it. He held his hands before his face as if he could see them in the darkness. And, then, amazingly, he did see hands.

Sherry's little hands were reaching for him . . . reaching for him as Sherry always did when she wanted him to lift her out of the pool. He reached out to grab her. But before he could touch her, the hands changed and belonged to someone else.

These hands had long, thick fingers covered with callouses. Les wrinkled his brow as he stared at these hands. A jagged scar about the size of a walnut surged up in the palms of these new hands. And blood, not water, dripped from them.

They reached for him. Les reached back. The scarred hands dissolved and Sherry's hands reached for him again and then Sherry's white hands and the blood-red hands reached for him.

Hands dripping with water. Hands covered with blood. Water, in the water. That's what Sherry said to him in the hospital. And that's what Nelson told him at the Jordan River. It began in the water. The work of Jesus. The work that Nelson said kept going even today. It began in the water . . . the redeeming work of Jesus.

But it didn't end there. It moved on from the water to the cross. The hands that dripped with water in the Jordan then dripped with blood at Calvary.

It all blended together . . . his baptism and Sherry's drowning. Somehow, the two were connected . . . not because of the water, but because of the One who came out of the water and walked to the cross.

Les wondered. . . . As Sherry drowned, did she somehow see it all? He didn't know. He never would. And what if he didn't? What if some of it remained a mystery? Like Tebbs said it would. Could he believe without understanding it all?

The hands reached for him, the hands of water and blood, the hands of Sherry and of Jesus and then the hands touched him. And as they did, a light pierced the charcoal darkness of the death pit that covered him, and a humid warmth flowed over him and into him and he knew the truth. The truth that he would never understand it all. That mystery would always shroud God. That faith demanded mystery. That faith embraced mystery. That faith depended on the known and the unknown. That his faith depended on knowing Jesus and trusting Jesus and following Jesus.

Les held the hands that held him, and he prayed that God would accept the faith he offered, and that in his dying moments he might find peace. The hands holding his disappeared.

Les dropped his hands to his sides and breathed a deep sigh. Then he blacked out. When the sun raised its head over the rim of the desert four hours later, Les didn't wake up with it.

Chapter Sixty-two

Katherine said goodnight to John about 10 P.M. and tried to reach Colonel Harper. She phoned Reverend Tebbs at 10:35 and asked him to pray for Les. She talked to Walter and Beatrice at 11 and told them of her anxieties. Still wound up, she drank coffee and watched the moon crawl over her kitchen window and disappear behind the trees. She tried to go to bed and sleep but couldn't, so she trudged back to the kitchen. Right after midnight she understood why sleep had eluded her.

A white van pulled up in her driveway and two uniformed soldiers banged their doors against the silence of the night and marched up her concrete walkway. Having heard them drive up, Katherine didn't wait for them to ring the doorbell.

With quaking hands, she opened the door.

The soldiers saluted her.

"Would you like to come in?" she asked, her voice squeaky.

They refused. One of the men, the shortest of the two, took off his hat and spoke quickly. "Ma'am, we're here on official business of the U.S. War Department. We need to report to you that we believe your husband was in the barracks hit by the Scud missile last night."

Katherine blinked her eyes in surprise. At least they weren't telling her Les was dead. She took a deep breath and held to the door. "You believe he was in the barracks?"

"Yes, but we're not certain. He was temporarily quartered there, but no one has found him yet. It's possible he's not there, but chances are good he is."

Katherine wrapped her sweater tighter to her shoulders. "And if he is?"

"Well, ma'am," the short one hesitated for a skip, then rushed on to finish his duty. "If he is, then he's obviously buried under the wreckage. The rescue teams are clearing it pretty fast, but they're not done yet; we're trying to contact all the families of the missing." He stopped and waited for her response.

Katherine nodded. "When will I know?" she whispered.

The short officer shrugged. "Can't say for sure, but probably by morning. They're moving through the rubble as quickly as they can."

"Will someone contact me when they know something?"

"Yes, ma'am, as soon as we have word, we'll get back to you. Any other questions?"

Katherine shook her head.

"We'll contact you as soon as we can." The soldiers turned and started to walk away. Then the short one pivoted back to her. "Ma'am," he said.

"Yes?"

"I'm sorry for your trouble. Hope your husband turns up okay."

"Thank you, sir," said Katherine.

The soldier slipped his hat onto his head and marched off with his companion.

Katherine turned too and trudged inside. She felt like an eggshell licked clean of its contents.

As she moved zombie-like toward her bed, an unexpected thought crawled through her mind. The key.

The key to his trunk in the attic. Les had told her she could use it if he died. As if dying of thirst and knowing where to find water, she instantly wanted to see what was in the trunk. It would somehow connect her to him. No matter where he was, alive or dead, the trunk would bind her to her husband and make her feel less alone.

She racked her brain. Where had she put the key? In her jewelry drawer in the dresser? Yes, that's where it was.

Katherine rushed to the dresser and pulled out the drawer. She thumbed through the beads and earrings until she found it—the key to the trunk in the attic. She would see what it held. Les had said she could—if he died. And, she sadly admitted to herself, right now she had little doubt that he was, indeed, dead.

Chapter Sixty-three

The soldiers scratching through the wreckage of the barracks at El-Khobar found themselves growing more and more desperate. They had already uncovered over twenty dead comrades and the more dead they found, the more desperate they became. As the hours shifted toward morning, they began to wonder if they would find other survivors. Between the smoke, the shattered barracks, and the heat of the earlier fire, they didn't see how too many more would have made it.

A crane operator, his arms quivering with exhaustion from a night at the controls, dropped the hook of his machine under the middle of a steel girder. He eased the crane arm into reverse. The hook snuggled under the center of the girder. The operator joggled his controls. The hook lifted the beam. Slowly, ever so slowly, he eased it away from what remained of the left corner of the destroyed barracks.

As the beam moved to the left and out of range of the rescue workers on the ground, a swarm of men descended on the rest of the carnage. They pushed away ceiling plaster, hauled off bricks and mortar, and cleared a path to the center of the building.

Chain saws buzzed as they cut away broken wood, and shovels scraped as they cleaned refuse off the floor. A staff sergeant, his face grimy with sweat and soot, leaned down to push away a section of tile that had fallen into a heap on the floor. Moving the tile, he saw a hand. He grabbed the hand and pulled. It was attached to a body.

"Hey, get over here," he yelled. "I found one over here." The sergeant waved to his buddies and five of them ran to him. Together they attacked the pile of soggy rubble. Within minutes they reached the bottom of the wreckage. A body lay on the ground at their feet.

An Army medic bent down beside the body. "Looks bad, homeboy," he murmured. He probed the man's throat, searching for a pulse.

"You find another one?

The medic glanced up at the deep voice. The whitest teeth he'd ever seen flashed a smile back at him.

"Yeah, but we may be too late. Just found him."

"Any pulse?"

The medic shook his head. "Hold on a minute, let me see." Seconds passed. Then more.

The man with the big smile squatted down beside the medic and tilted his head sideways, scanning the injured man's battered face. He touched the man's cheek. Lifted his hand to his mouth and spit on his fingers. Wiped away some of the grime from the comatose man's forehead with his spit. Saw the scar on the man's forehead.

Wait a minute! It was Les! He had found Les!

"Is he alive?" the man asked the medic, his voice unsteady.

The medic held up a hand. "Yeah, he's alive, but maybe not for long. His pulse is weak but, yeah, he's alive. . . . Hey, guys, we got us a live one here," he shouted. "Let's get him ready to move."

Beside the medic, Nelson Reed dropped from his squat to a full kneel. He lifted his eyes and raised his arms to the night sky and nodded his head at the stars. One prayer answered. But oh, so many more to go.

Chapter Sixty-four

Katherine groaned as she lifted the heavy top of the dusty trunk and laid it back against the wall. Taking a seat on a stool beside the trunk, she leaned over to look inside. For a few seconds, she only sat and stared, not touching anything, trying to size up her emotions before she explored this odd assortment of trinkets. Though eager, she didn't want to disrupt anything. She sensed she was on hallowed ground. But, looking at the top layer of mementos, she couldn't understand why. What made this so special? Why did Les keep all this a secret? Nothing unusual here from what she could see.

His high school and college yearbooks. Katherine lifted them out of the trunk and thumbed through them. Most Likely to Succeed in high school . . . she knew that. Diplomas and plaques . . . starting in the first grade Les had won plenty of them.

Pictures of his family. Katherine flipped through them. Most were ones she had seen. She laid them aside quickly and picked up another stack. One she hadn't seen was on top, Les with his dad and his dad's arm around him. But Les had a scowl on his face.

Not surprising—Les and his dad were never close. Les blamed his mom's death on his father.

Katherine kept digging. Baseball cards! She didn't realize Les had saved them. But here they were—stacks and stacks of them. Looks like his favorite player was Mickey Mantle. One, two, three, . . . sixteen different Mantle cards. She spotted a thick, hardbacked book in the corner of the trunk. Pushing away the cards and papers resting on top of it, she tugged it out and onto her lap. A family Bible.

Katherine opened it and ran her fingers over the front two pages, touching the names listed on them. The family tree from his mother's side. Four generations that ended with his mom.

Katherine searched through the crinkly pages of the big book. She recognized a few of the passages. Near the back of the book, she licked her fingers and turned another page. A letter, browned at the edges as if toasted, lay on top of the page.

Forgetting the Bible for a moment, Katherine picked up the envelope. It was addressed to Les Tennet. Katherine examined the handwriting of the address but didn't recognize it. Odd. The letter had no stamp. She lifted it to her nose and smelled it. The tint of aged smoke still clung to it.

She turned it over. The seal was torn. For an instant, she paused. She closed her eyes and sighed. Should she read it?

Opening her eyes, she reached inside the envelope and pulled out the yellowed stationery. Her eyes darted across the words.

Les,
No use pretending anymore, boy. Your mom's the only thing that kept this family together and she's been dead a long time now. Yeah, you're my son, but I've never been your father, not really. I know that and it's chewed me apart inside. I'm tired of it all—the guilt, the loneliness . . . So, by the time you read this, if you ever do, I'll be finished with it all. It's not you, boy; it's me. Don't ever blame yourself. Blame me. And don't forget, I love you. Sounds funny to hear me say it, doesn't it?
Dad

Choking out her breath, Katherine dropped the letter back onto the opened Bible. Through watery eyes, she glanced down and saw a newspaper article under the stationery. She picked up the article and read it.

Mr. Robert Tennet, a 45-year-old St. Louis native, was found dead in his bedroom this morning after his house burned down at about 2 A.M. Mr. Tennet, a local mechanic with Hopson Automotive, apparently set the house afire himself, shortly before ending his life with a self-inflicted gunshot wound to the head.

Police reached this conclusion after discovering the remains of a gasoline can in the living room and a .32 pistol by Mr. Tennet's body. No foul play is suspected.

The only survivor is a son, Les Tennet, 18, a freshman at the University of Missouri. Funeral arrangements are incomplete at this time.

Like a boxer punched in the ribs, Katherine doubled over and grabbed herself around the waist. Les had always told her that his dad had died of a heart attack the year before they started dating. But oh, how much more sense it all made now.

Three hours later, an hour before she planned to wake John and tell him his father was probably dead, the white van stopped in her driveway again and the same two men piled out of it and strode to her doorway. But this time smiles decorated their faces and the short one blurted out the message the second she opened the door. "They found him alive, Mrs. Tennet, alive under the wreckage. He's in serious condition, but he's stable and they think he's going to make it."

He kept talking, telling her someone would soon call from Saudi with an update on Les' injuries, but she barely heard him. The sounds of joy cascading through her soul washed out the sounds of his words.

Chapter Sixty-five

Seventeen days later, the last day he spent in the hospital, Les found himself alone with Macy Spencer. She pulled up a chair beside his bed. "So, you're going home next week," she said, her green eyes moist.

Les nodded. "Yeah, unless His Insane tries some silly stunt, I'm St. Louis bound. What about you?"

"They say I'll get a new duty station probably within a month. They're shipping everyone out pretty quickly. Don't want the Saudis to think we're here permanently. I'm looking forward to receiving my next assignment. Army lifer, you know."

Les grinned and reached over with his good arm and took her hand. "Macy, I feel like I need to say something to you. You know, the day you told me about Sherry I, well, you know what I did. I'm—"

"We both did it, Les," she interrupted. "I didn't resist anything. So don't blame yourself. We were both vulnerable, alone, needing someone to lean on."

"I'm not really blaming myself, Macy, not blaming anyone, just trying to make sense of it all. You know I care for you. You're one of the most fascinating people I've ever met. If I weren't married—"

"But you are."

Les paused and sat up in bed. "Yes, I am," he said. "And I'm going to try to make a go of it. It may not work out, but I've changed over here. If Katherine will have me, I want to save our marriage."

Macy squeezed his hand. "She'll still have you. She's crazy if she won't. You're a good man, Les Tennet. Just a bit confused for a while, that's all. Maybe, as a result of all that's happened in the last few months, you and Katherine have grown. All of us should have."

"Too bad it takes so much pain for that to happen," said Les.

Macy nodded, then dropped his hand and stood up. "Be happy, Les," she said, her eyes glistening. "That's all I want for you."

"And you too," he said. "I'll write you and tell you all about it."

"I'll look forward to hearing from you."

She smiled at him, then turned and left the room.

He didn't see her again. Five days later, the Army shipped him home. His concussion had healed and, though he wore a cast on his left arm and had a fresh, seven-inch scar just behind his right ear, courtesy of a falling ceiling beam, his doctors had given him a clean bill of health. With all the fighting over, Colonel Harper had quickly processed his papers.

Roger saw him off as he boarded the plane. "See you in St. Louie, my friend. We'll get Nellie and Macy to meet us there and we'll go to the top of the Arch and have a drink to our success."

Les hugged his friend and patted him on the back. "Can't wait, Rog. I already miss you guys."

"Hard to believe it's over, isn't it?"

"Yeah, hard to believe Nellie went home a week ago. I never got a chance to really talk to him. Now, I'm leaving too."

"And you're leaving me all by myself. Even Macy's gone."

"They shipped her out to Turkey."

"Yeah, the relief effort for the Kurds," said Roger.

A loudspeaker barked out the last boarding call. Les said, "Time to go, buddy. The plane's about to leave without me."

Roger took his hand and the two nodded their affection.

"I'll keep the light on for you," said Les.

"And the bottle chilled."

Laughing, Les left his friend and climbed on the plane; as the jet lifted off, Les waved goodbye to Saudi Arabia. The yellow sand of the desert stared up at him for several minutes, then disappeared as the plane gained altitude over a layer of white clouds. Les lay his head back against the seat and closed his eyes and fell asleep. Though he transferred planes in Frankfurt and in New York, he never fully awoke again until the wheels of the jet touched concrete at Lambert Airport in St. Louis.

Chapter Sixty-six

Easing himself off the plane with the rest of the jubilant military returnees, Les stood up on tiptoes and scanned the crowd, searching for John and Katherine. He spotted John's tall frame thirty yards to his left. Katherine stood beside him. Both of them waved. With a grin as tall as the St. Louis Arch, Les raised his right arm and saluted them with a thumbs-up sign.

His broken arm raised to protect it, he threaded his way across the flag-draped tarmac, shifting and turning, moving as fast as possible toward the two people he loved the most in all the world. He knew it wouldn't be easy to make amends; knew it would take a long time for them to trust him; knew he would still falter and stumble and fall. But, he promised himself as he reached them, from now on his failures would come from trying to do too much for them rather than from trying to do too little.

They came together in the midst of the cheering crowd and, for a second, froze and stared. Les opened his arms and stepped toward them. Then, like hundreds of other soldiers on the sun-soaked runway, he gathered them up and hugged them as if he never again wanted to let them go. And he didn't. He was home.

For long seconds they stayed still, holding each other.

"Thank God you're home," whispered Katherine, her head

still buried in his shoulder.

Les stayed silent for another blink, trying to make the moment last as long as possible. Then he saw someone standing a few feet behind Katherine. His brow furrowed. What in the world?

He loosened his grip on Katherine. She turned around, saw the man, smiled, and said, "Les, I think you already know this man, don't you?"

Les nodded. "Yes, Katherine, I do. He's the one who found me in the wreckage at El-Khobar."

The man flashed a smile that split open the sky. Les said, "This is Nelson Reed. But what I can't figure is what in heaven's name he's doing here."

Katherine laughed. "Well, Les, I don't really know the answer to that question. He called me from Chicago last week. Said he wanted to see you when you came in. So, I told him you were due to arrive today. That's all I know."

Les slowly nodded his head and stepped to Nellie. The two men shook hands. Les pivoted back to Katherine and John. "Did he tell you he was a chaplain?"

Katherine's eyes squinted. "A chaplain?"

Les kissed her on the cheek. "Yes, sweetheart, chaplain. Does it surprise you that I have a chaplain for a friend?"

"Well, a little," she said, extending her hand to shake Nelson's. "Don't you think it should?"

Les chuckled. "I'm sure it should," he said. He snuggled his good arm around her waist and lifted her off the ground. Then he started laughing and his laughter drowned out the roar of the crowd around them and it echoed off the buildings and made it sound like the whole world laughed with him.

John and Katherine stared at him as he stood there on the tarmac with the wind fussing through his black hair and his head tossed back and his mouth open. "You think that's surprising?" he laughed. "Let me tell you both, you ain't seen nothing yet!"

Chapter Sixty-seven

Six days later, on a Saturday night, Les led Katherine and John up the steps into the attic. The pale light bulb hanging from the ceiling seemed brighter tonight, as if the glow from their faces helped it light up the dark corners of the room.

Les had described his night of hell to them—the night he spent trapped and almost died under the rubble of the destroyed building. But, as he told it, the night of hell led him to a glimpse of heaven—to a glimpse of Sherry and Jesus and also to a glimpse of himself, of what he had been and of what he could yet be. That glimpse had opened his eyes, and when he thought his life had ended, it had actually just begun.

He and Katherine had shared their fears about their new faith with each other and with John—both were ignorant spiritually, and afraid of failures sure to come. They knew they couldn't pressure John to any decision; they also recognized their experiences as something more than the normal.

They knew that faith alone wouldn't solve their problems. Their marriage had a long way to go. They needed to communicate more clearly, to develop more intimacy, to become less selfish.

Les still faced the malpractice suit. Snowball's wife hadn't dropped it and Les had spent almost two days with Ned List since his return, preparing for the first depositions. And John's trial loomed over them all—a dark shadow of uncertainty.

Yet, with all their fears, Les and Katherine had also talked of their hopes. They could learn together, they could love John more fully, they could survive Sherry's death with new faith, they could focus on what mattered.

Now, Les motioned them to take a seat. Once they were still, he opened the trunk, pulled aside the clutter on the top and picked his way to the baseball cards underneath. When he reached them, he turned to John.

"John, I want you to have these," he said, grabbing them by the handfuls and laying them in his lap. "I meant to give them to you before I left, but well, you know how things were then."

John nodded and picked up the cards. For several seconds, he flipped through the pictures, reading the statistics, looking at the pictures. Then he raised his eyes to Les.

"Thanks, Dad," he said. "I know these mean a lot to you."

"Well, at one time they did," said Les, "and now, for some reason, they do again, and I want you to have them. Kind of a reminder, I guess, a reminder that I was a kid myself once."

He lowered his eyes back to the trunk. To the right corner. To the thick black book lying there. For a beat, all three of them stared at it; then Les lifted it up and opened it.

"My mom used to read from this," he said softly. "And now her son will."

"And her son's wife," said Katherine.

"And her son's son," said John, surprising them both.

Silence rested on the room again, but this time the silence didn't threaten. It comforted instead, and they embraced it.

Katherine broke the silence. "I only wish Sherry were here," she said, "to see us all together." Silence hit again. Then Les concluded, "Kath, you may think I'm crazy, but I think she is."

Katherine put her hand over his and John added his hand. Then they all stood and, carrying the Bible with them, walked back downstairs.

The next morning, right after 8 o'clock, the phone rang. Les picked it up in the kitchen.

"Hello," he said.

"Dr. Tennet?"

"Yes, this is Dr. Tennet." He recognized the voice, but couldn't quite place it.

"Dr. Tennet, this is Tom Clemons."

Les wanted to hang up but knew he couldn't. "Yes?"

Clemons hesitated, then rushed ahead with the words as if saying them fast would lessen the pain. "Look, I received a call about an hour ago from Tina Spicer; you probably recall her from the preliminary hearing. She and her parents were at the hospital. Her brother, Jamaal Spicer, OD'd on drugs last night and died about two hours ago."

In a hurry to get dressed and not sure what this had to do with him, Les didn't care to hear about Tina Spicer's brother. But he knew Clemons hadn't called without reason, so he stayed calm. "Well, I'm sorry to hear that, lieutenant, but what does that have to do with John?"

Clemons cleared his throat and proceeded. "Well, Spicer told me some interesting news. According to her story, her brother killed Trevor Mashburn and—"

"Her brother!" Les interrupted. "Her brother killed Mashburn!"

"Yeah, seems so," coughed Clemons. "Accidentally. He was trying to shoot John. Had a real hatred for your boy. Seems John hurt him a couple of years back in basketball and wrecked his knee. Kept him from playing college and maybe pro basketball. Plus, John dated his sister and he hated him for that too. Didn't like a white boy dating her, you know that routine. So, as Tina and Trevor and John left the game together—"

Les cut him off again. "You say Tina was with John *and* Trevor? I thought John and Trevor disliked each other."

"Well, they did, but Tina had met with both of them during the game to help them patch up their differences."

"So they were leaving . . . " Les now wanted to know the rest of the story.

"As they were leaving, Jamaal drove by and took a shot at John. And hit Trevor instead."

Clemons paused. Les asked him another question. "But Tina Spicer said she and John had argued, that he left before Mashburn ever showed up."

"She lied."

"Why didn't she tell you this earlier?"

"That's obvious, don't you think? To protect her brother."

"So why tell it now?"

"Because her brother is dead and it can't hurt him now and she doesn't want John to go through any more grief over this. She said this has caused enough grief for everyone already."

"I can agree with her on that." Les paused for a second, then continued. "So where did John get the gun?"

"Easy. Jamaal tossed it and John picked it up."

Les sucked in a drawerful of air. "Does this mean the case against John is ended? he asked.

Clemons practically spat out the words. "Yes, I expect so. I'll have to get Spicer to make an official statement, but unless she backs away from this story, then that's the end of it."

Les exhaled and the air from it stirred the hand towel hanging on the rack by the phone. A swirl of questions surged through his mind. Why hadn't John told them this? Why hadn't his son confided in him, trusted him? A surge of anger welled up for a moment. John's silence had put them all through hell. But then it dawned on Les. John didn't tell him because he didn't trust him to believe his story. John stayed quiet because of the broken relationship between father and son.

Les took a deep breath and turned his thoughts back to Clemons. "Well, thank you for calling, lieutenant."

"You're welcome," said Clemons.

Both hung up. Leaping the stairs two at a time, Les called John and Katherine into the hallway, put his arms around them, and poured out the good news.

Chapter Sixty-eight

Nelson Reed eased himself into the warm liquid and took three long steps into the center of the water. His blonde hair glistened in the light flowing in from the window behind him as he pivoted with a right quarter turn and faced the crowd gathered below.

Reaching to the ledge in front of him, he opened a small Bible and read, "If anyone is in Christ, behold he is a new creation. Old things have passed away, all things have become new."

Then he turned to his right and motioned for Les and Katherine to enter the water with him. Katherine edged down the steps first, her bare feet almost covered with the white robe she wore. The water climbed up her legs as she entered it and reached almost to her chest as she stopped in front of Nelson.

He positioned her carefully—her profile at a right angle to the watching congregation and to his chest. He faced the people.

Beside them both, but behind the curtain and hidden from view, Les stood and watched.

Nelson smiled and turned to Katherine. "Katherine Tennet," he asked, his deep voice making the water quiver. "Do you come today to profess your faith in Jesus Christ as your Savior and Lord?"

Katherine spoke firmly. "I do."

Nelson lifted his right hand into the air as a sign of blessing. "Then I baptize you in the name of the Father, and of the Son, and of the Holy Spirit. Amen."

Gently, he lowered his hand and placed it in the small of her back. Then, he bent her backwards, into the clear liquid, into the water. Like a mother's arms, the water parted and let her enter. "Buried with Christ in baptism," said Nelson as he dipped her under, "and raised to walk in newness of life," he continued, as he lifted her out.

With water streaming down her face, Katherine moved across the baptismal pool to the opposite side. Then she turned and looked back, waiting on Les.

Nelson nodded to Les and he followed Katherine's steps into the water. Nelson positioned him. Looking sideways, Les sucked in his breath and spotted John—two rows back and to his left. John nodded to him. Les smiled.

Nelson asked him, "Do you come today to profess your faith in Jesus Christ as your Savior and Lord?"

In that instant, Les relived it all once more. His mom's face flickered across his thoughts—but her face was smiling now, not struggling for life. And he saw his dad's too—and Les breathed a word of forgiveness to him. And then Sherry's face—the angelic glow of one who would remain forever innocent. Seeing Sherry's face, Les looked over at Katherine and then down to John once more. The tears rolled out of his eyes. He said, "I do."

"Then I baptize you in the name of the Father, and of the Son, and of the Holy Spirit. Amen."

Nelson plunged Les' body and head and face into the pool, and Les relaxed backward into the water. This time he meant it because now he understood—it all begins in the water.